ELLE HARTFORD

Cold as Snow

The Alchemical Tales #2

Before we begin,
I'd like to acknowledge the giants whose shoulders I stand upon:
be they authors of fairy tales,
humorous satire,
Golden Age mystery,
classical myth,
or Victorian drama,
their influences have shaped these characters and this story.

Contents

Author's Note

Cold as Snow is book two in The Alchemical Tales series, taking place just a few months after the first book, *Beauty and the Alchemist.* If you haven't had a chance to read the first one, don't worry! Our narrator, Red, will catch you up on everything you missed. The mystery itself is stand-alone.

The Alchemical Tales blend cozy mystery with cozy fantasy and retold fairy tales. I had so much fun exploring twists on the old story of "Snow White" for this book, and I'm excited to share Red's further adventures with you!

Welcome

Long, long ago, a coven of witches created a world just
beyond ours—a realm of fairy tales.

In Beyond, humans rub shoulders with mythical creatures,
and magic mixes with science.

There are only three rules:

Happily
accept that we share the same home

Ever
remember that what you take, you must also give

After
struggle will always lead to new beginnings

So, if you are ready . . . you are welcome here.

* * *

Belville & nearby forest

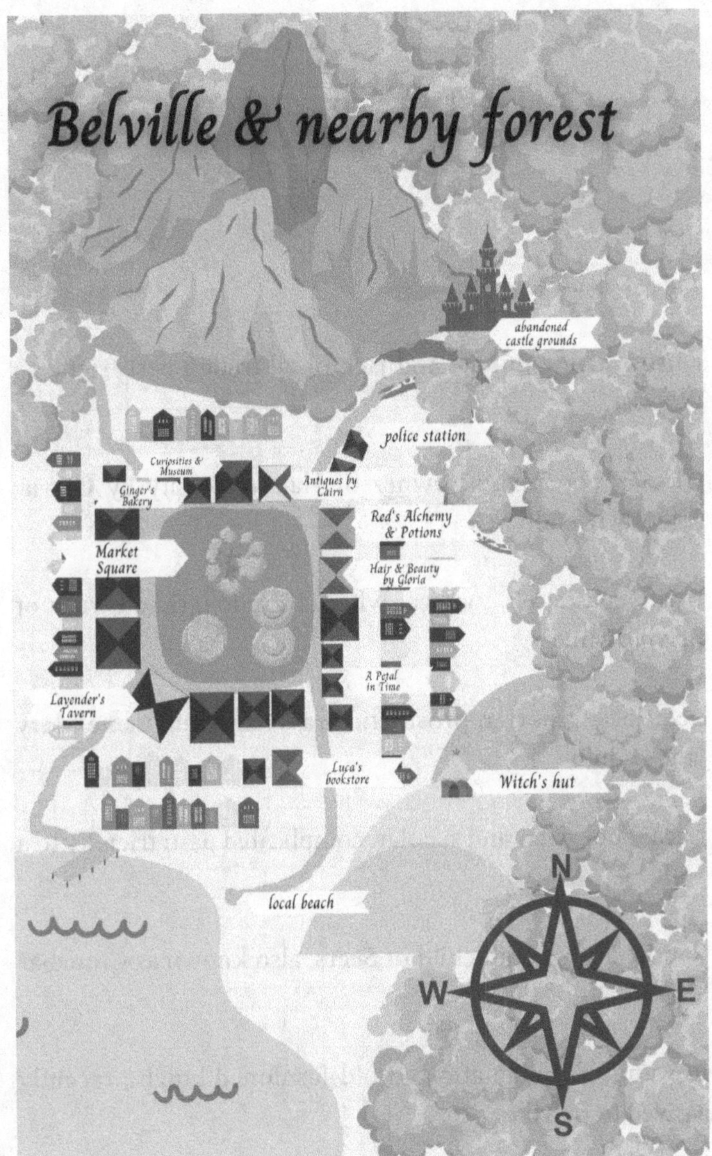

Cast of Characters

law in Belville

Trent: young Witch, lives in a Hut outside of town; eager to help

William: canine familiar, capable of protection magic and plenty of sass

1

Winter in the Air

I should have been opening my shop, but my first thought was to find—and potentially thaw out—my neighbor, Gloria.

Sounds dramatic, right? I was in a dramatic mood when this all began, that's for sure. My mother always told me that in daily life, the difference between comedy and tragedy came down to attitude. Attitude, she said, was the main way we protect ourselves. And Gloria's attitude was much more formidable than mine, so it would have made sense to think that she could protect herself.

But even so, I felt responsible for her.

"William!" I called down the stairs, still stumbling in the dark. "William, will you go out and check next door?"

"No. I shouldn't even be up this early," came the distant reply.

I ground my teeth. The thing was, in a world like Beyond—a world where you had gleaming magitech cities, thorny fairy tales, undersea kingdoms, and fairy magic all on the same earth—people like my mother who liked to talk about "attitude" were probably right. Folks in Beyond often liked to say that we were all re-living variations of the same old stories.

Given that my winter morning had begun with a crack in the kitchen window and dusty snow and icicles all over my tiny studio apartment, I felt like our street had been hit by some arctic pirate story.

That was probably exaggeration on my part. But still, a broken window was cause for concern.

"Morning, Red. *You* look a sight," William added as I appeared at the top of the stairs.

I glowered at my companion, a magical talking dog. When I'd simultaneously stubbed my toe and discovered the mess in my kitchen earlier, my cursing had been enough to send him down into the shop for cover.

"Unless by 'sight' you mean 'vision of beauty and grace,' I suggest you keep your mouth shut," I growled back. The menacing effect was probably marred by my limp as I came down the spiral staircase from my apartment above the store, but I didn't care.

William made a noise which I chose to believe was a cough.

Around us, the shop was dark and quiet. Flickering street lamps and the dull hum of a winter wind beyond the big bay windows reminded me that not all was peaceful, though. The problem with being from a tropical climate was that I never, ever seemed to get used to winter.

Especially not a winter wind that brought intruders along with it. "Go and check Gloria's, won't you, please? If you don't run out and do it, then I will, and we both know how well I fare in the snow."

William watched me for a split second, fuzzy ears cocked

and his black fur giving him the appearance of a shadow in the gray morning. "If you're that worried, then fine," he decided, bounding down from the chair he'd perched on. In a moment, he was out the back door, leaving an icy blast of wind in his wake.

Nonetheless, my alchemy shop was snug and cozy—unlike my apartment. I leaned against the wall behind the sales counter, taking a moment to calm myself down. *I'm sure it was nothing, and she's fine,* I thought, looking around. All the rows of potions and alchemical ingredients and reference books stood perfectly in order. A citrus smell from my cleaning potions lingered in the air, mixing with the evergreen scent of a new line of sparkling candles I was testing out for the season. The staircase from the apartment came down in the rear corner of the shop; in front of me was the sales counter, and behind me, I'd painted the accent wall behind the counter a lovely green. Through an interior window, my lab beckoned.

While waiting for William's report, I shouldered my way through the side door and into my true refuge. My lab had once been a small working kitchen, with stone tiled floor and sturdy appliances. Shortly after I'd bought the building and set up my shop, I'd added the interior window so that I could keep an eye on the sales floor while restocking potions or making custom orders. It was orderly and peaceful.

Except that this morning, a faint glow flickered from my burner. I narrowed my eyes at the magical flame. *Really? Is something else going to go wrong already?*

"I started some hot water," William said helpfully, bounding back in through the back door. "You know, in case your battle with the kitchen didn't work out."

"Thank the goddess," I muttered, pulling on an apron and

heading over to the workbench at once. Usually I was very careful about keeping food out of the lab, but I did keep extra mugs and freshly bagged tea in one of the cupboards just in case. Every rule had its exceptions, after all. Pulling out an elf-made ceramic purple mug and a packet of the strongest black tea on hand, I asked, "So, how is Gloria? Was her shop broken into, or anything? I'm guessing since you're back so fast, she was okay."

"She wasn't even there," William informed me, shaking himself dry of snow and continuing into the shop. As he reclaimed his seat on the stool behind the counter, he added through the interior window, "I just talked to Johann. You know, the new guy who's her assistant in the salon now? He lives above it in the apartment the fairies used to use. He said it was quiet all night there. No broken windows."

"Well, that's good. And yes, I remember Johann, thank you very much," I grumped. Normally I wasn't one to start my mornings so antagonistically, but also normally, my mornings didn't involve break-ins—even tiny ones. "He's been in Belville for nearly a month now."

"Two," William corrected helpfully. "He came right after the fairies left."

The business with Gloria and the fairies was probably why I was overprotective of her. Well, the fairies and a blackmailer named Owl and a certain adventure with a local haunted castle, too. Everything had turned out fine—the fairies, who had been manipulative and cruel as Gloria's assistants in the salon, had gone, and Owl's murderer had been charged for her crimes. *And that was two months ago already?* I shook my head, still trying to get a grip on my morning.

"I know what you're going to say next," William sniffed, his wet black nose in the air. "But the break in the window wasn't those fairies, and it wasn't my ward's fault either."

I sighed, certain that he was right. William had originally been a sorcerer's familiar with a specialty in protective magic when I found him on the road years ago. He continued to work the magic that he'd been created as a familiar to do: wards—basically magical shields—which protected us and our building.

"Yeah, I guess that makes sense." I focused on pouring a stream of steaming water over my tea leaves, pursing my lips as I did so, even though I knew William wasn't even looking at me. "If it was the fairies coming back for revenge, there'd be a lot more glitter around, anyway."

"Well, it wasn't. I keep telling you, Red, they're long gone by now." William snorted. "It was a fey spark against a natural limitation of my spell, if you must know."

I set down the kettle. "Run that by me again, in layman's terms, please."

William sighed and shook his floppy ears as though I was being obtuse on purpose, as though he didn't know very well that our arrangement had *always* been that he took care of the magic, I took care of the science. "Something very small and naturally magical, like a pixie or a soot sprite, was trying to get past the ward at a place where it was already weak. And why was the ward weak, you ask? Well, because *someone* had to go around last season making friends with all kinds of ghosts and shadows, didn't she? And what did her new friends see fit to do when they wanted a word? Did they ring the doorbell like *normal* visitors?"

"It is too cold for another lecture about Jade," I groaned.

"Ha!" William shook himself again. This time he nearly

knocked himself from his perch on the stool, which was too small for his furry butt.

This had become a recurring conversation between us in recent months. William would allude to me getting myself "in trouble" while helping Gloria and the local scholar, Luca, clear up Owl's murder. I would make some protest, such as helping friends was a good thing; everything turned out just fine; our shop sign *did* advertise that I could find lost objects, as well as make potions; or that he himself had been quite involved with that investigation. Then William would make some eloquent comment about me being too trusting and too easily duped by mysterious shadows named Jade, which he somehow managed to boil down into one expressive "Ha!"

Never mind the fact that Jade had turned out to be an alter ego of Luca's, and therefore completely incapable of harming so much as a homicidal fly.

William had to scuffle to realign himself on the stool, and I smirked at him as I passed a wide-mouthed mug of tea out to him through the window. With tendrils of deep blue magic, which curled like galaxies in the dimness of the shop, William accepted the offering. He slurped it down without hesitation, despite the fact that it was scalding hot.

We non-magical folk had to be a bit more cautious. I cradled my own mug against my fingerless lab gloves and mused. "Jade came to that window two months ago, as you so gleefully pointed out about Johann and the fairies. Don't you check and strengthen those wards all the time?"

Now it was William's turn to growl. "Are you accusing me of negligence?"

"Hey, stand down," I said, putting up a hand. The last thing I needed to add to my morning was a magical brawl. We were already running a bit late in opening the shop. But, with the storm outside, I doubted we'd get too many early morning customers anyway. "I'm just trying to figure out what happened. I thought your protections were supposed to be unbreakable."

"And they are. I said something *wanted* to enter. Did you see any signs of a creature of any kind actually entering through the window?"

"No," I admitted. I'd checked for footprints, claw marks, ransacked foodstuffs, and anything else suspicious while cleaning up the kitchen, but hadn't seen a thing. "So what are you saying, the weather could get in but the creature couldn't?"

"Weather doesn't count," William said, his buried snout in his mug.

"Great, then *you* can be the one to sweep up snow and scrape ice off the sink next time," I informed him.

William snorted. "You could've just waited for it to melt."

"Oh, and make an even *bigger* mess?"

"Tell me you closed off the window, at least."

"Of course I did. I'm grumpy and tired, not careless." I stuck my tongue out at him. Over his shoulder, I caught sight of a smudged shape in the street. It seemed to be a person looking in our window. A glance at the clock on the wall confirmed that we were, indeed, running late. "Thanks for humoring me and checking on Gloria, at least. We can figure out the rest later," I told William, setting down my tea. "For now, you get the lights and the safe, I'll get the doors. Anyone brave enough to come out today must be desperate."

2

Mine, Mine, Mine

I'd said anyone out in this weather must be desperate, but I'd overlooked the fact that some people didn't mind the snow as much as I did. And on top of that, enthusiasm in some can be just as dangerous as desperation in others.

"There you are, Red!" Officer Thorn's voice cut through the mumble of afternoon business.

Without turning to look, I knew that the good Officer herself would be cutting her way through the few shivering customers picking over warming powders and elixirs of protection. I set the rest of my newly-made vials of quicksilver down in my corner display of magical elements and rose to face her.

Despite some ancient magic in my blood, I'm human—so when I rose, I made it to about five foot nine. That was nearly a foot shorter and perhaps a hundred pounds lighter than Officer Thorn, who was half orc. Once she alluded to the fact that her siblings hauled freight and worked as bodyguards for a living. She, on the other hand, opted to join the police guild. Her gorgeous black hair, mossy green skin, and shiny uniform all appeared completely impervious to the winter weather outside.

"Where else would I be?" I asked her, raising an eyebrow. Thorn was one of my oldest friends in Belville, and she knew full well how I felt about frostbite, so there wasn't any need for me to glance at the gray world outside the window to make my point. Instead, I looked over the lanky form tagging along behind Thorn's massive shoulder.

"Off to the mines," Officer Thorn replied with a wink. Perhaps her chipper attitude served as a buffer from the weather. I looked back at her quizzically, waiting for the pun—because with Officer Thorn, any strange utterance was usually a pun—to reveal itself. *I'm already at work,* I reasoned, *so she can't possibly mean . . .*

"Did you forget?" Officer Thorn crossed her arms and glanced at our silent observer, who still seemed to be attempting to hide in her shadow. This feat was made difficult by the fact that the unnamed third party was even taller than Thorn. To this person, Thorn said, "See, I told you. You may think Belville's just a small town, but it's three jobs together trying to keep everyone around here in line. Aside from the mine and the usual crime that comes with trade, the shopkeepers can't even keep dates straight."

"Said 'shopkeepers' can still hear you perfectly well," I retorted, and groaned as I remembered. The day before, I'd received a note about a mysterious new discovery at the mine, along with a request to serve as a third party authenticator for it. "You're talking about the meeting with Lark today to go over the new ore, right? I *didn't* forget, I just thought the meeting would be canceled because of the weather."

I'd also thought that perhaps, as a bit of a reprieve after my morning, the universe might let up about this whole "trekking out to the mine to adjudicate some weird rock samples as the local expert" thing. But apparently my luck for the day was consistent.

"Come on, Red," said Thorn, grinning a wide grin full of pointy, sparkly teeth. "If we canceled plans because of a bit of bad weather, we'd never get anything done."

"Well, we could make Lark leave her precious mine and come over *here* for once," I muttered rebelliously.

"Lark prefers not to leave the mine during business hours—says it's not worth the hassle navigating the trails with her chair, and she hates being driven. Now, have you two met?" Thorn ignored my grumblings and stepped back, nearly knocking over a freestanding shelf of dried flowers. The person behind her startled violently and *did* in fact knock over a vase of moonflower. Several customers sniggered as they left.

"*I* haven't been introduced," William barked from the sales counter.

A glance around the shop showed me we were now alone, so I waved off our clumsy visitor's apologetic murmurings and bustled to the back corner to get the broom. As I took care of the cleaning, Thorn spoke loudly enough to be heard throughout the room.

"This is Maeve," she informed the shop at large. Maeve shuffled like a giraffe trying very hard to impersonate a lamp post. "She's here to learn the ropes. After that business with the murder and the castle and the books, the Guild thought we might use an extra hand out here in the sticks, so they'll be sending trainees from time to time. Gets 'em a bit of practical experience. What do you say, Maeve? Tell them a little bit about yourself."

"Um," said Maeve. I finished my sweeping and stood up, leaning on my broom as I craned my neck to look at Maeve's face. Maeve seemed also to be stooping to look at me. "I'm, um, a new trainee. At the police guild. Over in Pine. You can call me Maeve. Or 'she.'"

Such specifications are sometimes useful in Beyond, where you get people in all shapes and persuasions. But from the way Maeve clasped her arms around herself, I wondered if she had told us that because she was more worried about her appearance than she needed to be. Her uniform, a darker and more somber version of Thorn's military-esque outfit, fit well and looked well cared-for. Whereas Thorn never wore any kind of headgear, Maeve had opted for a large woolen beret. Neither her height nor the hat completely obscured the fact that her head was smooth and bald, her skin a dull gray.

Across the room, William set his paws up on the counter and the edges of his black fur glowed, a sure sign he was using magic. "Bit of Reaper in you, is there?"

"William!" I reprimanded. "Not everyone wants to tell you their inner secrets."

"It's, um, not really a secret," Maeve assured me, although the tuck at the end of her long mouth—as though she was biting her lip—made me think I'd been right, that she was worried about her appearance. Reapers are to the spirit world as wood elves are to forests: they walk the line between life and death. They could be found all across Beyond, because they were necessary everywhere—they helped souls move on to the next stage, whatever that might be. But just because they were ubiquitous doesn't mean they were well-loved. Not everyone in Beyond was comfortable with mortality. And it didn't help that Reapers often had a skeletal appearance.

There wasn't anything frightening or ghoulish about Maeve, though, aside from the fact that she looked about two feet too tall for her frame. And that could mostly be chalked up to a lack of confidence.

"It's my Da," she continued at a mumble. William pricked up an ear, perhaps to hear her better. "I don't—I don't have any magic though. They ask you about that in training. Ma told me once when I was a child I had kind of, um, a sense for it. And that for a minute I was holding a bird and, uh—"

"By all that's Just, trainee, there's no need to babble," Thorn interrupted, not without kindness. "The dog is William, and like Red said, he doesn't have any right to know your business. The important one for you to meet is that one there, with the goggles and the broom." She gestured at me. "That's Red. She's my *un*official assistant," Thorn explained with a toothy grin, ignoring William's huffs. "Official assistant, meet unofficial assistant."

"I'm an alchemist," I corrected as I shook Maeve's cool hand. No amount of saying this ever persuaded Thorn not to treat me like police backup, but I kept trying anyway. "Hence the goggles." I ran my free hand self-consciously over them, always perched on my forehead. Say what you will about fashion, but nothing could beat the convenience of carrying my most useful tool around with me on my head. Plus, the goggles kept my long dark hair out of my way, and helped obscure the glittery strands that might draw attention to my mystic heritage. "Welcome to Belville, Maeve. It's not usually this snowy," I added with a smile. "Winter came early this year, it seems like."

"Please. There's barely a foot out there," Thorn protested.

She made it to the front of the shop in three short steps and yanked the door open, letting snow come swirling in around her knees. Turning back with a grin, she added, "Get your cloak and boots, Red. It's time for us to leg it."

***

I left William to handle any remaining customers for the day—or, more likely, to plot his revenge against Officer Thorn. He hated it when people referred to him as simply a "dog." Grabbing my warmest cloak, a lush purple felt lined with enchanted blue velvet, along with knee-high boots and my tool belt of Useful Things, I followed the officer and her trainee out into the snow.

Belville is the quintessential small town. Nestled deep in the rural district known as Pastoria, Belville was the sort of place where everyone knew your business and any strangers who did more than pass through with the trade caravans became Public News Item Number One. That said, Belville didn't lack for much—while technically the town was surrounded by forest, a lake lay along the southern outskirts, and along the northwestern border forested cliffs give way to what locals know simply as "the Mine."

The Mine was huge. In fact, as someone who frequently dealt in rocks and minerals, I knew well that the complex in the mountainside outside Belville wasn't just *one* mine—it was a dozen, or even more. The whole operation was run by a coastal elf named Lark. She originally brought her business to town because she was building a railway out to the seashore—at least, that's what she told people; her tactics had sometimes clashed with the town's desires, though, and Officer Thorn might have said something different. Since summer, Lark had been expanding her system of caverns and tunnels. Most folks in Belville were happy to see their business increase, even if they were a little leery of miners who came in from out of town. More miners meant more people buying lodging, food, and clothing, particularly during the winter months. But I had my reservations about the new ore Lark and her miners had found.

"I'm saying this for the last time," I told Thorn for perhaps the fifth time in the past twenty-four hours, since news had hit town of Lark's latest discovery. "The miners did *not* find a vein of 'Quintessence.'"

"How do you know if you haven't inspected it yet?" Thorn yelled back cheerfully. She led the way as the three of us hunched along the mountain trail to Lark's headquarters. Maeve took up the rear.

"Because there isn't any such thing as an ore of quintessence," I retorted. Above my head, snow-laden branches watched impassively. For the moment, finally, the storm had abated. "A quintessential ore, sure. That you could have. But you'd get that ore after days, or even *moons* of alchemical preparation. Quintessence is a product of distillation—sort of like the spirit inside the physical item. It's *not* something you find just lying around in a tunnel."

"It wasn't just lying around in a tunnel," Officer Thorn reminded me matter-of-factly. "A team of outside contractors here to help with the mining spotted it in a slag heap. No one's sure where in the mine it actually came from. That's part of the problem."

"The *problem* is that it's a natural impossibility," I muttered.

"You keep saying long words, Red, but all I hear is professional jealousy."

I snorted. Even the breath coming out of my lungs tasted like ice. "How can I be professionally jealous of Lark or her contracted miners when none of them are alchemists?"

"Um," said Maeve.

Thorn and I both stopped at once, our boots crunching in the silence. It wasn't anything about Maeve's tone that gave us cause for alarm; it was simple surprise, because Maeve hadn't spoken since we'd left the shop. Now, we were halfway up the mountain, a mere moment away from Lark's semi-permanent camp. The trail ran below a cliff ledge, which would soon give way to the plateau we'd be climbing up on to in a minute.

But Thorn evidently felt there wasn't a need to rush. She squinted up at her lanky assistant.

"I just, had a feeling," said Maeve. She shuffled, drawing attention to the fact that despite her size, her feet didn't sink into the snow drifts. Now *there* was something I could be jealous of: not having to clean snow out of every crevice of your boots when you got home.

"Had a feeling about what?" Thorn asked, one hand on her hip. "The ore?"

"No. That, um, that weird shape over there."

Maeve gestured several yards down the trail behind us. Trees shaded one side, while snowdrifts piled against the rock wall on the other. Pulling my goggles down over my eyes and activating the zoom feature, I could see some specks of brown and neon green among the pure white lumps.

Brown made sense; minor rock slides happened on the mountain all the time. But neon green? Not at this time of year. I hesitated uneasily for a moment before retracing our steps, following the trail Thorn's large feet had plowed.

"Good eye, Maeve," Thorn said as she fell into step behind me. When the three of us huddled around the suspicious drift, Thorn was the one to reach out and brush away the snow.

And when Thorn's hand revealed no bit of plant matter or forgotten equipment, but a crumpled tunic and a cold body, I wondered if Maeve's *eye* was what had sensed the disturbance after all.

3

White as Snow, Black as Night

"Whoever it is, they're dead," said Maeve. Officer Thorn and I exchanged a glance as we bent over the unfortunate snow drift. Belville sat squarely in a rural county called Pastoria, where many people chose to hunt for their food or care for a farm. As such, dealing with death was a matter of life for most locals. However, soft-spoken Maeve sounded suspiciously teary.

"Correct," Thorn agreed, straightening. "And in this weather, they'll keep, for a minute. Here's what we're going to do. Maeve, you come with me. Lark's offices are just up around the bend. Let's go see what the miners know about this, shall we? Red, you stay here and keep an eye on things until we get back. Make sure nothing's disturbed. We'll just be a moment."

"You owe me," I informed Thorn, thinking, *a little bit of snow in the kitchen this morning was nothing compared to being told to stand in a snowdrift while Thorn has a chat.*

About a death. I shivered, hoping the poor soul had gone peacefully.

"All the hot tonics and pasta you want tonight at Lavender's,

17

on me," the officer promised me as she steered her assistant down the trail. "Consider it a reward for a job well done!"

"A job I haven't done yet, and was never hired for," I muttered under my breath. Still, I couldn't help but perk up a little at the thought of dinner. Lavender ran the local tavern and made *wonderful* food.

As Maeve and Thorn vanished around the corner and up the hill, I contemplated my situation. In the face of this unfortunate death, my trials at home didn't seem so significant. What was a vengeful fairy, a little ice or a broken ward here and there, really?

Unless the broken ward wasn't an accident. I puffed out a cloudy breath, glancing over the body beside me. Part of me couldn't help but wonder if the same applied here.

Judging by Thorn's cheerfulness as she'd left me behind, I figured she assumed the death was an accident—maybe someone had fallen from the cliff above during the storm. It wasn't at all impossible; in fact, it was likely. But I hesitated to make the same assumption. It's not that I'm a pessimist—far from it. It's just that when I was an apprentice alchemist, I'd had one maxim drilled into my head every day: *never make assumptions. Let the experiment show you what is true.*

I couldn't see much of the lifeless person beside me, though. *They must have been a miner,* I thought, because who else would be so far out on the mountain? Thorn had only uncovered enough to make sure that the person was beyond hope of saving, and I didn't want to uncover more—partly out of respect for the dead, and partly out of respect for Thorn's evidence-gathering later. Though my friend the police officer could come across as abrupt and bull-headed, I knew she took her work seriously.

There's nothing more to learn right now, I decided. Rather than dwell on morbid details, I took in the scenery. The tree trunks across the trail returned my gaze patiently, as though they were simply waiting for me to go away before resuming some secret party. Knowing the forests around Belville, maybe that was an option. As I breathed deeply, the clear scent of snow and spice of fir came to me—along with something else; some other scent, something almost like lakeweed, just underneath everything else. I breathed again.

And as I held my breath, trying to identify the strange smell, my ears caught a snippet of song.

"Waiting for the day your ship will come in. . ."

It was a low voice, muffled, but definitely there. Somewhere above me. I craned my neck, letting the hood of my cloak fall back as I looked up the cliff face.

"The tide's gonna turn . . ."

"Hey!" I called, stepping back onto the trail for a better view. "Hello?"

"Eeeek!"

Snow crunched and heavy boots thudded as someone thirty feet above me did a double-take. After a moment, a dark, bearded face appeared over the cliff. Had it not been for the snow, I don't think I would ever have seen him: from a distance, he looked like he was made of rock.

"Who's that? 'Sat you, Raven? You pulling a trick on me?"

"Hi," I said again, trying not to chuckle at his surprise. "Not pulling any tricks—sorry to scare you. I live in town. I didn't think anyone else was out here."

"Of course we're here," the singer retorted. "Where else should we be?" Then, as though a thought had occurred to him, he added, "We aren't late for the shift, are we? I *told*

Pigeon that we oughta get going—"

This time I did laugh. "Slow down! I don't know anything about being late." The last words went ashy in my mouth, though, as I thought of Thorn and punniness and the whole reason I was standing alone on the mountain trail. I chose my next words more carefully. "You work at the mine, I suppose?"

The head tilted to one side. "Don't you?"

"No, I'm—"

"Then why are you out here?"

Before I could explain—before I could decide how *much* to explain—another voice called across the ledge. "Who are you talking to, Goose?"

"Come over here and see this, Snow," the singer—Goose—replied. "There's a person down there on the trail. Maybe she's seen Raven."

My eyes fell to the form in the snow between me and the cliff. "Er, maybe. Do you two have a moment to come down here and talk?"

* * *

The last thing I wanted to do was spring a dead body on someone, but I knew every bit of evidence now would help Thorn later. Plus, I didn't want to lie to my new acquaintances. And by the time it occurred to me that I should have kept my mouth shut from the beginning, Goose had already scrambled down to meet me.

Goose, it turned out, was a dwarf. The rock-like appearance of his face and gruffness to his voice made sense now, as did his work in the mine. I'd heard rumors that dwarves once had lived only in caves because if sunlight hit them, they'd turn to stone. These days, though, dwarves walk freely; whether because of magic charms to protect them from sunlight, or because the whole story had been bunk in the first place, no non-dwarf could say for sure.

Standing proudly as high as my shoulder, with a broad grin reminiscent of Thorn's, Goose contemplated my boots, cloak, and various tools. "You *aren't* a miner," he decided.

"Nope. Actually," I said, figuring I may as well get one of two hard parts out first, "I came up here with Officer Thorn."

The person trailing after Goose—Snow, if I had to guess— went very still at this comment. This was just another sign that the two were outsiders. No one in town was afraid of Officer Thorn, because everyone knew better than to cross her in the first place.

Snow watched me over Goose's shoulder. She only accomplished this by standing several yards back along the path, because whereas Goose was maybe five feet tall, Snow was more like four. As with Goose, Snow's heritage needed no explanation. She was, in fact, oddly reminiscent of the fairies who had bullied Gloria—aside from her coloring. Her bright orange, thickly woven miner's clothes did nothing to hide her slight frame and icy pale skin. Her eyes were so blue I could see them clearly despite the distance, and her hair was the kind of deep black that looked cobalt in the light, like the very depths of night. Snow was clearly an elemental fairy.

Three guesses as to her element, I thought wryly. *I don't need nosy William for that.*

"Have you seen Raven?" Goose asked me as I sized up my visitors. "He looks like me. Last we saw him, though, he was wearing green."

Green. The detail struck a heavy chord in my heart. "Listen,"

I said to them both, as kindly as I could. "There's a chance I've seen him, but I'm not sure. And it might come as a nasty shock for both of you. Do you want to—"

"He's there, isn't he," a new voice cut in. From behind Snow, another dwarf had emerged. He immediately came down the path and put an arm around the fairy, the look on his face both terrified and concerned.

Snow shifted. "What makes you say that, Pigeon?" she asked the newcomer, her voice bright and deft like cut ice.

"Why else would he be gone, and the police be here, right by our camp?" Pigeon returned. Goose was staring back at him now too, and it was clear to me that Pigeon had some authority in their group. He pointed past me. "Raven's in that drift, isn't he? He—he must have fallen from the cliff. Oh, Snow, I *knew* coming to a mine we'd never seen or dealt with before was a bad idea!"

Snow caught her breath with a gulp and buried her head in Pigeon's blocky shoulder. Goose turned to me again, but he didn't move forward. "Raven—fall? But he wouldn't! None of us would ever do a clumsy thing like that!"

I bit my lip. Before I could offer sympathy, though, Officer Thorn—with Maeve and a veritable crowd in tow—came round the corner behind them.

"As far as we know, he did," Officer Thorn announced grimly. "And the best thing you can do now is help me figure out how or why it happened."

* * *

An hour later and the crowd of us hadn't moved from the trail. Officer Thorn held her ground.

"I understand he's one of your crew, but I need to take him to the station for an examination. No, Lark, I'll have no argument from you about this. And I expect everyone to give statements, understood? Yes, I *know* I said it was probably an accident. It probably was. But this fellow here—Goose—says it couldn't have been, and that strangers have been seen wandering around his camp. You have to respect that. We have to make sure we follow procedure."

Thorn turned from a belligerent mine owner and sullen miners to nod at her assistant. Her assistant, however, was staring rather dreamily at Snow. Snow was staring stonily at the cliff above Raven's body.

"He's our brother," Goose sniffed. "We stick together."

"He was my *employee*," Lark interjected. The elf sat regally in a magic, purpose-made wheelchair that made me sick with inventor's envy every time I saw it. Floating atop a revolving orb of clear sea water, the machine had every hallmark of merfolk technology. It was far from an inconvenience; Lark treated it like a mobile throne. Still, the fact that she'd made her way down the trail—despite her clear preference to stay at the mine—showed she was taking this very seriously. "And as such, I expect to be kept abreast of your investigation. I have the mine and the rest of the miners to consider, you understand."

Officer Thorn nodded stiffly. "Of course."

"And I expect you to investigate *quickly*," Lark added, her aquamarine eyes flashing. "We have several important deals to fill, plus the new ore awaiting adjudication. This is not a time for any *strangers* interfering with our business."

At that, her sharp gaze turned to me. I returned her look coolly; it seemed like any thoughts of new ores were eons ago. *But maybe it's not so irrelevant after all,* I thought. This "mysterious stranger" information had come from a distraught Goose; Snow and the other dwarves had been mum on the subject, and Lark had expressed outright disbelief. But Officer Thorn had said that a group of outside contractors had been the ones to find the ore . . .

What if Raven—or all the dwarves and Snow together—were the ones who found the ore? I wasn't sure what the implications of that could be, but I didn't like it. I don't particularly believe in coincidences, and making such a discovery—then winding up dead—seemed like awfully bad luck.

To add to that, Lark was waiting on me, as a neutral third party, to certify the new ore. Once she knew what it was and where in her mine it had come from, I reasoned, that could be very good for her business, too. *If this ore really is so unique, it could be worth a lot. I wonder if the stranger—or the dwarves—were somehow already tied up in potential deals for it.*

If they had been, Thorn wouldn't have a hard time finding motives for murder.

And even if they hadn't, there were more important things going on.

"I'm not looking at any ore until we can lay Raven to rest," I declared. I avoided using the word 'quintessence' on purpose, and I could tell it rankled Lark. But what I really wanted to do was buy Thorn's investigation some time—and maybe afford Snow and Goose and the others a little protection as well. "It's a matter of respect."

"Not to mention I'll be needing Red to help with my own examinations," Thorn chipped in. She winked at me before turning back to Lark. "You can be sure we'll go exactly as fast as needed."

"If that's the case," said Lark, "I see no need to remain out here in the snow. You may take charge of the body for now."

With one last glance at me, she turned and retreated up the trail. *Did I imagine it, or did she look a little impressed?* I wondered. Ever since Thorn and I had stumbled into the mine the previous summer, Lark and the officer had had a push-me-pull-you relationship. I thought that perhaps they both secretly enjoyed the challenge.

In Lark's wake, Snow and six dwarves remained, including Goose and Pigeon. The atmosphere shifted to one of sadness rather than a standoff of wills. I realized that it had indeed started to snow again, and glanced curiously at the elemental fairy.

Snow ignored me and put her hand on Goose's shoulder. "They'll figure out what happened," she told him quietly.

"We won't let anything else happen," Pigeon added, his own hand still on Snow's waist. Clearly, the group was a close one.

"We will figure it out," Maeve echoed, faint but fervent. She was still staring at Snow.

Thorn nodded, approving of her assistant. "Is there anything else you folks want us to know upfront? For example, how was it that you happened to find Red?"

Goose snuffled in his sleeve. "We were just walking back after—after lunch."

"I heard Goose singing," I explained to Thorn. Judging by the shuffles and grunts of his fellow dwarves, this was not an uncommon experience. I glanced down at Goose with a small, sympathetic smile which he did his best to return. "I started talking to him, so he came over, and the others followed him down the trail."

Thorn nodded again, still focused on the mining team. "And

now that it's just between you all and us, can you think of any reasons for Raven's fall?"

There was much shuffling, shaking of heads, and blowing of noses. The dwarves' heads turned to Pigeon as if by force of habit. Pigeon said at last, "I s'pose you know we're new here, Officer. We don't want any trouble. I'll tell you frankly that not all of the miners take kindly to an outside team coming in, and some of 'em have prejudices about dwarves, even. But that's not to say it was on purpose. Our camp is right at the top of the ledge. It's the only space they'd give us. Most likely—" his voice broke. "Most likely, poor Raven just wasn't thinking or looking where he stepped."

Officer Thorn exchanged a look with me, and I knew what she was thinking. Lark's business was primarily a charity operation, mining materials for wheelchairs like the one she used and shipping them to the coast, where elves made each chair by hand. Most of Lark's employees bought into that cause and had become exemplary residents of Belville. Still, it was known across Beyond that some groups of people did not get along—trolls and dwarves being one such example. I wasn't aware of the history myself, but I knew there was bad blood there. And some of Lark's advisors were trolls.

"Would that have been a common occurrence?" Officer Thorn asked carefully. "Raven not looking where he was going?"

Pigeon hesitated, then nodded.

"He'd get distracted sometimes," Snow agreed, in a whisper.

For the final time, the officer nodded. "If that's everything, we'll get out of your hair for now. You know how to find me if you think of anything, right? Anyone in town can point you to the police station. I'll have Raven back to you as soon as possible. In the meantime, don't any of you go anywhere, you understand?"

Pigeon hesitated again. "But—"

"Of course we're not going anywhere," Snow interrupted. The flash in her eye as she lifted her head to look at Thorn echoed Lark's. "We're here to do a job."

"It's alright," Maeve hastened to say. "It's not like she suspects you or anything. We just need to, um . . ."

As one, the dwarves stepped back, rumbling. Thorn sighed.

"At present, we're treating this as an *accident,*" the officer repeated. Moving to Raven, she crouched carefully; though I knew she wore a back brace, anyone else would have thought she was simply dedicated to proper athletic procedure. With surprising delicacy, she picked Raven's body up out of the snow. None of us spoke as white flakes swirled around Thorn and the empty place at the base of the cliff.

"Don't you worry," Thorn added as she turned, indicating to Maeve and me that it was time to go. "We'll get to the bottom of this."

She waited until we were around a bend in the trail before leaning over to me with an apologetic grunt. "Not the best word, eh? Still, it is a *little* funny . . ."

"It isn't funny and you know it," I reprimanded, glancing back at Maeve before focusing again on Thorn. "Will you be okay carrying him?" He might have been short, but the dwarf was solid, almost as though he really had been hewn out of stone. He must have weighed three hundred pounds or more. I'd seen her carry bodies before, but no one built so . . . sturdily.

"This is nothing," Thorn assured me. "Did I ever tell you about the time my sister bet a troll she could beat him at a lift match? She ended up lifting him *and* the weight, which was made of a local stone that . . ."

Safe in the knowledge that Thorn *had*, in fact, told me that story before, I let my mind wander. The forest was quiet again, under the spell of a fresh blanket of snow. Through the treetops I could see smoke rising from the chimneys of Belville, the curls of gray accentuating the stillness of town. It didn't feel like the kind of place for murder.

Except that, as we discovered the moment we stepped out of the woods, Belville wasn't nearly as quiet as it seemed.

4

Stranger Danger

First we heard it from the baker, a kindly werewolf named Ginger. Then we heard it from Priya, who ran the local museum-aka-curiosity shop. When my neighbor Gloria met us on the corner of the market square, Thorn finally stopped her determined march to the police station.

"Not *another* of you with a complaint about a stranger to make," said the officer to Gloria, with good humor. "Can't you see I'm busy?"

Had Thorn said something so cavalier to Gloria a few months ago, Gloria's response would've been to stomp off. She probably would have been smoking as she did so, too. Literally smoking—Gloria is phoenixkin, which means that even though she's an elf, she has phoenix characteristics. Mostly that includes burnt orange skin, a red feathery crest instead of hair, and a temper best described as "fiery."

But today, Gloria merely crossed her arms and glared at the three of us. "Why is it you're always 'busy' or out of town when things are happening?"

"What things?" I asked quickly, hoping it wasn't more broken windows. Or querulous strangers.

Gloria's black eyes shifted to me. With one last sharp huff, she softened a little. "The miners happened, that's what. They came in just after lunch, looking to pick up Lark's order. Standing order for heavy-duty soaps and products they use at the mine," she added before Officer Thorn or I could ask. "That's not the important part. The important part is that they were harassing Johann, giving him a hard time about his looks, and if that knight hadn't stepped in it would've gotten ugly."

While Thorn looked over her shoulder at Maeve, making a series of faces which seemed to indicate *did you write that all down, assistant? I have my arms full*, I adopted Gloria's crossed-arm pose.

"What do you mean, 'ugly'? And what knight?"

A smile flickered across her face only briefly. "No idea. But he came in and told them off, real official-like, for making fun of Johann, then made sure they paid for the order properly. And it's a good thing, because if he hadn't I might have clocked them," she added sharply as she noticed that Maeve had finally produced a notebook. "I want a complaint sent up to Lark. And whoever that knight is, he should be thanked."

"You didn't get a chance yourself?" Thorn asked, shifting her grip on her burden.

Gloria huffed smoke. "He left at the same time the miners did. Said he had errands to run."

"Hmmm," said Thorn, looking thoughtful. "I wonder what exactly they were."

"There's been trouble in a few other places," I explained to Gloria. "At the bakery there was an argument, and Priya wanted to report a suspicious artifact. But they didn't say anything about miners."

"Could've been the knight himself," Thorn remarked. "We'll find out in time. Right now, frankly, none of this strikes me as more important than Raven here. If it's all the same to you, Gloria, I'll leave you in Maeve's hands. Red, I expect to see you at the station later." The officer turned to leave, but pivoted at the last moment. "Don't you have anti-theft charms up, Gloria?"

"I—those were a fairy thing." Gloria's cheeks grew crimson and she pursed her thin lips. Officer Thorn shrugged and continued on her way. *At least she knew better than to press the point,* I thought, thanking the universe for small blessings.

"I can talk to Trent for you if you like," I told Gloria quietly. I knew she wasn't a particular fan of our local Witch. "And in the meantime, William might be able to include your shop in his wards."

"It's just some soap, for ash's sake," Gloria exhaled, her breath practically sizzling in the frozen air. "I'm sure Lark will sort things out. As long as she doesn't send those goons again, I'm happy. I mean, thanks for offering, Red. Really. But you don't have to keep looking after me."

I hadn't realized that was what I was doing, but I appreciated her point. "Hey, I'm still trying to prove to you that having an alchemist for a neighbor isn't so bad," I joked.

Gloria cocked her head at me and almost smiled again. "You're not so bad. The mouthy dog that comes and goes at all hours of the night, on the other hand . . ." She shrugged, and we both chuckled. More soberly, she added, "Speaking of, though, you might want to check if William saw that knight too. Just in case."

"Did you?" asked Maeve suddenly. "See him, I mean. Um.

Can you give me a description?"

Gloria nodded slowly. "Sure. But you should probably speak to Johann first."

As Maeve moved toward the salon, I said to Gloria, "He made quite an impression, huh?"

"I just want to make sure justice is done," she returned. Nudging me with her elbow before she, too, went into the salon, she added, "You taught me that."

I stood there a moment, surprised. It wasn't that I'd expected Gloria to be personally interested in the knight—over the fall, Gloria had confided to me that she was aromantic and asexual, both common phoenixkin characteristics, and I knew firsthand that she didn't make friends easily. But I also hadn't thought she was taking a page from my own book. The idea gave me a warm feeling.

Setting that aside, I paced the few steps to my own store and went about questioning William.

* * *

"What are you talking about?"

William's dark eyes followed me as I paced around the counter and into my lab, shedding my cloak and starting up some water for another pot of tea. When I hesitated, trying to think of how to tell him everything that had happened so far, he added tartly, "I don't see why your ghost boyfriend would be visiting me."

"I do not, and never have had, a ghost boyfriend," I replied through gritted teeth. Thank goodness the shop is empty. I stared at the tea kettle, wondering if we should close up early. *How is it not evening already?* "And I wasn't asking about a ghost anyway. Everyone in town is up in arms about some stranger, it seems like. Gloria says he came by the salon at just the right moment and stood up for Johann. However . . ."

"'However' what?" William prompted.

"Well, I was just thinking that a stranger was seen around the miners' camp, too. Um," I said, realizing I hadn't caught William up on the situation with the dwarves. "I was just thinking, he could have been involved in something."

"In 'something.'" William deadpanned. "Sounds scintillating. Do tell."

"Stop that."

"Is it as scintillating as the fact that a certain bookseller stopped by the store again?"

I made a face at him and focused back on my mug. "Will you hush for a moment and let a person make some tea?"

"You could have had some of the tea out in the book corner. There haven't been any customers to drink it."

I actually had forgotten about that pot, which I liked to keep on hand for folks as they waited on orders. Making tea blends was a little hobby of mine, and offering free cups was a good way to advertise. I considered William's suggestion for a moment, trying to remember which tea I had put out that morning. One of the new matcha mixes, I recalled. I'd steered away from a strong black tea lest I end up drinking it all day and becoming jittery.

"No thanks," I told my annoying companion. "This one's just about to boil, anyway. Then I'll tell you all about it. You just have to wait one more minute."

From the recesses of the shop, someone coughed politely. "I don't suppose you're making an earl gray?"

* * *

My hands froze over my mug and open pot of loose tea. It *was*, in fact, a fragrantly floral earl gray. But somehow the tea didn't seem important.

"Sure she is," William said, his tail thumping against the legs of the stool he'd once again claimed. "She'll make you some."

"No problem," I agreed. My voice was distinctly more reluctant than William's. I've never understood how someone who can be so scornful can also put up such a good face in front of customers.

If in fact this *was* a customer. Trying to look nonchalant as I set up the cups, I scanned the shop through my lab window.

What daylight there had been, filtered through snowfall like cotton balls, had faded over the western side of town. The light from the chandelier, a concoction of crystal and multicolored flame, mixed with the spotlights and candles throughout the shop. Into this soft light, a tall man stepped very gently, as though he thought the tile floor might take offense.

At first glance he seemed human, maybe with fairy blood: pale, long features, dark hair. There was a grace to him that wasn't quite normal, and he was dressed like he'd stepped right out of a story book. Delicate chainmail winked at his neckline, sandwiched between layers of dark silk; silver-plated boots flashed from below the hem of a regal blue cloak.

"Thank you for your generosity, miss." The stranger addressed me quietly but with a clarity that reminded me of someone, though I couldn't put my finger on who. "As it happens, I have with me a little stock which I think you might appreciate as a token of my gratitude."

Is that so? I bit my tongue, reminding myself not to be too impressed by courtly manners. This guy was *definitely* out of place in Belville, and while his cloak was regal, it was also *huge*. He could be hiding any sort of "stock" or, more worryingly, weapons.

But he also *had* to be the knight Gloria had been talking about.

William sniffed the air. "Strangers bearing magical gifts. Isn't that usually a sign of a storm brewing?"

The knightly man bowed. "The weather is indeed precipitous, sir."

This exchange flew right over my head, but it must have amused William. The familiar barked out a laugh, tail wagging, as I emerged from my lab with two mugs of tea in hand. I set one on the counter for our visitor, who stepped forward and took it readily.

"You don't have to give us anything," I told him, inhaling steam from my own cup. "We're happy to serve."

"As am I, miss." The stranger drank from his mug, sighed gratefully, and added, "It was my intention upon seeing your alchemy shop to bring this to you. I have far too much for my own needs, but I hate to see it go to waste. I am certain that you will make good use of it."

One gloved hand disappeared into his cloak and reemerged holding a finely woven basket, about the size of a bunch of bananas. Its open top sparkled gold, indicating a spell which he removed with a wave of his hand as he set the basket on the counter.

William put his paws up on the counter and made some comment about containment spells which I ignored as I leaned in for a closer look. Our mysterious visitor had brought us a batch of unspoiled, unbroken, absolutely immaculate iceflower.

I straightened with one eyebrow raised. Iceflower is very difficult to pick correctly—it shatters easily, even for experienced gatherers like me.

"You harvested this?" I asked, interrupting the magic-nerd talk.

"I did, miss. You'll notice it was picked today, and is still quite fresh."

"Hmm. Then why'd you get more than you needed?"

"Jeez, Red," said William. "Now which one of us is the rude one?"

I frowned. I couldn't help my reaction; my old alchemical teacher, Paracelsus, had always drilled into us apprentices that a good gatherer never takes more than they need. It wasn't professional.

The man arched one fine eyebrow right back at me, as though he knew exactly why I was upset and found it amusing.

"Forgive me, miss," he said, with another slight bow. "Unfortunately, I don't deal with materials as precise as potions. It is often prudent to be amply prepared."

"What *do* you deal with?" I asked.

"Drinks, miss."

Drinks? I frowned. Who ever heard of a magic bartender? Particularly one wearing armor? Is *this the guy Gloria was talking about, after all?*

Before I could ask for clarification, the bells above the shop door jangled, and William called out a greeting.

"Hi William, hi Red, glad you weren't closed yet," the incoming voice said in one long breath. Even before I looked past Sir Bartender, I knew I'd see Luca, bookshop owner and local historian extraordinaire. "Listen, can you guys tell me something, friend-to-friend? Have I done something to Ginger? I went over there to get some double-chocolate cookies after I closed up shop and he spent the entire time yelling, really shouting at me, I couldn't even tell what he was talking about!"

"Cinnamon, sir," said the magic bartender. He pivoted and bowed impeccably, but Luca had already barreled past him, coming to rest against the sales counter with his green eyes wide.

"Cinnamon?" he repeated.

"Cinnamon," the stranger said emphatically, "does not belong in baked goods primarily flavored with chocolate."

Luca glanced at me. I shrugged. I adored baking, but I knew an argument not to meddle in when I saw one. I'd also just remembered who the stranger's voice reminded me of: Jade.

Perhaps he noticed my preoccupation, because Luca's gaze slid to William, who was even less help. Finally, Luca said uncertainly, "But . . . I never told him anything about spices. So it isn't me Ginger's mad at?"

"I think not, sir," said Sir Bartender. "I regret to inform you that *I* have been the cause of the disturbance."

5

Confessions

"**M**y name is Rowan," the stranger continued, as though we might need this information to understand his inclination to argue with bakers. William sneezed. "*Sir* Rowan, isn't it?"

"Yes, sir."

Aha! I thought, watching our visitor bow to William's correction. *I knew he was a knight.* I'd met a few of them on my travels. They were pretty much as one would expect: wandering, dragon-chasing, bowing minstrels mostly, in my experience. Many of them could cast little spells or carried magic objects, too. Usually they were attached to some local prominent family or ancient castle. I watched Sir Rowan, wondering if he'd tell us his allegiances.

My friends, however, were not so circumspect. "Hi, I'm Luca," our local historian said brightly. His habitual wide smile had returned, his green eyes and white teeth flashing against his dark skin. In his long black scholar's robe and hood—the only outfit I had *ever* seen him wear—he was just as striking a figure as Sir Rowan, if a little shorter and bubblier.

"I run the bookshop a block off the Square. I don't know everything about Belville, but I'm learning! If you have any questions, just let me know."

Sir Rowan acknowledged this introduction with a small but kindly smile. "I am certain you are too humble, sir. If you'll forgive me for pointing it out, the state of your robes speaks volumes to your dedication."

William, still presiding over our meeting from behind the counter, snickered. Scholars and booksellers across Pastoria dressed alike and belonged to a larger community, rather like Witches. But I doubted that was what Sir Rowan meant about a "state." In some places Luca's outfit was more gray than black, as he was too interested in reading his books and scrolls to bother dusting them.

"And you, miss, are naturally the owner of this establishment," said Sir Rowan, pivoting to me. I set my tea on the counter as I nodded. He continued, "Am I correct in presuming you are also the expert in finding lost objects, as advertised on your sign?"

I hesitated. To be precise, the sign hanging above my shop door read *Red's Alchemy and Potions,* with a recent subscript, *and object finding services.* "I wouldn't go so far as—"

"Red's wonderful at solving old mysteries," Luca enthused. "She helped me with a whole set of books, and a necklace besides. Are you in town to find something? What are you missing?"

"I doubt he's in town to start fights over cinnamon," William rumbled.

Sir Rowan cleared his throat, a genteel noise of disagreement. "I have already found what I am looking for. However, I may need your assistance in retrieving it. In fact, I would like to hire you, Miss Red."

* * *

While I flipped the sign on the door to "closed" and Luca eagerly rearranged the chairs in the shop's reading nook, Sir Rowan watched gravely. He remained standing before the three of us as we sat and listened to a tale which he insisted Luca listen to as well.

"I serve a very ancient family of water fairies on the shores of the Lake of the Green Dale," he began, naming a lake I didn't recognize. "Twenty-two years ago, the daughter of this family formed a—ahem—a regrettable alliance with a neighboring rival, an alliance which did not result in an official marriage, but nonetheless produced a child. Naturally, the matriarch of the family was much distressed. However, the daughter kept her child and raised it for eleven years before, most regrettably, passing away. At that point, it was no longer practicable to keep the child in court with the rest of the family. On my advice, the matriarch sent her grandchild to live a very different life in the nearby woods. Since that day another ten years have passed, and the matriarch has decided that it is time for the child to reclaim her place in the family. Thus it has fallen to me to hunt down her whereabouts."

As Sir Rowan spoke in his archaic language, I translated in my mind. The daughter of a powerful family had a fling with someone the family didn't approve of, ended up with a child, and did her best to raise it despite a lot of push back, it sounded like. Knowing that water fairies could live extremely long lives if they weren't injured or ill, I had a bad feeling about what might have happened to the mother. *Life in that court sounds fraught,* I decided. *Maybe it was better for the child—the girl—to live somewhere else. But why the change of heart from the matriarch?* I wrinkled my nose as I thought of this and recalled the word Sir Rowan had used. "'Hunt'?"

"The word was an unfortunate one," Sir Rowan acknowledged. "It would be better to say that I was asked to find and retrieve her. The matriarch has had time to reflect upon her actions and regret them. My task has been a difficult one, however, as no one has heard from the child in the intervening years. Shortly after being placed with a local shepherd, she left to find her own . . . companions, and even a line of work."

"We don't do *people,* though," William said, looking at me. "Objects are enough trouble as it is."

"Oh, I have already located the child, and any responsibility for convincing her to return home lies with me alone," Sir Rowan assured him.

"In that case, why come to Red?" Luca asked.

At this, Sir Rowan turned fully to me. "Would I be correct in thinking you have been on the mountain this afternoon?" I nodded reluctantly and he continued, "Then I have faith that you realize the nature of my problem. Matters at the mine are complicated by the discovery of a material mistakenly named 'quintessence,' and while that complication ensues, the child and her companions are loath to leave."

Despite my doubts, I smiled wryly. "I've been *trying* to tell Thorn that they're wrong about the 'quintessence' thing. But I haven't seen it yet."

"Of course, my own powers of judgment in this field are nothing compared to yours," Sir Rowan told me gallantly, "but in my opinion, the material in question is nothing more than corrupted ore."

"Ore corrupted by what?" As a historian first and foremost, Luca was out of his depth with mineral talk. The look on his face was one of puzzlement as he tried to keep up.

"By something you would recognize, perhaps," said the knight, looking down at the scholar. "You are surely familiar with an old tale regarding the origin of the mountain on which Belville rests?"

In the expectant pause, Luca glanced around at us. "Well, there's a bunch of them, stories about the mountain, I mean. But there is a recurring theme of terrible dragons—specifically, the guardian of the Tree of Life, often depicted as an apple tree. They say the guardian retreated here at the beginning of the world and built itself a great fortress as a home, and that fortress is our mountain now. . . . And that anyone who goes too close will be incinerated. Most of the stories are pretty insistent upon that fact, actually."

"A fortress for the Apples of Life," said Sir Rowan, summarizing very neatly while managing to leave out the most concerning bits.

I was a lot less nonchalant. "You're saying you think a mythological tree guarded by a dragon has corrupted the mine?"

"No, miss." Sir Rowan turned back to me, and for a moment I could swear I saw him smirk. "Begging your pardon. I'm saying that a very real magical object has corrupted a certain vein deep in the mountain. I am certain that, were a dragon present, the miners would have discovered it by now."

"That *is* a good point," Luca mused, a faraway look in his eye suggesting that he was thinking over all his old scrolls and histories as we spoke.

"I don't do dragons," I told Sir Rowan pointedly, just to make things extra clear.

"Naturally, miss," he responded with a slight bow. "Were a dragon present, that would, of course, be more in my line. However, I can assure you, there is not. Perhaps it has left the Apples, thinking them well protected; perhaps it was never there at all. Nonetheless the Apples *are* present, and you are more equipped to find and identify them than I. Therefore I am asking you to put an end to this controversy at the mine by finding them. Once you have done so and matters at the mine are concluded, I am confident I can complete my task."

"Convincing Snow to go home," I clarified, keeping a level eye on him. "I've met her."

"Naturally. She and her companions are camped along the trail leading toward the mine, of course," Sir Rowan allowed with a slight bow.

His immediate acknowledgment of the geography—the geography where Raven had fallen to his death—concerned me. And as he bowed, I could have sworn I got a whiff of lakeweed.

But Gloria had insisted that Sir Rowan had helped her and Johann, and I couldn't ignore that, either. I decided to test him a little bit. "Have you met the other miners, too? Today at the salon?"

"I did encounter some miners while procuring soap and other necessities," he answered patiently. "They did not strike me favorably."

"Uh huh." I thought about this as I watched him, conscious that William and Luca were watching me. I wanted to give Sir Rowan an answer, but I didn't want it to be one I'd regret. *Look into the ore—which I was going to have to do already—and share information with him and Snow and the miners; well, that's fine. All the talk about dragons and court life is disconcerting. But he's clearly not one to talk without reason, and from what Gloria said, he'll stand up for what's right.*

And if I don't help him, he'll probably just get involved on his own. Or even, I thought, glancing at my friends, *draw Luca or William into it.*

"Sure," I said at last. "I'll look into the ore and share the report with you. But it'll take a little time, because I promised Officer Thorn to help with the investigation of Raven's death, first."

"That is all I could ask of you, miss," said Sir Rowan gallantly. "I promise you will be amply compensated by the fairies I represent. I'll check back with you tomorrow, if that is acceptable."

"That's fine," I said, holding out my hand to shake on it. *This way I can help Gloria even out the score, and at the same time help keep my friends safe.*

* * *

A little while later, after Sir Rowan had taken his leave and I began to long for dinner, Luca was still asking questions. "What do you think, Red? How do we find the ore in the first place?"

I sighed. William huddled over the safe, glowing as he ran through the last security checks before closing the shop. "Like I told Sir Rowan, I'll cross that bridge after helping Officer Thorn with Raven." In the dimmed light of the shop, I made an exasperated face at Luca.

Luca, who had much better vision in the dark than I'd remembered to give him credit for, saw my expression and chuckled. "I just think it sounds like the kind of thing that'd be perfect for you. I mean, aside from the dragon. But really, how likely is it that a *dragon* has been hiding right next to Belville all these years? And anyway if it was, a knight would know, right?"

"I sure hope so," I admitted. "To be honest, it's the story he told about the family that makes me worry, more than anything else. Especially since it was so vague."

"But he said where he came from," Luca interrupted.

I snorted. "'Lake of the Green Valley' or whatever? Is that even a real place?"

"Well, *that*'s not a place, but the Lake of the Green Dale is," Luca laughed again. "People know it as Lake Greendale these days. You know, right over by Pine? It's a huge lake, so I know you've heard about it. It's supposed to be really nice actually. I'm pretty sure that's what he meant, anyway."

Knowing the collection of old maps he had squirreled away in his shop, I was willing to bet Luca was right. "Okay, so do you know what family he was talking about, then?"

William stopped glowing abruptly. "Done. And you know, you might not want to pry too deeply into the backstory of a knight like that, Red. They used to call them 'huntsmen' for a reason."

"That's the strange thing," Luca was saying meanwhile. "Supposedly there's a whole underwater palace for a society of water fairies inside the lake, but they never get involved with the locals. I bet they only ever do business through representatives, like Sir Rowan."

"Kind of like the Drus?" I asked Luca with a small smile, referring to his heritage as a very secretive kind of woodland elf.

But rather than replying chirpily, Luca faltered. "Yeah, I guess—yeah, something like that."

Oh dear, I realized belatedly. *Good going, Red, remind him about the family he's lost . . .* I could have smacked myself on the forehead. The thing was, I was never sure how much Luca actually *remembered* from his time in Drus society. Or the times when he was cursed to live as Jade. "Sorry," I said hastily. "I didn't mean to—"

"It's alright," Luca was saying. "Actually, I—"

But I felt too guilty to listen. I kept talking, interrupting him. "I think we better call it a night," I decided. "I still have to check with Officer Thorn, and I'm already tired and saying silly things. It's been a long day."

6

Cross Examination

It had been a long day, but it wasn't over yet. Luca left quickly, but I still had to catch William up on everything that had happened. By the time I made it to the police station as Thorn had asked, it was well into the evening.

And I still hadn't eaten. And it was *still* snowing.

The police station squatted at the edge of town, a few blocks from my own store along one of the main roads into the Square from the forest. With its overhanging shutters and wooden beams, the station somewhat resembled the forest it kept watch over. Its tiny front yard and bench were buried in snow, but a magic spell kept the path to the front door clear.

As I shut the front door behind me, wind swirled around my snow-encrusted cloak. Officer Thorn looked up from the front desk—the primary piece of furniture in the station's main room—and opened her mouth at once. Knowing from experience that she was about to reprimand me for being late, I held up a hand. A hand carrying a hand-knitted bag, which in turn carried two large traveling mugs of tea.

Thorn fell upon the tea without a word. Her silence

47

indicated that she'd been working as hard as I had been, and doubtless had some interesting stories to tell. I waited until I'd hung my cloak on a nearby hat tree and shook the snow from my boots before asking. Meanwhile, the wood-paneled, rather severe little police station filled with the scent of vanilla and ginger as Thorn downed her cup of warming tea.

"I know I should have got here sooner," I said. Thorn shrugged as she sat on her desk and wiped her lips, and the gesture made me smile. "I have a good reason, though. I think I met your rabble-rouser. And Johann's savior."

Thorn tilted her head, her pointy ears sticking out like the wings on a child's paper plane. "Showed up at your shop to argue with you about cinnamon, did he?"

I laughed as I sipped from my own mug, which I'd made sure to keep a hand on lest Thorn drink it down too. "No. To be fair, he owned up about that pretty easily, and he confessed to running into some miners at the salon, too."

"He sure gets around," Thorn said. "So who was it?"

"Someone in very nice armor, that's for sure. He said his name's Sir Rowan, and that he serves a clan of water fairies over in—what was it?—Lake something or another. He's here to look for Snow."

"For snow?" Thorn rose one eyebrow and I knew she was thinking about how to turn that into a pun before she realized who I meant. "Oh, *that* Snow," she said, not concealing her disappointment. Her eyes narrowed. "Quite the coincidence that a fancy out-of-towner shows up and then one of the girl's companions ends up dead. And she didn't mention anything about him or any fairy parents. I take it that 'we' includes the meddling scholar?"

I winced. Luca and Officer Thorn had a checkered past,

mostly because she'd suspected him of murder for about five days.

But now, Thorn simply chuckled. "Figured. Neither you nor that dog of yours are very good about local geography yet. Stopped by the bookstore for some gossip before attending to your duties, did you?"

"I did not! Luca was there when Sir Rowan came in, and he insisted on talking to all of us. Sir Rowan did, I mean. Also, looking at dead bodies isn't a duty, it's a favor I'm doing for you. In exchange for food, I might add!"

Thorn pushed herself off her desk, landing quite lightly for someone so large. "When there's a potential murder, *everyone* is duty-bound to help. That's on page two of the Guild guidebook."

"Well, I didn't go to the police guild, I apprenticed as an *alchemist*," I muttered rebelliously as I fell into step behind the Officer.

"The other dwarves gave me full permission," said Officer Thorn, speaking loudly so that I understood that she hadn't heard my complaint, "to go through the Guild checklist. I already did, of course. Maeve and I went through it while we were waiting for you."

"Where is Maeve?" I asked, realizing suddenly what had been missing from the station. I'd already gotten used to Maeve's shadow hovering over Thorn's shoulder. As we crossed the main room, passing by Thorn's office and the basement stairs, I looked in through the doorways as though Thorn's assistant might be hiding somewhere.

"Getting the rest of the employee records and accident reports from Lark. Ought to be back any time," Thorn said.

I paused on the threshold of the back room, which served

as a mortuary for the station. "You sent her out into the forest alone?"

"She's got to go sometime, hasn't she? Besides, it's not the full moon." Officer Thorn turned and grinned at me toothily. She was joking: Belville was usually quite safe, and our one family of werewolves—Ginger and his kids—were more interested in cake than carnivorous hunts, no matter what phase the moon was in. Still, I always preferred to be safe rather than sorry.

"Like I said, we already took a look." Thorn gestured in front of her. She stood in the corner of the small room opposite the door; between us lay the one piece of furniture, a large table, currently holding up the deceased dwarf. Along the walls around us, shelves held miscellaneous tools and bottled charms, and many books—no doubt copies of Thorn's infamous guidebook. She relied on its checklists to make sure her surveys—be they of bodies, sites, or objects—were thorough. Even so, she preferred to have me look things over, too; as the kind of person who's most comfortable when speaking aloud to (or perhaps berating) someone else, she lacked her usual confidence when it came to methodical searches.

"No injuries aside from those caused by the fall," she continued, "and nothing of note that we could find in his pockets. Didn't even have his mining gear with him. But neither Maeve nor I have special vision, so I'd like you to take a look with your magic glasses. And maybe that magnet you used last time."

"They aren't magic, they're alchemical," I muttered good-naturedly as I pulled said convenience down over my eyes. My goggles *are* a bit magical, truthfully. While I liked to think of myself and my tools as scientific, the glass in my goggles did have some magic enhancements, things like an automatic zoom and enhanced night vision.

With an outward breath, I reminded myself to focus on the task at hand. By applying pressure at the wrists of the fingerless gloves which, like my goggles, I nearly always wore, I activated a mechanism that made griffon-talon tips close over my fingers. Setting aside my scarf and satchel of tools, I moved toward the body.

Raven was quite typical for a dwarf, physically. He wore miner's clothes like the others had, thickly-woven brown pants and a neon green tank top. That made sense to me; working miners preferred bright colors that were easily distinguishable from dark and shadowy caves. His heavy steel-toed boots, too, were no surprise. I moved carefully, not wanting to look too closely at any injuries. I wouldn't have anything helpful to say about those, anyway. Though I did make a few medicinal potions, I tended to avoid the healing arts and sciences.

A careful scan of the body revealed nothing helpful. Obliging Thorn's other request, I fished a strong, rectangular magnet out of my bag and ran it over the body. I'd already lifted my head to tell Thorn I'd had no luck when I felt a tug toward the dwarf's waist.

"Something there?" Thorn saw my reaction and was on it immediately. I let the magnet guide my hand toward the hem of Raven's shirt and Thorn inspected the area for me. After a moment of running her hand over the fabric, she pulled something free with a triumphant "Aha!"

I finished my magnet scan, just in case, and then tucked the tool away. Officer Thorn, in the meantime, examined her find.

"It's a money pouch," she said, holding the small, dark object aloft. On close inspection it turned out to be a leather rectangle, only as long as her pinky finger. "Made to fit in the clothes perfectly flat in a secret pocket. We never would have found it."

"Why would it have iron in it?" I pursed my lips. My magnet was only a magnet, after all, and couldn't find hidden money-pouches unless they were magnetic too.

"The lacing's reinforced with iron," Thorn said, leaning over the table to show me. "It's an old superstition. My grandda had one just like this. It's to ward off fairies and other tricksters stealing your money. Outdated these days, of course," she added, seeing my look at her description of fairies. Sure, we had dealt with some tricksters in the past, but police officers were expected to be neutral.

"So, what's inside?" I asked, turning to more practical matters.

Thorn undid the lacing carefully and upended the pouch over her broad hand. Nothing but a slip of paper fluttered down.

"Promissory note," she said as she caught the paper and turned it over. "Signed by one Frost of Poole." That combination of names must have meant something to Thorn, because she said it exactly like the concluding line in the second act of a dramatic play.

It meant nothing to me, but before I had a chance to point that out, a cold gust of wind blew Maeve in through the station's front door.

* * *

For a little while, the station was a whirlwind of pandemonium as Maeve attempted to make her report, I tried desperately to keep up with the conversation, and Officer Thorn ordered everyone around. It wasn't until Thorn and I had departed for dinner, leaving Maeve to watch the front desk, that I managed to get any sense out of the officer. And even then, all she would talk about was food.

Though there were several places to eat in Belville, not least my own cozy kitchen, Lavender's was a perennial favorite of Thorn's—and I couldn't blame her. Lavender's Tavern reigned over Market Square. It was halfway across town from the police station, diagonally across the Square from my own shop, but it was well worth the trek. The two-story wooden building had become stately with age rather than old, its dark timbers framing warm windows and paisley curtains. No matter the season, Lavender always had a few guests staying in the rooms upstairs.

Lavender herself was the sort of person who was unfailingly warm and inviting without ever giving away anything about herself; everything I knew about her was more rumor than fact. Some said she and her tavern had been around since before the founding of the town. Some said she was half angel, or even all angel, and that's why she had feathers caught in her silvery hair and eyes the color of her name. Some said her food was actually a blessing in physical form.

That last one might have been true.

With her white apron billowing around her ample body and her clear voice, Lavender was the one person I knew who could give Thorn a real run for her money. Lavender's authority was undisputed as she informed us gaily that we were very late for dinner, and that we would have to sit at the bar and eat leftover gnocchi and consider ourselves lucky.

"So spill," I told Thorn, once we were settled on our stools and the steaming mug of cider in my hand had thawed me. At both ends of the room around us, fires flickered in massive hearths. A few small groups of guests and locals lounged around tables, most savoring their last drink of the evening. The smell of hot chocolate wafted through the air, mingling with ash as the fires slowly subsided and lemony soap as Lavender's employees began to clean up the kitchen. "Who is Frost and why would he or she or they be paying Raven?"

"He," said Thorn, her eyes fixed on the door to the kitchen as though our food might escape before we knew it. "Ask Luca about the ice fairies of Poole and the water fairies of Greendale."

I would, but in the meantime, I could catch the gist. I remembered Sir Rowan's talk about a 'rival family.' "Let me guess. They're engaged in a centuries-long feud with the water fairies?"

Plates of gnocchi appeared, doused in basil and butter, and Thorn beamed. "Something like that," she said, fork in hand, her mouth already full of pasta. "And with your knight in town representing the other side, and a mysterious ore and a dwarf dead, I don't like it. This is delicious."

I smothered a laugh behind my napkin, because *I* at least had manners. She was right about the pasta, but I protested about the rest. "He isn't *my* knight. Not every mysterious person who turns up in town is automatically *mine*, you know. And I thought you said it was an accident?"

Thorn sat back, wiping at her mouth. "It is, for now. The thing is, Red," she said, lowering her voice, "I went up there on that cliff. There weren't any prints, except the ones left by that dwarf you met. Goose."

I saw her problem. No signs of altercation made for a very uncooperative crime scene. Snow the snow-fairy probably walked on top of snow drifts, like Maeve, but Sir Rowan in all his chainmail probably did not, and the dwarves certainly didn't. "Wait, what about Raven, the one who fell? Had he left prints?"

"Nothing I could see. But he'd been missing since this morning, so the snow could have covered them."

I waved a ball of delicious potato dough in her direction, frowning. "Do you really think it would have covered *everything* in that time, though? Dwarves leave wide trails, from what I saw."

"Maybe he was snowshoeing."

"And what, the snowshoes splintered into teeny tiny pieces when he went over the cliff?" I raised an eyebrow.

Officer Thorn had the grace to look sheepish, a fact she nearly hid by leaning over her plate. "Or maybe they were stolen."

"In which case we still would have seen prints at the bottom of the cliff," I retorted. "It has to be a cover up."

"Or it could have been an accident, like I thought," Thorn said testily. "Aren't you the one always telling me not to leap to conclusions?"

I sighed. I'd finished off my meal, and sat for a moment looking at the bar without seeing it. I hadn't meant to fight with Thorn. I wondered if I could get Lavender to make me some of that hot chocolate. "Oh no," I said aloud, as another thought struck me. "I forgot you weren't there to hear it. Sir Rowan essentially said that Snow's father came from the rival family, which we now know is the Frosts."

"Does Snow know that?" Officer Thorn asked pointedly. "And do the Frosts know about Snow?"

I pursed my lips. "I don't know. I mean, I suppose she knows she's different from the other water fairies. But all this information came from Sir Rowan, not her. I really don't know much at all."

"Don't you worry," Thorn said with a burp. "We'll figure out more tomorrow. You're coming with us when we go to talk to the rest of the team. Including Snow."

All thoughts of hot chocolate flew out of my head. "Me? Why?"

"Because you've seen Sir Rowan, and I haven't. Now, I'll make inquiries," Thorn said, anticipating my protest. "I'll ask Lavender right now. But unless he's *very* foolish, he's probably nowhere to be found. And that makes you our leading witness."

7

Let it Go

Though Officer Thorn might have been lacking in the social graces department, she knew her town (and the criminals passing through it). Neither hide nor hair of a knight in blue could be found in Belville overnight, exactly as she predicted. And so I was indeed on the hook.

Unfortunately for me, my morning got off to another rocky start. There wasn't any broken glass and snow in the apartment, at least. But as I bumbled around the kitchen in the winter dark, I found evidence of just how distracted I'd been the day before. The butter crock, which I usually kept on top of the icebox (I could never decide if I should put it in or leave it out, and somehow keeping it on top was a compromise), tilted dangerously on the edge of the sink. All my brightly-embroidered kitchen towels lay in a heap at the corner of the ceramic stove. And every single cabinet door lining the corner kitchen seemed awry.

Not to mention I couldn't find the brown sugar for my morning tea. Mug in one hand, teapot in the other, I pursed my lips and glanced around the kitchen again. "How in Beyond did I make such a mess yesterday? Was *I* the one that did this?"

William snored in his window seat in the opposite corner, so I figured the apartment was safe. I shook my head and opted for honey in my tea instead. By the time I'd packed up my travel mug (charmed never to spill), wrapped a cheesy bagel in a handkerchief, and donned my boots, Officer Thorn was knocking at the back door.

I ran downstairs to let her in before she froze in place. The day was dawning crisp and clear and much colder than I'd like. Of course, I needn't have worried too much about the Officer; dressed in her usual uniform, hatless, she seemed like she couldn't even feel the cold. The same could be said for Maeve, wavering behind her shoulder. I bit back an envious sigh. *Maybe their uniforms have some kind of spell on them. Maybe I should look into that . . .*

"Just let me put up a sign on the shop door," I said to them both by way of hello, waving a paper note in one hand. "William's opening the shop for me, but I have a feeling he'll be running late."

"Lateness in assistants is no good," Thorn said firmly. "Unless they're zombies."

Maeve gulped audibly.

I groaned at the pun on "late" as I raced through the shop. Once my task was done and I'd joined Officer Thorn and Maeve on the back patio, I explained, "I woke him up early yesterday, so I wanted to give him a reprieve this morning."

"Why'd you wake him yesterday?" Thorn asked as we made our way around the shop to the street.

"I thought something got into the apartment," I told her, and explained the kitchen escapade. In hindsight, it seemed almost funny; it certainly struck Thorn that way. Her guffaw rang out across the silent Market Square.

I harrumphed, even though I couldn't hide my grin. "I guess you haven't had any other reports of housebreaking?"

"By an invisible, tiny, flying thing? No," Thorn chuckled. "Come on, double time. We've got a lot to do today."

And with that she hastened up to marching speed, leading us down a side street that would take us to the mine path up the mountain. Around us, the snow had turned crystalline, and the smoke rising above the peaked roofs felt ethereal. It would have made for a very good contemplative walk, if it weren't for the sad reason behind our errands. I tucked into my bagel as I tagged along behind Thorn, thinking about the dwarves and the feuding families of fairies.

We made it halfway up the trail, under heavy pine boughs and the beginnings of morning light, before the silence was broken. To my surprise, it was Maeve who spoke.

At first, she just cleared her throat. But when Officer Thorn turned around, the assistant gathered her courage and said, "Um, there's—there's another way if you want to take it. A shortcut. I just thought . . . since you said . . ."

"Lead away," said Thorn, though as she continued to eye Maeve thoughtfully as we veered off the main path. "How did you come to know about this, assistant?"

"Last night, I . . ." Maeve shrugged, batting a low-hanging branch away from her shoulder on the much narrower trail. "The dwarves showed it to me."

This seemed to be all she had to say on the subject. Officer Thorn turned back to look at me, now that I was at the rear of our little party. The look in her eyes seemed to say, *only a few days in Belville and this new recruit's already taking initiative!*

I had a suspicion that Maeve's initiative had more to do with being love-struck than eager to please as a police officer, but I kept that to myself. After all, the shortcut *was* quite handy. In one breath-taking scramble, we climbed up the far side of the cliff I'd stood under the day before. It was tough, but worth it: we arrived behind the dwarves' camp just as they were leaving for work.

Maeve, who had led us up the trail, sped up and slipped between the heavy canvas tents. Thorn and I followed, breaking into the semi-circle and nearing a dying fire in time to see Maeve chase down Snow on the road to the mines. All around us, dwarves were gathering tools and washing out breakfast bowls and yelling at each other. It sounded as though we'd walked into a circus of elephants, not a camp for six dwarves and a fairy. I looked on, unable even to hear my own thoughts, as Maeve and Thorn singled out Snow and sent the dwarves to work. Or they tried to, at least: the leader, Pigeon, insisted on staying with Snow, "for moral support."

Eventually the other five dwarves rumbled off down the road in a cloud of icy dust, and I heaved a sigh of relief. *They said this was the only land available to camp on, but maybe the noise was another reason to keep them apart from everyone else,* I thought, grinning to myself. I hated to think that yet *another* reason might be the attitudes of Lark's trollish advisors.

"Right," Officer Thorn said, rubbing her hands together. She gestured, and the five of us shuffled around the fire pit, taking seats on various stumps and rocks which the dwarves had arranged into the classic primitive camping kitchen-dining room combo. Snow waited until the last moment and sat opposite the officer, a sullen, distrustful look on her gorgeous face. Her work clothes today were vibrant pink and left her arms bare—arms which had no more muscle tone than mine, despite the very heavy-looking pickax strapped to her back. When Pigeon sat beside her, she leaned into him as though tempted to hide behind him.

"We've got some questions for you," Thorn continued. "And Pigeon, you may as well chime in as well. First off, do you know anything about a deal with the Frosts?"

Snow's distrustful look slid into confusion. "You mean a deal between Lark and the Frosts?"

"We haven't had anything to do with them," Pigeon added gruffly.

Officer Thorn shifted and tried a different approach, focusing on Snow. "When was the last time you talked to your family?"

Snow straightened, frowning, her eyes fixed on the Officer. "The people *here* are my family."

"All right then, when was the last time you talked to your parents," Thorn tried again, unruffled.

"Basically never." Snow hesitated, then waved one paper-white hand. "I never even knew my father. My mother, she—she had other things going on. She passed away about ten years ago, if that's what you want to know. But I don't think I ever really *talked* to any of the rest of the family. Why?"

Maeve shuffled on her boulder, but Thorn quieted her with a glance. "Understood. And have you had any contact from anyone representing either parent during the past ten years?"

"No."

"Are you sure about that? No one at all?"

Snow stood abruptly. "Listen, it doesn't matter, okay? All of that is in the past. It's over. I never fit in there, and even if I wanted to, I'm not going back. My place is *here.*"

She sat again, as though her vehemence had unnerved her.

I found I could sympathize. I, too, had left my home and didn't plan to return any time soon. Of course, in my case, leaving had been voluntary; Sir Rowan's story, if it could be believed, indicated that Snow had been turned out. I couldn't imagine the hurt she must feel. And, looking at her wavering eyes and resolute chin, I was reminded that she was still very young—barely out of her teens.

"What matters is the truth," Officer Thorn insisted. "I'm not here to tell you to choose either way. But yesterday your teammates were talking about strangers around the camp, and I need to know if you knew who they were."

"Snow," said Pigeon. I couldn't tell if the word was meant to be a warning or a reassurance.

"I—I may have seen someone," Snow admitted at last. "But you can't tell any of the Flock, okay?"

"That's what you and the dwarves call yourselves?" As Snow nodded miserably, Thorn looked pointedly at Maeve, who took a long moment to realize she was supposed to be writing down details. As she hastened to pull out a notebook and pencil, Thorn went on, "I won't tell anyone unless it's absolutely necessary. Now. Who did you see, and what did they say?"

"His name's Rowan. He stopped me in the forest outside camp a day ago," Snow sighed. "Not yesterday, the day before. Around dinner time. He's worked for my mom's family for, I don't know, forever. But I don't really know much about him and I don't want to."

"Tall, blue armor, dark hair?" Thorn turned her commanding gaze on me, and I leaned forward, confirming the description with Snow. She nodded along absently, though she seemed uninterested in anything I had to say.

"Sure," she agreed as I finished. Then a thought seemed to occur to her and she added hastily, "But he isn't a murderer or anything. He just wanted me to go back."

"Go back?" Pigeon seemed ruffled by this. In fact, his immediate and almost brotherly concern for Snow made me smile.

Thorn tilted her head. "I didn't say he had anything to do with Raven's death."

Snow's lips went flat as though they'd literally been zipped shut, and pink bloomed on her cheeks. Maeve dropped her pencil. In the ensuing pause, I realized that Snow really had no reason to protect Sir Rowan or her family, unless somehow *she was involved* in their actions.

I cleared my throat. "Snow, am I right in thinking you have power over snow drifts and ice?"

"Not ice," she said, her voice cracking. "It's too hard. Not water either. My mother always wanted me to, but it just slips away from me. I can only—only—"

"We shouldn't bother her," Maeve said, her voice barely above a mumble.

But Thorn had caught on to my train of thought. "You can shape snow. Does that include making an area of churned-up snow look flat and undisturbed?"

Snow's face crumpled. She clutched her arms around herself, as though hiding an offending weapon—her own hands. "I didn't mean to. I thought—I thought he'd just come by to talk to me again, that morning. He won't give up until I say yes, at least, that's what *he* thinks. I just thought he'd been by camp to talk and I didn't want anyone to know because it'd only upset them," she said, her words ending in tears that bounced down her cheeks, tiny twin trails of ice.

Pigeon enveloped her in a side hug at once. Maeve leapt up as though to offer Snow a handkerchief, but she made it all the way across the fire ring only to realize that her pockets were empty. She stood there beside the hunched fairy, gangly and awkward, until I tossed her the cloth from my breakfast. It was reasonably free of bagel crumbs, and I figured it'd save Maeve some face. For just an instant, Maeve beamed at me gratefully, catching the handkerchief and passing it down. Snow didn't so much as look up as she took it.

Officer Thorn stood too, her face grave. "The snow around the campsite was trampled the morning Raven fell?"

A hiccup escaped Snow, and she nodded.

"Did you recognize the prints?"

Snow paused, and with her ensuing head waggle communicated uncertainty.

Officer Thorn sighed. "This Sir Rowan character. He didn't say why he wants you to come home so bad?"

Snow shook her head.

"And you haven't heard anything from anyone else?"

Another shake.

"Although—wait," Snow said suddenly, lifting her head. "I did hear from Lark. Yesterday night. She wanted to—to—"

"Extend the olive branch," Pigeon finished for her.

"Yes, that's it," Snow said, nodding. "She offered us some other things to do around the mine. To help—with expenses, that is—"

"She's paying out for Raven," Pigeon clarified, no doubt referring to Lark. "But she said as how we might need the extra money on top of that, if we're thinking of leaving."

My ears pricked up. *Maybe Lark* wants *them to leave?*

But my thoughts were confused when Snow went on, "She

said we didn't have to go back to the mine if we didn't want to. We could do—do errands around town."

"A fine idea," Officer Thorn said, looking not unkindly at the distraught fairy. "Why don't you have Red here help you with that? And in the meantime," she added, turning to Maeve, "it sounds like we need to question everyone else more thoroughly. Come along; we're headed to the mine first."

8

Mirror, Mirror

As the others left, Snow mumbled something about a list and disappeared into a tent. Rather than stare after her—especially since she probably wanted to wash up a bit—I looked around the camp. In summer weather, it would have been quite nice. Notwithstanding the dangerous cliff, of course. The drop was about twenty paces from the semicircle of tents, which were snugged up against the mountainside. The lack of trees on the narrow ridge meant that the site had a great view of Belville, though.

"I've got it," Snow said reluctantly as she emerged behind me. I turned, doing my best to look friendly. She added, "I guess it's good that you'll know where to go to get this stuff. But who even are you, again? You're not a police officer?"

"Definitely not," I told her. She'd lifted her head at last, her blue eyes scanning my face warily. "I'm an alchemist. I have a shop down in town. I just help out Officer Thorn sometimes."

"An alchemist?" Snow's brow wrinkled. "Like with potions?"

"Some potions, yeah," I confirmed, thinking that either Snow wasn't very highly educated, or was very sheltered, or both.

Not that any of those things were her fault, young as she was. "But also minerals and powders. Scientific doodads, and the occasional—"

But Snow had stiffened. "Rowan does potions. Are you—are you with him?"

"No," I said again, half wondering if I needed to make myself a pin saying "free agent!". The other half of me wondered quite a bit about Sir Rowan. "He did talk to me a bit yesterday, though. He said something about making drinks?"

"Drinks, potions, whatever." Snow shrugged.

As some of her tension eased, I took the opportunity to start guiding us down the path into town. As we walked, Snow still wouldn't quite look at me—but she did keep her head up, at least. Seeing that she'd lost interest in suspecting me, I ventured a question of my own. "Are you sure he wasn't involved in what happened yesterday?"

"I don't know. I mean, he wouldn't ever kill anyone. Unless my grandmother told him to," Snow said, making the realization as she spoke it aloud. She turned to me with wide eyes. As I'd suspected, she was walking on top of the snow, which put her almost level with my shoulder. "You don't think Grandmother sent him to go after the Flock, do you?"

"If she did, he definitely didn't say anything to me about it," I answered. "Does that seem like something they would do?"

Snow bit her ruby lip. "I don't know what they would do. I don't know them any more."

I could sense lots of unshed—and shed—tears behind that statement, and I hesitated. The wandering child in me ached for her. Very gently, I said, "Are you sure about that, Snow?"

"It was so long ago. I was a different me back then. I've changed. *They* might have changed," Snow said, casting her eyes down.

"One thing alchemy has taught me," I said, keeping my voice even and neutral, "is that no matter how much something changes, there's still a little core left of itself."

Snow seemed to ponder this, and we walked along in silence until we reached Market Square.

It turned out that the first errand Lark had included in her list for Snow was a stop by the hardware store. I led Snow across the park, toward the southeastern corner of the Square. There, an old brick building leaned against its neighbor like it was trying its best to claim just a *little* bit of park-front property. The sole picture window was jammed full of all sorts of practical things—albeit some for a different season entirely: wheels, tools, portable chairs, umbrellas, buckets, and even a child's sandcastle mold jostled for room. Plenty of dust was in evidence, too, and the letters painted across the window, *Tools & Hardware for Generations*, could have used a little attention. I smiled almost apologetically at Snow as I gestured her through the front door.

Perhaps understandably, she gestured back for me to go first.

When at last I gave up on being polite and stepped up into the store, I collided with Luca, who'd been on his way out.

"Red! Red, I'm so sorry, are you okay?" He put his arms around me like he was worried I'd topple over at any moment.

"I'm fine," I said, still trying to clear the stars out of my vision from Luca's forehead banging into mine. Blushing, I did my best to shuffle myself and him out of the way of a gray-haired gnome and her pint-size grandchildren. Snow drifted in after me, as silent a shadow as Maeve.

"You aren't fine, I've knocked your goggles all askew," Luca was still saying. As he reached up to set my goggles right, he managed to pull my ponytail loose and hit my nose with one of his oversize sleeves.

"It's *fine*," I protested again, trying to knock his hands away. "Snow, why don't you go up to the counter and get what Lark ordered? Luca, shouldn't you be at your shop, anyway?"

"I ran out of ink this morning," he said, finally stepping back just enough that I could fix my hair. In his defense, there wasn't much room to step back into at all: thin, over-stacked shelves ran throughout the store, all the way up to the door. Judging by the handles poking me in the back, we'd landed in the "shovels and tools" section. *At least Snow is getting something done,* I thought, hearing her place her order off to the right. Meanwhile, Luca was still talking.

"It was on my list to pick up yesterday, of course," he explained, "but with everything that happened at your shop, and meeting—um—everyone, I kind of forgot, well and I *had* been hoping that you carried ink at your store, maybe even a special kind I could use, but of course I forgot to ask, and I noticed today it was just William in, and I didn't want to bother him, so—"

"You need special ink?" I summarized as Luca's voice trailed off. I watched him as I tied up my hair. Ever since he'd taken over the bookstore—and been reunited with his alter ego, Jade—his voice didn't trail off as often as it used to. *Wonder what he's so worked up about?* "What kind of special ink?"

"I don't—I don't know," he said. "I just thought you might have some. Since you have so many other—interesting things."

"'Interesting,'" I repeated, still watching him. His eyes seemed intensely green, more so than usual. My gaze fell down to his collar.

Which, much like my goggles, was askew. "Goodness, Luca," I teased as I reached out to fix it. "Is this the state you run your errands in?"

"Only when people insist on running into me," he grinned back.

Snow cleared her throat. "I got the stuff."

"Good," I said, still trying to wrestle Luca's robe into place. As I finished, I added, "Luca, this is Snow. Snow, Luca. Sorry about all the—uh—commotion."

"Nice to meet you," Luca said, sticking out his hand.

Snow shook his hand limply, then resumed staring at me. "I have to go to the salon next."

"Okay, I guess we should go then." I turned to Luca with one last smile. "We'll let you get back to your shop. And let me think about that ink, okay? I think I can come up with some recipes you'll really like."

However uncertain he'd seemed before, Luca seemed cheered by that thought. After dealing with suspicious deaths and family dramas and unfriendly miners, that cheerfulness felt special. As Snow and I began the short walk to Gloria's, I mused over that, smiling to myself.

"So are you two, like, a *thing*?" Snow asked.

"What?" I nearly slipped on a patch of icy sidewalk. "No, um, Luca's just really nice. He's like that with everyone. So, what'd you have to pick up from the hardware store?"

The fairy shrugged. "Bunch of oil."

At once, the wheels in my head were turning. *For the machinery at the mine? But they'd probably buy that in much bigger quantities than the hardware store carries. Maybe for Lark's chair? I wonder what kind it uses. That's just so cool that—*

But my (admittedly nerdy) train of thought took an abrupt

turn into the land of metaphor. *Oil. What if the payment Raven had received was to 'grease the gears,' so to speak, on some deal at the mine?*

Before I could say anything, we'd arrived at the salon, so I set the thought aside to examine later.

"Welcome to Gloria's Hair and Beauty," Johann called out as Snow and I walked in—much more smoothly than we had at the hardware store.

I paused at the counter, and Snow did the same. We were the only visitors in the salon's little entryway; in fact as soon as the door snapped shut behind us, it felt like we and Johann might be the only people in the world. Despite big, bright windows, none of the noise or chill of the Square seeped in. Instead, Gloria's salon was an oasis of leafy potted plants, black tiled flooring, and sleek white walls splashed with artful decorations.

Snow seemed drawn to one such art piece, so I let her slide past me before I leaned my elbow on Johann's tall desk. "Hey, how's it going? Sounds like yesterday was a big day."

"You're telling me," Johann returned with good humor. Though he was much older than me, he had a very youthful look, probably due in equal parts to his vampire heritage and the fact that Gloria had given him a new haircut shortly after he'd arrived in Belville. A returning law student completing his studies via correspondence course while he helped out Gloria in her salon, Johann had often told me that he knew nothing about beauty but he knew a lot about supporting his friends. Judging from the glow to his brown skin and the shine in his black hair, Gloria was teaching him quite a bit.

"Gloria told you all about the encounter with the miners, then?" he continued easily. I nodded, and he went on, "It was so strange, really. I've never had any problem like that in Belville before. Even my aunt—you know her, right? She's retired and lives over by the lake—she said she's never heard of miners causing trouble in town, either."

Johann leaned easily against the back of his chair as he said this, which I thought bespoke a lot of confidence. He was a little shorter than me—perhaps five foot eight—and more inclined to cushion than muscle, so I doubted he'd ever entertained thoughts of facing off with the bullying miners directly.

"Snow's actually come in their place today, I think," I said, looking over at my charge.

"Ah, that makes sense. They didn't leave with everything they came for yesterday," Johann volunteered. Now we were both staring at Snow.

But Snow had her back to us and was staring resolutely at a silver hand mirror which had been tacked up onto the wall beside Johann's desk.

"Red, I thought I heard you," Gloria said, emerging from the rest of the salon. To Johann, she said, "Don't let me stay out here more than ten minutes—we've got a treatment going at station three. Now, Red, are you here with that new hair mask? Because—"

"Sorry," I said, holding up a hand to stop her before she got too excited. "I'm just here with Snow, who has some errands to run for the mine. Um . . . Snow?"

My attempt to catch Snow's attention was only partially successful, but Gloria was unruffled. She leaned against the desk beside me, and said to the fairy's back, "That mirror is supposed to be some pretty powerful magic."

At this, finally, Snow wheeled to look at us. "Is it?"

Gloria shrugged and glanced over at Johann. "I got it from *him*. Some business-warming gift, eh?"

"And exactly who else do you think should have it?" Johann returned primly, breaking into a smile at the end. He and Gloria had met years ago, in school, and it was evident when they spoke together. To Snow and me, he explained, "It's of ancient dwarven make, actually—quite a rarity these days. Instead of showing you how you look on the outside, it reflects how you think of yourself on the inside. After all, for as much good work as Gloria does, isn't it the inside that ultimately counts?"

I was intrigued by this, myself—I'd never noticed the mirror before. But Snow wavered, her wide blue eyes looking more torn than anything else.

"You don't exactly like it, do you? What you see," Gloria clarified, watching Snow. Where Snow's eyes and lips trembled, it occurred to me that Gloria—herself incredibly beautiful, and having just weathered a murder investigation a few months before—looked steady, and tired. She went on, "Or maybe you like it *more* than what everyone else sees, even though you think you shouldn't."

"I—the picture in the mirror is so much darker. It looks broken," Snow said at last. Her gaze darted to mine, and no doubt she could see my confusion. "Everyone thinks I'm so pretty. That's the only good thing they ever used to say about me. But in this . . ."

"It shows how you feel," Gloria repeated gently.

"*You* know," Snow guessed, glancing back to Gloria.

Gloria nodded, her regal red plume of feathers arcing gracefully through the air. "I used to think I hated everything. The truth was, I hated myself. And when I looked into that mirror, it was like looking at a ghost in a horror story."

"'Used to,'" Snow echoed, biting her lip as she snuck another peak at the mirror. "It changes?"

"The image changes as you do," Johann said kindly.

Snow considered him carefully, then twitched as though she almost looked back but decided not to at the last moment. Instead, she pulled Lark's list from her vest pocket. "It says they left behind some soaps," she said, focusing on the written words.

Johann slid easily back into business mode, retrieving packages for Snow, while Gloria sidled up next to me. "What in Beyond is going on at that mine?"

"I don't think it's the mine," I whispered back. "I think it's her past coming back to haunt her. And—she just lost a close friend."

"Either way," Gloria said, shaking her head. "I just hope she has someone to look out for her."

"Several someones, I think," I answered, thinking of the dwarves—and of Maeve. And wondering, once more, about Sir Rowan.

"Still," Gloria remarked as though sensing my hesitation. She looked at me pointedly. "One more never hurts, right?"

9

Coming Around the Mountain

After our stay in the salon, I insisted we swing by the bakery for some pastries and chai. Snow, it turned out, had never had chai tea before, and I was very proud of myself for introducing it to her—even if we did have to add a lot of milk and sugar to it before she found its spices palatable.

Plus, because of the tea, Snow warmed up toward me enough to magically clean off a bench in Market Square for us to sit on together as we ate.

"That's your store, right?" she asked suddenly, after blowing on her tea for a few minutes. She pointed to the opposite corner of the Square.

I hastily swallowed a bit of chocolate roll. "Yep, that's mine. It goes without saying, maybe, but you can come there any time you need anything. William—that's my assistant, a magical familiar—and I live on the upper floor."

"The dwarves look after me," Snow said absently, still staring at the shop's window displays, which were tiny at this distance. After a long gulp of tea, she added, "And you were coming up

75

to the mine to look at that strange ore, Lark said."

She didn't exactly say it as a question, but I recognized that she was sounding me out. I wiped sugary crumbs from my mouth and nodded. "Belville's pretty rural, so I get asked to do a lot of that kind of stuff. Just weighing in with a scientific opinion, really. It's not like I would deal in the ore myself, unless for some reason Lark wants to sell it locally and doesn't want to deal with customers herself. Were you the one who found it? Or your team, I guess?"

"I was." Snow nodded and took a bite of her own mini currant tart. She must have enjoyed it, because she became much more talkative. "Me and the Flock work together, yeah, but *I* was the one who found the ore. It was just sitting off to the side of one of the slag heaps, where they dump all the rock that they're not going to sell. But I could tell there was something strange about it. The snow wasn't sticking to it."

I thought about this for a moment as I sipped my drink. *I thought someone said it was a dwarf who found it, but then, just like Snow said, the dwarves are pretty protective of her—I guess I can see why they might not have spread that she was the one to find it.* "No snow on it, huh? Was it warm?"

Snow hesitated. "I thought it might be—at first. But if it was, it cooled down really fast after I touched it. Things usually do," she added, more to her pastry than to me. "I never really could control my magic."

"You've got plenty of time to sort that out," I assured her. "It isn't going anywhere. And besides, warm or not, it's still strange either way."

"That's what I thought," she agreed. "That's why we took it in. We thought it was best, since—"

"Since what?" I asked, setting down my napkin.

"It's just, things are a little tense around the mine," Snow explained. "They have been since we got there. I know Pigeon thinks it's because there's trolls and the trolls don't like the dwarves. But I kind of thought—from the way Lark reacted about the ore—"

I cocked my head as I guessed, "You think the ore is what's making the miners tense?"

"Something like that. It's not like I think the ore itself is making them tense. But like, maybe there's something to do with whatever vein it came from? Because really, why wouldn't they be able to trace where it came from in the mine? Why haven't any of them spoken up and said 'oh, I found that'?"

This was perhaps the most I'd ever heard Snow speak, and I smiled as I thought it over. As far as I could make out, her reasoning made sense. *Maybe there's a branch of the mine that makes the miners uncomfortable—for whatever reason,* I thought, my head filling with thoughts of dragons' lairs. *Would a nearby dragon make a rock hot?*

Visions of fire breath and enormous teeth filled my mind, and I found I didn't want to think about this too much.

"But I didn't tell the Flock about that," Snow added. "I didn't want them to think I was too focused on the ore or something."

"Why would that be bad?" I asked, frowning. "I mean, you *all* are a bit curious about it, aren't you?"

"Yeah. I mean, sure, we all are, but it's a little different—it's a little different for *fairies,*" Snow said, whispering the last word like it was a curse.

She glanced at me meaningfully from the corner of her eye, but the meaning sailed straight over my head. I spread my hands apologetically. "Sorry, Snow—I mostly do science, not magic. I'm not super familiar with fairy things. Why is it different?"

For a moment I thought she wouldn't answer; she sat still, staring at the snow in front of her. But at last she blew out a breath. "Fairies don't like metal," she said. "Everyone knows *that,* at least, right?"

I thought about this. I did, theoretically, know that about fairies, but I hadn't often encountered it practically. *Maybe that's why they have an at least partly-human knight to do their sword-wielding and mail-wearing,* I thought. Slowly, I nodded.

"So instead of metal, if they want something to last, they use rocks," Snow continued. "Well, the ones I know do, anyway. The water fairies. It's like, rocks take on whole new meanings for fairies, because they like to use natural stuff to build with. They can get a little weird about it, to be honest."

"Hmmm." It struck me as a tiny bit funny that Snow disparaged the water fairies but also had apparently found fulfilling work as a miner, but I didn't voice my thoughts.

"But I *am* focused on it," Snow said more forcefully. Icy tears collected at the corners of her eyes as I watched her, and I wondered if this was something she'd realized while gazing into Gloria's mirror. "I am. I can't let it go. There *is* something strange about the ore—something—something magical, even. So I told Lark myself. I told her, I'm not leaving here until they figure out what it is."

* * *

Snow was quiet again as we walked back up to the mine, and I did my best to give her space to work through her thoughts. I almost wondered if I should have escorted her at all—she surely knew her way back—but soon had reason to be glad I'd come.

We were within sight of the mine headquarters when we heard the commotion.

Snow dropped her packages and left me in her icy dust. Even though she'd been derogatory about her own powers before, it was apparent that she'd mastered one common trick of fairies: sprouting a pair of magic wings and flying away. Ice-blue butterfly-like wings bore her toward the mine.

Normally, I'm no slouch either, when it comes to speed. My heritage blessed me with swift feet, far swifter than the average human. However, I did not have Snow or Maeve's ability to walk on top of snow drifts, and running through them proved very annoying. I'd made it halfway down the road to the mine and already nearly tripped three separate times when I noticed movement in the trees to the right. My eyes caught sight of a wisp of blue. Abruptly, I changed direction.

"Hey!" I called, charging off the path and up the mountain. In about six quick steps, I collided squarely with Sir Rowan, who had been about to mount something that looked an awful like a shimmery blue horse.

"Hey yourself, miss," Sir Rowan replied, managing to pack a lot of consternation and disbelief and polite impatience into three words.

"Hey nothing," I said, still a little winded and confused by the suddenness of events. I staggered to my feet and put a hand out to help Sir Rowan to do the same. To my surprise, he accepted. "What are you doing out here? Officer Thorn wants to talk to you!"

"I appreciate that fact, but I regret to say that I do not share her desire," Sir Rowan said. The horse-like animal, which was shimmying near his left shoulder, snorted.

"Well, that's too bad," I informed him. "I said I would help you, and I will, but you have to help *us*, too. We *do* have justice here in Belville, you know. You can't just run around doing whatever you want."

At this, very annoyingly, Sir Rowan smiled. "Am I to understand, miss, that running into people is considered acceptable?"

"If they're criminals, yes."

"Do you have any evidence to suggest I am a criminal?"

"Where were you yesterday morning?"

"Gathering iceflower."

"Uh huh. And why are you in town at all, Sir Rowan? I mean, why *now*?"

"The Matriarch decided that it is Time," he answered, impassively.

"'Time?'" I parroted back, exasperated. "Snow's what, eighteen?"

"Heavens no. Teenagers? No. The young lady is twenty-one."

I paused. Around us, the forest resumed normalcy: birds tweeting, cold breezes blowing. "You know twenty-one is still young too, right?"

"If you'll pardon me pointing it out," Sir Rowan said, bowing slightly, "Everything is young to the fae."

"Well, now she's both young and yet old enough to know you and your masters have never treated her well, and she resents it. Rightly, in my opinion. And you know what? You asked for my help, which means I can run into you whenever I like. Don't give me that look," I concluded sourly. "You're going to have to come with me to see Officer Thorn."

"Of course, miss," Sir Rowan said. "And where is the

Officer?"

"At the mine. Where," I recalled suddenly, "it sounds like something very bad has happened."

10

Doubling Down

The mine's main entrance was cut deep into the mountain. In the chasm out front, flanked by two outstretched walls of rock, Lark's camp and headquarters sprawled. Further back, where the walls met, a hole large enough for three carts to pass through side-by-side marked the beginning of the actual mine. To one side of the entrance, carts which ran on a rudimentary rail system waited, some filled with debris waiting to be dumped—most likely, down the slope just beyond the camp.

At that moment, though, hardly anything about the mine was recognizable. The place was in pandemonium. Miners, some towering, some hulking, ran in every which direction; from one of the central shacks (the main office, I'd bet) a siren blared; and the air was thick with gray stone dust.

Sir Rowan quickly tied his mount's reins to the last of the trees remaining outside the camp, and we strode in together. *Because if he didn't go in under his own steam, he knows I'd drag him,* I thought, grinning to myself despite the chaos. But my humor quickly dissolved into worry as I realized I could see no sign of Officer Thorn or Maeve.

"I doubt she's in an office," I said to Sir Rowan, having to yell to be heard over the shouts of the miners. "She's probably in the middle of it. Whatever *it* is."

Sir Rowan nodded as though this made perfect sense. Then, to my surprise, he began to lead the way. I couldn't help but be jealous of his regal cloak and over-six-foot stature. Those, combined with the sense of undeniable purpose he carried everywhere he seemed to have in every situation, served to part the miners like a muddy sea.

I jogged in his wake, hard on the hem of that cloak. I didn't even glance at the miners, some of whom were definitely staring. Cursing my average height, I tried to get glances around Sir Rowan's shoulders, but the nearer we got to the mine, the louder and cloudier it got. Even had all the miners and the knight gone invisible, I doubt I could have seen anything more than a few paces away.

And I wouldn't have believed it if I had.

Sir Rowan stopped abruptly and, rather than plow into him a second time, I leapt around his side. This jump had me colliding with Maeve, who bumped into Officer Thorn, who turned to look over her shoulder with a grim expression on her face.

We were about twenty paces inside the mine at that point. But I didn't need night vision or my goggles to see that a heavy mine cart, full of rubble, had gotten out of control and slammed into the rock wall. And the number of onlookers, not to mention the presence of Lark's hired nurse, told me that the mine cart had taken someone with it.

"There you are," Officer Thorn said, not at all in her usual jocular tone. "Aren't you supposed to be with Snow?"

"I was, but she ran over here as soon as we got close," I stammered, pulling myself upright and dusting off my clothes, then hugging my arms around my body. I'm not all that sensitive to magic, but the bad luck in the air felt palpable.

"We should find her," Maeve said, her thin voice only audible because we were all standing within arm's reach of each other.

"We will, but we have more to worry about," Officer Thorn said, turning back to contemplate the ruined cart. Under the nurse's direction, two large, muscled orcs were pulling it free of the rubble while several other miners loaded the debris into another cart nearby. "This isn't good, Red."

"Do you know what happened?" I asked, feeling like the question must be a silly one, but at a loss for what else to say.

Thorn turned away from the scene, so that she, Maeve, and I formed a compact huddle. "It wasn't an accident," she said, her usually brash voice only reaching the two of us.

I gulped. "How do you know?"

Officer Thorn looked sternly at her assistant. "Maeve, tell her. How do I know?" Apparently, in policing, everything was an opportunity to learn.

Maeve bent over awkwardly so she was talking at my level. "Um, the carts are usually on rails, and the rails don't go near the walls. And, um, to hit the wall like that, it must have been going *really* fast."

"Not to mention that a cart loaded with rocks like that would have been too heavy to jump the tracks. It should have just fallen over," Officer Thorn added, nodding her approval at her assistant. Maeve hastened to scribble this fact down.

I was still unwilling to go where they were headed. "You aren't saying someone picked a loaded cart up off the rails and—and what, pushed it? Why would they do that?"

"Why and how, we don't know yet. But if I was them, I'd've picked up the cart first, then loaded it," Officer Thorn corrected. "It'd take someone strong to manage it. And even *stronger* to give it a push to make it go that speed. But look around, Red. The place is full of people strong enough to manage that."

I glanced at Maeve, who was still writing furiously. The dust in the air had settled in the tracks of tears on her cheek.

"So it wasn't an accident," I said, giving in. "And someone was—murdered?"

"Another of the dwarves, from the sound of it," Officer Thorn said. "Though we've yet to pull out the body. This is one I don't want you looking at, Red."

"Understood." I shivered, grateful for the officer's discretion.

"There she is. Poor Snow," Maeve whispered.

My head jerked up and, following her gaze, I glimpsed the young fairy surrounded by a ring of dwarves. *The remaining dwarves*, I thought, shivering again. *Seems a lot less likely now that Raven's death was an accident.* "Oh, Officer, I found—"

But, in looking around for Sir Rowan in order to make introductions, I found that I'd lost him. "He got away," I said, and cursed.

My vehemence startled Maeve, who stepped back and looked around over my head. "The person who was with you? He just walked off," she said.

"And you let him?" Officer Thorn tugged at her ear, clearly exasperated. "Who was it, Red?"

Maeve, meanwhile, chewed her pencil. "I thought, um, he was just guiding you . . . "

"It's okay," I said first to Maeve. To Thorn, I explained, "I met Sir Rowan in the woods and made him come along to meet you. I have no idea why he was out there, but he seemed alright with coming along. But now—"

"Never mind, Red," said the Officer with a wave of her hand. "I'll meet him soon enough. There's enough to do here."

"But don't you think it's suspicious?" I asked.

"Sure," said Thorn, turning back to look at the crime scene. "But no one here has mentioned seeing a knight around. And I doubt any human would have had the strength to do this. We're looking for an orc, a troll—or something even bigger."

* * *

Thorn insisted that she and Maeve would handle the scene alone, and I didn't protest. Instead I pushed my way out of the mine, shouldering past concerned miners, moving quickly lest Lark or one of her lackeys spot me and ask questions. The only thing on my mind was getting out of there.

Just like Sir Rowan did. I pulled up behind one of the shacks for a moment and considered this. I'd only been talking to Thorn and Maeve for ten or fifteen minutes; he couldn't have gotten too big a lead on me. Especially if he had lingered and poked around the mine for any reason.

Determined to salvage some part of this encounter, I pulled my goggles down over my eyes and took a quick glance around. With the zoom feature, I hoped to pick out even the tiniest of indications that the errant knight was still nearby.

The area around the mine was a mass of heaving gray, though. Not a speck of blue to be seen. Hoping that some form of luck might be on my side, I rushed to the edge of the chasm wall, which gave way to the road leading away from the mine.

And with my goggles still dangerously zoomed in, what did I see but a flash of shimmery blue.

Sir Rowan's horse. It was still right where he'd left it, and the man himself had just mounted. I tucked myself behind a boulder, watching. Confronting him directly hadn't worked very well the first time; this time, I decided, a little more discretion was in order.

It was time to put my shadow skills to the test—with Maeve's example for inspiration.

The knight wheeled his horse and took off through the trees. The horse ran easily through the forest, keeping up an impressive speed, but that at least was no problem. Turning off the zoom on my goggles, I set off after them, running just fast enough to maintain a steady distance between us.

I quickly realized we weren't headed back to Snow's camp, and was glad. Instead, the horse turned sharply up the mountain, climbing the slope as though it was nothing.

I need to stop hanging out around magical creatures, I thought as my breath started coming more raggedly. At least the horse and rider couldn't run on top of the snow. By keeping inside the horse's trail I made the ascent easier for myself, but only barely. I could run fast, sure, but running straight *up* was hard.

For once, though, I had reason to be grateful for the recent snow storm. The snow had been heavy and persistent enough to fall even between the thickest of trees—and the trees *did* thicken as we left the mine behind. This area of the mountain rarely saw loggers or settlers, or in fact anyone except the occasional hunter. By this time I was staring mostly at my feet and at the trail in the snow, and the tree trunks rose thick as kegs around my feet, which made me think of Lavender's tavern which was *not* helpful. There were no real trails; hiking wasn't a popular pastime in Belville, except with me (gathering ingredients) and my neighbor Gloria (who was, let's face it, a little eccentric at times). I hadn't been this high on the mountain since summertime, and even then I only made the trip for some very rare glowing mosses.

Sir Rowan seemed to know where he was going, though. His trail dodged around trees and bushes, but didn't deviate in its primary direction. Unfortunately for me, that direction remained *up*.

My boots slipped in the snow and a voice in my head— one that sounded suspiciously like William—said *you know, you could just walk along the horse's trail, rather than run up the mountain like an alpine goat. It's not like the trail is going anywhere.*

But would it? Given all the talk of snow magic and water fairies and ice fairies and winter storms lately, I realized I didn't want to take any chances. Besides, the horror of the scene at the mine had filled me with energy. Running was hard, but it was a lot better than walking along with plenty of time to think about what I'd seen and what might happen if I arrived at another scene late.

The bushes around me began to thin out. We'd climbed high enough on the mountain that the ecosystem was changing. In another few ragged breaths, I realized that the trees were thinning out too.

Where is he going, I wondered, *straight to the top of the mountain?*

And then came another unwelcome thought. *It's going to take me ages to get home.*

But just as fast as the thought came and went, Sir Rowan's

trail turned. Following it with a few quick steps to the right, I squeezed between a couple of aspens and nearly fell straight into a clearing.

My shadowing skills, if they were to be tested, would have to be tested at an elementary level.

"Miss Red," said Sir Rowan, his voice very pleasant and smooth and full of breath, which I knew mine wouldn't be. "How kind of you to drop in."

"Ugh," I told him. The frustration in that one syllable, I felt, was sufficient to describe my feelings about his comment and the entire silly goose chase.

Since there was no point hiding in the trees, I emerged into my third camp of the day. This camp gave the distinct impression that, if camps were people, it would look down a very long nose at the other two. In a small clearing ringed by aspens, Sir Rowan had set up a large, stately tent and a sophisticated cook fire. Nearby trees served as hangers for bags and supplies as though they'd been grown for the purpose. And at the far end, perhaps fifteen paces away, Sir Rowan's horse munched happily on a bucket of hay hanging from a silver poplar. *Does it even have a special traveling tack room? I* blinked. *That horse camps better than me. And I spent* years *on the road.*

And that horse, I realized, now that I'd regained some breath, smelled distinctly of lakeweed.

"I confess I have not yet had time to brew a cup of tea," Sir Rowan continued, gesturing me toward an ornately carved bench set up by the fire, which was crackling happily. "You are possessed of an unusual speed, it seems."

"Thanks," I said, although Sir Rowan's comment fell far short of being a compliment. I passed him with my nose in the air and dropped on to the bench. While he bustled about with gleaming copper cookware, I stretched my legs and warmed my boots. "What kind of horse is that?"

"Nessie is a water horse," Sir Rowan said, as though the commonplace nature of my question pained him. "Summoned by a special spell, and given birth from water and foam."

"*Lake* foam?" I asked, lifting an eyebrow.

Sir Rowan held my gaze for a moment, and the series of looks that passed across his face made it clear he understood what I meant. "You have, I take it, noticed Nessie's presence before. Perhaps around the miners' camps? Until yesterday, I was camped in their area, farther down the mountain. After the day's unfortunate events and a troubling sighting, I decided it best to move up here."

"A sighting?" I asked, distracted.

But the knight didn't answer. "If I may perhaps make a suggestion, miss," Sir Rowan said, not looking at me, "in the future if you wish to conceal your movements, you might consider stepping on fewer twigs."

"Ugh," I repeated, with feeling. But as my feet thawed and my heart slowed, I became slightly more eloquent. "I'll take that under consideration, sure. But seeing as I don't make a habit of *running away from the police,* I don't think it'll be all that necessary."

Between us, the kettle dangling above the flames whistled.

Sir Rowan pursed his lips. "It seemed to me that Officer Thorn and her Reaper assistant were busy."

"Her name is Maeve. Don't be rude," I retorted.

That got his attention. Sir Rowan stepped back, his blue eyes wide and, for once, fixed on my face. "I would never, miss."

"Well, you are. A polite person would have waited outside the mine, instead of retreating to their hidden mountain lair. What is this all about?" I asked, waving a hand around me, not so much at the campsite as at the general air of secrecy. He might be able to explain away the fact that I'd smelled Nessie the morning we'd found Raven's body, but he couldn't explain away everything.

For a moment, Sir Rowan was quiet. He busied himself with measuring tea leaves out of a pouch from inside his cloak, and then readying tea cups taken from a traveling trunk. When there was nothing to do but watch the tea steep, he finally went still, and at last dropped onto the bench opposite mine.

"The last thing my employers would wish is to be involved in a scandal," he said, as though commenting on the clear blue skies above us.

"*Another* scandal," I pointed out, since the star-crossed lovers story of Snow's origin had sounded pretty scandalous to me.

From his seat, Sir Rowan bowed to my correction, his eyes on the tea kettle. "As you say, miss."

"You asked for my help, and I'm on it," I pointed out. "And Snow has given you her answer, for now. So why are you still . . ."

"Lurking around corners like the big bad wolf?" Sir Rowan glanced at me with an unexpectedly self-deprecating smirk.

Despite myself, I grinned. "Something like that."

"I don't suppose I could convince you I was gathering ingredients, miss?"

"Magic drinks is a whole other conversation we need to have," I said, shaking my head. "But not now. No. What gives?"

"'What gives,'" he replied, reaching to pour the tea, "is a

certain amount of suspicious activity among the dwarves."

"Uh huh." I cradled the cup he handed to me, smelling it carefully just in case. *Cinnamon, fennel, cardamom, ginger.* Nothing too dangerous. In fact, as Sir Rowan handed me a small pot of honey and a silver cow-shaped container of cream, I realized he'd made chai. *Yum.* Even though Snow and I had just had chai in the Square, I could always go for another cup. Still, though, I raised an eyebrow expectantly at him, letting him know he wasn't off the hook.

Sir Rowan cleared his throat. "I spoke to Heron this morning. I happened to catch him on his way to work; he lagged some distance behind the others, and was glad enough of an excuse to chat. Heron," he added quietly, "was the victim of that rather ostentatious attack."

I paused, saying a mental prayer for the deceased. "Do you know all the dwarves by name? I thought you only just met them."

"I did. However, I find it best to be prepared," Sir Rowan said enigmatically as he stirred his tea. I waited until he added, "Heron told me a story you might find interesting, miss. He intimated that Raven had recently come into a great deal of money, and that it was connected to something they'd found in the mine. It can only be surmised that he meant the very ore I came to you about. A very valuable ore, I believe, which others at the mine might wish to have complete control of."

I could see where he was going. "You think that someone is murdering the dwarves over jealousy or greed because of the new ore? Even though the vein itself hasn't been found?"

Sir Rowan paused meaningfully, and then said, "I understand that the mine owner is known to be somewhat . . . ruthless in her methods."

"Lark?" I hesitated, taking a sip of my tea. Lark *did* sometimes operate in gray areas of the law—areas as gray as the rock dust at her mine. Officer Thorn seemed to have a professional respect for her, though, and I trusted the officer's judgment. I did not, however, fully trust Sir Rowan.

Although he did make a very nice chai.

"That doesn't explain why you wouldn't want to see the police," I said. Tea notwithstanding, it annoyed me that he'd made a liar of me to Thorn. "In fact, that's something I'd think you ought to tell Officer Thorn."

"And I will, Miss Red," said Sir Rowan mildly. "But if you'll recall, it was your idea to meet the Officer at the mine. I personally would have preferred to pay her a visit at her station."

"Why's that?"

"Heron also mentioned the reason he wasn't in a hurry to get to work," Sir Rowan told his tea cup. "And, while I believe the Officer will find his reasoning relevant, I didn't wish to bring it up while in a crowd in the mine itself. You see, Heron informed me that he and his fellow dwarves had faced some rather unpleasant racial discrimination from their coworkers. Coworkers who are, he informed me, rather prone to violent outbursts."

11

Shadowy Reflections

When I'd finished my tea and managed to dry off from my run in the snow, Sir Rowan offered me a ride into town. I accepted for three good reasons: it would be much faster than walking; I was dying for some chili and biscuits back home; and it would get Sir Rowan in the vicinity of the police station. I couldn't be sure Officer Thorn and Maeve were back in town yet, but at that point, every attempt to get the stubborn officer and the slippery knight together counted.

Sir Rowan's horse, Nessie, carried us both easily. I never had been a big horse rider myself, but by the time I reached home, I was thoroughly impressed. Sliding from horseback in front of my shop, I paused to give the creature a pat on the nose.

"Miss Red," said Sir Rowan very solemnly before you left. "You have already heard Snow's story. You may find it worth your while to look into the ice clan—the current family members have assumed the name Frost. They are, I believe, the only local family wealthy and interested enough to have paid off the dwarves."

I nodded noncommittally and thanked him for the ride, not mentioning that we *had* found one of their promissory notes on Raven. The evidence was strong, but I couldn't help but think how convenient it would be for Sir Rowan if his employers' greatest enemy turned out to have a hand in the murders.

The minute I turned and walked into the shop, William was on me like frost on window panes. "Where have you *been?* Why didn't you invite Sir Rowan in? What happened at the mine?"

I wondered why he bothered asking, since apparently to him, all my answers were crystal clear.

Instead I glanced around the shop. It was late afternoon by then, and we were well into the post-lunch lull. A family was clustered around the display of warming powders, and in the front corner, a wizened couple pored over mineral samples. William, stationed at the back counter, had a twin soul seated next to him: Dusty, the local handy-gnome and gossip-monger extraordinaire.

I grinned. Dusty and William were best friends, and, aside from the fact that Dusty was an eternal optimist, very much alike.

"Hey Dusty," I said, ignoring William's interrogation. "I trust you haven't shown up because we've got a leaky pipe?"

"Stopped by for lunch," the gnome told me, holding up a cloth baggie filled to the brim with trail mix. On the counter beside him lay a banana peel and a glass water bottle. Though he was about as high as my thigh, Dusty seemed to be constantly snacking. Light brown skin hidden behind a cloth cap and baggy overalls wrinkled as he grinned at me with his usual good humor.

"I need some of that too. No, not yours," I laughed as Dusty thrust forward his trail mix. "I'm going to run upstairs and grab something. You'll be okay, right, William?"

William harrumphed. Meanwhile, Dusty leapt down from the counter.

"I'll come with you," he said. "William told me all about your window attacker."

"My 'window attacker'?" I hesitated, then chuckled as I realized what he meant. *Was that really only yesterday?* "Oh, yeah. We do need help replacing one of the window panes. Come on up."

Dusty trailed after me as we climbed the spiral staircase up to the apartment. My thighs were already yelling at me internally, sore from my run, which was a bad sign. But I brushed that aside, choosing instead to focus on Dusty's cheerful chatter as we hit the landing and I let us into the sunny kitchen.

"William told me all about what's been happening. First your window and that storm, then the strange knight and the dwarf at the mine. I was over at the smith's guild just now and heard another might've got murdered too, is that true?"

"Ask Thorn," I said absently. "What do you mean, 'that storm'? Was the snow storm yesterday unusual?"

Dusty shrugged. "Depends who you talk to. Meself, I think it's too early for a storm like that. We don't usually get two-footers until January at least."

"Great," I said dryly, thinking of all the winter storms in store.

"Anyway," Dusty said, hopping with ease up onto the kitchen counter and clambering over the sink, "looks like this break isn't half as bad as William made it sound. I thought an entire pane was missing or something, but that's just a little hole. Barely big enough to put your hand through."

"Please don't," I said, looking up from rummaging in the ice box to see Dusty stripping away my makeshift window stopper.

"What d'you think I am, foolish?" Dusty grinned at me.

"Of course not." I pulled a biscuit and a ceramic bowl of chili out of the icebox and leaned back against the kitchen island, hungry enough to eat both cold. "What bothers me is, how did it happen in the first place? I mean, I know William said his ward was weak there, but he was kinda cagey about the whole thing. Cagier than usual, that is."

Dusty turned from measuring the window pane to fix me with a beady eyed-stare. "You don't know why that is?"

"No," I said, gulping down a spoonful of chili like a guilty child. "Do you?"

Dusty chuckled as he turned back to his work, which I took as a "yes."

"Dusty! You have to tell me. I'm sick of people keeping secrets," I protested.

Again he paused, and this time he looked contemplatively at the half-biscuit in my hand. "Got any more of those?"

"Yes." I was already moving to get one, totally on board with this bit of bribery.

"Thanks." Dusty moved to sit on the edge of the sink, grinning around the edges of his biscuit. "Yours are the best. Don't tell Lavender I said that, though. Sometimes I can get her to give me some for free."

"Well, this one isn't free," I told him with a lopsided smile.

"Yeah, yeah." Dusty took a huge bite, and then with crumbs

on his chin he said, "The way I figure it, William didn't want to strengthen the ward on this window because he thought if Jade ever came back, you'd want to see him."

I set down my bowl before I dropped it. "Really? William told you that?"

Dusty shrugged one shoulder. "Might as well have. I can put these things together, you know. People forget how much a plumber overhears."

Lost in thought, I forgot to answer. Jade was a part of Luca now, and technically, always had been; for a while, Luca had been like the monster in Beauty in the Beast, his inner self trapped behind a strange, cursed appearance. There was no reason to think Jade alone would seek me out. And even if he did, he could knock at the door just like everyone else, corporeal or not.

No; the thought was illogical, and the fact that William had entertained it—because I didn't doubt Dusty's intuition when it came to our mutual friend—said . . . what? That William thought I must have very deep feelings for Jade?

Though no one was watching me, I blushed. Nothing like that had ever been said. In fact, Jade had always been very prim and proper. In some ways, I realized, Sir Rowan and Jade really were quite similar. Of course, Jade had never been so powerful, or self-righteous, or prone to handing out drinks or employed by a potentially dangerous fairy clan. Plus, Jade had good reasons to keep secrets, which Sir Rowan did not. But they did have similar manners. And similar tendencies to stay on the outskirts of society. *Maybe that's why I'm having a hard time keeping Sir Rowan at arm's length.*

Something tugged at my ponytail, maybe an errant fly or a bit of ice just now melting. I brushed the feeling away and cleared my throat. "Dusty, how soon do you think you can fix the window?"

"Might be a day or two," said the gnome, his voice muffled by his work. "Pane's an odd size. These old ones usually are. I'll have to get it specially made by Mayor Marguerite."

"Really?" This woke me fully from my reverie. I poked at my chili again. "The mayor blows glass?"

"Yep." Dusty stood, wiping his hands on his overalls. He'd replaced my temporary solution, though naturally, it looked much more professional now. "Everyone in town government started in trade, you know, and most of 'em keep it up."

"Huh." Small town life was surprisingly complex, and I always seemed to be learning more about Belville. But Dusty's comment made me wonder how much I didn't know about Lark and the other leaders of the mine. *And the families interested in it. I hate to say it, but . . . Sir Rowan might have been right. Although why would the Frosts be paying Raven and be responsible for killing him? Did he ask for too much, maybe? And how does Heron fit in?*

"Coming back down?" Dusty asked as he headed for the shop.

"Hm? Oh, yeah. I'm right behind you," I called, moving to rinse out my bowl in the sink. As soon as the day was over, I resolved, I would pay Luca a visit.

* * *

An hour later I stepped out the front door and locked it behind me. William had elected to come along; he was already waiting in the street.

In fact, he was happily gossiping with Johann.

99

"Hey," I said, joining the two of them on the sidewalk.

"Everyone in town has heard about Heron," Johann said by way of hello, laying his hand over his chest in a sign of respect for the dead. "How are Snow and the other dwarves?"

"To be honest, I haven't seen them since we found out," I admitted. "But they seem like a very close-knit group. I'm sure they're comforting each other."

"I hope so," Johann said. "Gloria told me she spoke to you about looking after Snow. Now that we know there's a murderer loose, we need everyone to be careful."

"Thorn hasn't said anything official yet," William reminded our neighbor with a rumble.

"True, but two fatal accidents in as many days, at a mine which up until now had a sterling work record? What are the chances?" Johann huffed, but since he was part-vampire, his breath wasn't warm enough to fog up the evening air.

"You make a very good point," I admitted. "I can only imagine how Lark feels about all this, too."

"If I was her I'd think about kicking the dwarves out," William grumbled. He turned away from us to contemplate the Square, which was oddly empty for dinner time on a work night. The shadows of the trees stretched dark blue over his black fur.

"But it isn't their fault they've been targeted," Johann insisted, ever legally-minded. "If she did that, they could have reason to register a legitimate complaint."

"Or she'd be saving them by sending them somewhere away from the murderer," William retorted.

"None of this has been proven yet," I said, interrupting what could become an all-night argument. William loved to debate, and Johann was always looking for a chance to improve his skills, too. "Let's not make extra problems just yet. We have enough to deal with as it is."

"Well said," Johann conceded.

"Hmph," said William.

Trying my best to suppress a giggle, I told Johann, "We're headed over to the bookstore, and I want to stop by the pizza shop before it gets busy. We'll catch up tomorrow?"

"Certainly. You know where to find me, and Gloria, too. She's always glad when you stop by." Johann waved us off before strolling back into the salon.

What a change, I couldn't help but think. For a moment, snow and wind notwithstanding, I recalled standing on this very sidewalk with the summer sun overhead and Gloria haranguing me from her doorstep—while the fairies looked on inside, no doubt. I was glad to let that version of our relationship go. *There certainly is enough to deal with in Belville,* I thought, bringing my mind back to the present. But the thought was a little warmer now. *And enough friends to deal with it, too.*

William and I continued on our errand. It wasn't fancy food, but the benefit of the pizza shop was its speed. Plus, the half-elf who ran it had traveled abroad for culinary training, and came back knowing how to make all the city food that I missed terribly. Things like skewers of grilled vegetables with exotic sauces, *wrapped* sandwiches instead of cut ones, and—suitably enough—pizza. I picked up two and William and I were back on the road. The bookstore was only a ten minute walk from the Square, and with the night growing colder by the second, we made it in record time.

"Sorry, it's actually past closing—oh." When we entered, Luca's hood popped up from behind a stack of books, followed quickly by a bright smile. "Hey, Red! Did you come over to work on the mystery of the magic ore?"

Aside from my own shop, Luca's bookstore had become one of my favorite places in Belville. As far as shops go, it was polar opposite of mine: whereas I believed in tidy, orderly rows, organizational systems, and everything being in its place, the philosophy at the bookstore had always been "wherever you can reach is good enough." Shelves lined the entire first floor of the building haphazardly, with books, scrolls, and sets of encyclopedias tumbling around every corner. No amount of light could compete with the ever-present dust. But the armchairs scattered throughout were imminently comfortable, and somehow Luca always knew exactly where to find what he needed. Eventually.

"Dinner first," William insisted, shutting the door behind him and nosing around for the lock.

"We brought food," I told Luca, moving into the store. "And yes, you could say we're here to work on the mystery. Mysteries. But I don't think anyone's going to call it that," I added with a laugh, trying not to think back on the embarrassment of running into Luca earlier, and of Snow's following question.

"Why not? I thought it had the beginning of some good alliteration. Come on, come on, we should sit back here in the old reading room. I just cleared it out. I found a whole collection of old fairy tales in there, can you believe it? I think I'm going to turn it into the fiction section. It has a fireplace though, and I got it going, so it's really warm now!"

"I don't think he ought to be allowed to have fires," William mumbled to me as we followed Luca through the stacks.

I chuckled but said nothing. Luca, like booksellers and scholars all across Pastoria, had inherited his bookstore from the previous scholar, who had inherited it from another scholar, and so on. It was no wonder the place was full of surprises. As to whether a person with the natural energy of a puppy on a sugar high ought to set fires, I had complete faith in Luca. He'd had some bad luck early on in his life, but things generally worked out for him now.

"I pulled out everything I could on the fairies of Greendale," Luca continued, his long black robe trailing over the furniture as he led us into a back room filled with picture books, the sparkles of a merry fire, and the fluffiest rug I'd ever seen. "There isn't much here, since this is Belville and all, a historian at Greendale or somewhere closer to the lake would have more. I hope. Anyway, I know that's not exactly what Sir Rowan asked us to look into, but I figured you might be curious."

"We definitely are," I assured him. "And it turns out there's another fairy clan we should look into, too. But first, pizza. Cheese or veggie?"

Luca plopped himself on the rug without delay, and William did the same. I followed, trying not to wonder when it had been cleaned last. *It's not the most rustic place I've been today,* I reminded myself, smiling as Luca helped himself to the boxes we'd brought along. And of course, even though he was an arcane familiar and technically didn't have to eat, William's magic curled around the cheesiest slice of pizza.

"I also looked into the myths about the mountain, like I promised," Luca continued. After a day of trying to talk to people who believed silence was the greatest virtue, I loved this quirk of Luca's more than ever. Once he got going on a topic, he'd eventually tell you everything you needed to know. "There's a bunch, of course. I mean, Belville's been here for centuries, so that's a long time for stories to morph into new versions, right? I think I got them all, but I still have to check the basement."

William's happy panting stopped. Had he been human, and naturally pale, he probably would have blanched. "This place has a *basement?*"

"Yup," Luca said happily, using the hem of his sleeve as a napkin. I rolled my eyes good-naturedly before throwing a handkerchief at him. "Owl never used to let me go down there. There's tons of cabinets. I think it's all family records and stuff, probably not for the fairies though, like for townspeople. You know, stuff he might have been using—"

Luca faltered, and I understood completely. Luca's previous boss, Owl, had blackmailed quite a few people in town before eventually being exposed as a criminal.

William sneezed in the silence. "Better in your hands than his, then."

"I—I suppose so." Luca beamed, recognizing this comment for what it was: high praise from someone like William. He recovered and added, "Would you like to hear what I did find? The stories about Belville, I mean. It's really cool stuff. I found a bunch of different versions, but they're usually called *The Curse of Belville Mountain.*"

12

The Curse of Belville Mountain

"So," said Luca, swallowing a huge mouthful of melted cheese, "most of them go like this."

In preparation for his story, he sat up straighter and cleared his throat. When he spoke, his voice was actually less breathless and excitable than usual; he sounded quite professional—if one ignored the pizza in his hand.

"Centuries ago, before Belville was officially a town," he began, and immediately interrupted himself to add, "probably shortly before the Drus and the elves settled in the forests, historically speaking. Anyway, centuries ago, there weren't very many people living around here. It was considered a very desolate and wild place, compared to the rest of Beyond.

"The mountain range all around us existed, of course. However, there's speculation that this particular mountain—the mountain Belville is at the base of—didn't. At least four separate stories I found *insist* that the guardian created the mountain as a secret hideaway.

"So, who was the guardian, right?"

"And more importantly, *what* are they," William grumbled. I shushed him.

"Well, literally making a mountain is no small thing," Luca went on, eyes alight. "That's the really interesting part of the story, if you ask me. Some sources suggest that the guardian is divine, or some kind of earth spirit. But actually, this might make more sense if we talk about the Tree first.

"Most sources agree that the Tree is, or was, exactly what Sir Rowan suggested—that is, an apple tree. Specifically, the Tree of Life. If anyone were to eat just one bite of an apple from the Tree, they would be forever young. Through the years, some people have thought, too, that they could use the Apples to turn other things into gold."

This time I was the one to interrupt—I couldn't help myself. I rolled my eyes. "Does it always *have* to be gold? There are so many other valuable substances in the world!"

"Only nerds know about most of the other ones," William reminded me, teasing.

Luca broke and laughed at us both before continuing. "So, the Tree is really valuable, right? And of course, no one has ever actually *seen* it. So no one knows what it looks like or how big it is. But here's the thing: this new ore at the mine isn't the first time that people on the surface have discovered evidence of 'corruption.'

"In the pixie chronicles—I checked those just in case, since the pixies have been in Belville longer than almost anyone— well, the pixies talk about settling on the hill beside the lake and having to clear away an 'evil presence' before they could make their homes. Now, pixies tend to only talk about positive stuff, so they're not really specific about this evil that they say they encountered."

William wrinkled his nose. "Why would turning stuff into

gold be considered evil?"

"Hold on just a moment—there's more," Luca answered. "Through the years that people have lived in Belville, there've been records of incidents—legends, really. People say they hear groaning from within the mountain, if they're camping really high up at night. Briefly, there was an old stone outpost *really* high up, near the peak of the mountain. Everyone who stayed there said that the winds were incredibly wild at night, and the water in the well sometimes glowed strange colors, and finally there were plants growing right through the walls. The place had to be abandoned. As they left, some of them said there was this huge, shadowy shape chasing them.

"That was the main sighting. People have also reported earthquakes around certain areas of the mountain, and for a while, the local druids had a belief that anyone who even carried an apple through the woods would end up paralyzed by a ghostly spirit. But nothing has ever been confirmed."

"Lot of overblown drama, if you ask me," said William, shaking his floppy ears.

I, too, was skeptical. "Paralyzing people and growing really big plants doesn't sound like a dragon to me. Of course, maybe that's all effects of the ore . . ."

"Because if the ore itself is contaminated by the Tree of Life, then wouldn't those make sense as side effects?" Luca rocked up on his heels as he spoke, eyes gleaming in the firelight. "To some extent, of course, William has to be right. Things like this get exaggerated over the years. But if you boil it down to the bare bones—"

"—Then you get a magic tree inside the mountain, and an unseen force protecting it," I finished for him, grinning. "In alchemy, we call that 'distilling.'"

"Potato, potahto," Luca replied with a wink. "So, what do you think? I think there's definitely something there."

"But is it something that's been pushing dwarves off cliffs or chucking mine carts around?" William pointed out.

"No, and it doesn't seem to be really connected to Snow or the water clan—aside from the fact that they all might want it. And Snow did tell me earlier that she thought her grandparents were a little 'strange' when it comes to magical ores," I agreed. "I'm with you, Luca, I do think there's something to the stories—and the fact that it's probably effects from a magic tree, not a dragon, is a big relief. But, for the second time, William might be right in suggesting that we focus on the suspects right in front of us before we go digging up more."

William groaned, but I didn't understand why. Luca and I had *both* just complimented him, after all.

I looked at Luca for clarification, and he chuckled at me. "Officer Thorn would have been sad to miss that pun. So, Red, does that mean that you're thinking Sir Rowan's request is going to have to wait?"

"Oh, I still have plenty to talk to him about," I said. "But I told him from the start that he'd have to wait while we focus on the dwarves' tragedy."

"Good," said Luca. He hurried to add, "I mean, I'm with you about where to investigate next. I was thinking, I could close up the shop for a day if you wanted to go visit Lake Greendale?"

I hesitated, because for one thing, it didn't seem fair to ask Luca to close his shop. He wasn't directly involved in any of this nonsense, after all, and that was a *good* thing.

As though sensing the reason I held back, Luca added, "I've

been open pretty much every day since Samhain, even on Rest Days, because every time I think of closing then someone comes by and wants a book—you know, since it's the season to stay inside and be cozy, and all. But after all the research I did today, I was thinking it's time to take a break. It'd be nice to get some actual fresh air."

"Well, in that case," I acquiesced with a smile, "the other thing I was going to say is, it seems like we're on pretty good footing with the Greendale fairies so far. Not relationship-wise, but what I mean is, we can be pretty sure we know what their aims are, since Sir Rowan is here and focused on Snow. I actually wanted to look into the other side of her old family—the Frosts."

"From Poole," said Luca, thoughtfully. When William tilted his head at the scholar as though to say, *what—do you know everything now?* Luca went on with a self-deprecating laugh, "they come up sometimes in the records about the Greendales. Kind of the way you might occasionally mention your nemesis, I guess? Anyway, I did come across their name when I was reading earlier. And actually," he added, green eyes brightening, "I have a friend—his name is Tomte—who goes up that mountain all the time—you know, because Poole is actually on the peak just south of here. Tomte runs a supply sleigh between all the little towns from here to there during the winter months. How about I see if we can hitch a ride with him?"

"When do you find the time to meet people when you've always got your head buried in books?" William asked, his voice half suspicious, half impressed.

"That's easy," said Luca, beaming. "Tomte brings me *new* books. I'm sure we can work something out!"

13

Social Calls

The next morning I found a note from Thorn to the effect of 'don't go to the mine, I'm watching it,' and from the huffiness in the words, I guessed that Maeve had insisted on watching the dwarves again, too. I wondered if Thorn suspected what I did—that Maeve had a crush on one of the newcomers to town. I'd sent a note of my own to Thorn, of course, detailing the proposed trip to Poole. She didn't comment on that, which I took as approval.

I packed up for a day of adventure, suppressing a yawn. After a late night of research with William and Luca, I hadn't been able to sleep. I kept waking up thinking I heard strange noises—noises like someone burrowing deep under the earth.

But that was ridiculous. And what *wasn't* ridiculous was Luca's willingness to help.

"How come I have to stay and watch the shop again while you go on a date?" William grumped when I woke him and gently pushed him down into the shop ahead of me.

"It is *not* a date," I protested, stumbling. "This is an investigation. We're helping Thorn and Snow."

William shook his fluffy tail at me. "Sometimes you ought to help your*self*."

I had no idea what to say to this, and fortunately I was interrupted by a tap at the window. I recognized the rapid pattern as one I often heard on my shop door. Turning, I saw it was indeed Luca, plastered to the glass. Knowing him, he was probably beaming wildly or making faces, but his face wasn't visible. Instead, the morning darkness combined with his flowing robes to make him look like a terrifying apparition.

"I am *not* going out there," William declared.

"Don't worry, it's me he wants, remember? Anyway, I'll try to be home earlier today," I promised, shifting my cloak and satchel in preparation to face the outdoors. "Thorn knows what's up, too, so you can call on her if you need help."

"Whatever," said William.

I slipped out the salon door, crossing from William's chilly send-off into Luca's bright enthusiasm.

"Hi Red! I hope you don't mind I came over a little early? I got everything ready this morning and I figured, why wait? After all we don't want to keep Tomte waiting! He said to meet him over by the tree in front of Lavender's. It's about an hour to Poole, did you bring something to read? Do you want to borrow one of my books? I have a whole collection on stories about the mountain range . . ."

* * *

Neither Luca nor I got any reading done on the way to Poole.

Luca's friend, Tomte, turned out to be considerate, humorous, and exactly as chatty as Luca himself. The old wooden sleigh slid along the forest road, which was no doubt full of birdsong and the crackling of icy branches; I mostly heard stories about the farmers living around Belville. I also enjoyed a very thorough history of Pine, the local county seat, seeing as our road out of town went straight to Pine and we only veered off to go up another mountain at the last moment.

As the road shifted, the sleigh laboring up and up, Tomte had to focus on his driving. Luca and I slid to the back to give him some space. I'd just gotten used to the quiet when Luca leaned toward me, his leg brushing mine as we sat side by side on the bench.

"Red," he said, his voice a little more soft and serious than usual, "You mentioned yesterday that you and Snow had gone to Gloria's?"

"Yeah, yesterday morning we were running some errands," I said. Without really meaning to, I echoed his manner, tilting my head toward his and lowering my voice. "Why?"

"I was thinking," he said, and paused. Then, "I guess you've seen the mirror they have in there? Right by the front desk?"

"I hadn't noticed it until yesterday," I admitted. "I guess I just head straight for the back, normally. You've seen it, then?"

Luca nodded. "It was there last time I went in for a trim."

His hand went to his neck as he spoke, dipping under his hood. I hesitated, thinking about this. Under his robe, Luca bore mossy green tattoos across his shoulders and neck, and he even had a horn protruding from his forehead—all leftovers from the old curse. A magic spell in his hood hid those things from public view, but of course he'd have to remove that sometimes, like for trimming his close-cropped black hair. I'd never thought about that before. I wasn't sure how it made me feel.

And more importantly, it was clear *he* had some strong

feelings about it.

"Did you look in it?" he asked, his voice even lower.

"No, I didn't even think to," I confessed. "Maybe I was a little scared. It seemed to strike Snow pretty deeply. Have you?"

"I did," he said, his gaze dropping to his hands in his lap. "I, um—well, I—when I looked in it—I think I saw—well, I'm pretty sure it was him . . . I saw myself—but myself when I was Prince Kalos."

The prince of the Drus who once lived in Belville, and were driven out by a curse. The weight of it hit me—a weight Luca somehow carried all the time!

"Um, do you—what do you think of that?" Luca asked me.

"Luca, what do *you* think about it?" I asked. The sleigh jolted against a boulder, but we remained focused. "It's not important what *I* think. It was your reflection."

For a moment Luca's green eyes met mine, and then slid away, looking out over the trees. "Honestly? It kind of scared me."

This confused me, because in the story of the Drus, Kalos had been the victim, not the aggressor. A little bit like Snow, actually. I leaned closer, letting my hand fall on top of his. "Why?"

"Because," said Luca, drawing a very deep breath, "because Kalos had answers. Maybe not always good ones, or the right ones, but still. People looked to him as a leader. But that isn't me any more. I don't have any answers at all."

"How could you say that?" I asked, my fingers tightening over his. "Luca, you have all kinds of answers. You're the one who arranged this trip, even. You're always the first one we go to when we have questions about Belville."

"Yes, but—but those aren't *big* questions," he said.

Ah. I started to get a glimmer of a feeling of what Luca meant. "You mean the *really* big kinds of answers, the things at the heart of everything else? But no one has those."

"Are you sure?" Luca's nose wrinkled. "What about—what about people like Sir Rowan?"

"Sir Rowan?" I repeated, bewildered. "I guess he *seems* like he has things figured out. But I doubt he has nearly as many answers as he wants you to think."

"And aren't you always looking for those big answers?" Luca pressed, regardless. "Things like who's behind a murder, and why?"

"Ye-es," I said slowly, drawing out the word. "But if you ask me, those are also kind of small questions. They're really important—don't get me wrong—but they're still not as big as *how can we help support each other?* or, more specifically in this case, *can we make sure that Snow and the dwarves are treated fairly?*"

When Luca was silent, thinking about this, I added softly, "And it's okay to not have those answers. Those are the kinds of things we'll figure out in time, right?"

Luca looked back at me, his eyes starting to light up once more, and the rush of relief I felt was so surprising and so loud in my heart that at first I didn't hear Tomte when he said we were getting close to Poole.

* * *

Despite knowing comparatively little about Poole, I liked it at first. It had the kind of snow-dusted, hot-cocoa-infused icy charm that could make even a desert dweller like me admit that winter climates could be pretty cute. Though Poole was on a separate, smaller peak than our own, it was nearer the top. Everything around us was ice and steep slopes. Small houses huddled along streets paved white, and evergreens presided over cozy town squares. The air smelled distinctly like candy canes.

"I think it's a spell," Luca leaned over and whispered when he noticed me take a long, disbelieving sniff. "Or maybe a curse."

Intriguing as that may be, I reminded myself we hadn't come to Poole for sightseeing and history. As we waved Tomte off on his way up the mountain, I said, "Should we stop by the local bookshop first? Do they have one here?"

"I don't think they have one. But," Luca said, his grin allaying my concern, "I brought along a map!"

"Of course you did." I smiled as I watched him fumble with his overloaded knapsack, thinking, *I'm glad he seems to have recovered.* And then, *it's a good thing we didn't have to walk here.*

"Here it is! But I don't think we need it, anyway." As he straightened, Luca pointed up the mountain, over my head. "I'm pretty sure that's where the Frost clan lives."

I looked up and had to agree. Luca had singled out the one house that wasn't clustered with the rest. Instead, its roof peaks rose above the town streets like a cluster of royal statues overlooking their land.

Climbing through the neighborhood streets toward our goal was a little harder than usual, thanks to my sore thighs. Fortunately, Luca was ready with a distracting—if increasingly breathless—string of "interesting facts" about mountain architecture. As he elaborated about timberlines and cross-beam support, I couldn't help but notice that the mansion above us wasn't living up to its grand promises. In fact, the closer we got, the more it looked like a jumble of statues knocked over a century ago and left to crumble in the snow. Eaves drooped, windows cracked, and as we came up to it, the fence seemed to be held up by snowdrifts and spiderwebs.

"Huh," said Luca, pausing in front of a once-ornate gate to catch his breath.

"'Huh' indeed," I agreed. Turning to him with a raised eyebrow, I asked, "I don't suppose you have an architectural name for places like this?"

"Haunted," Luca said promptly.

"Wrong season for hauntings," I retorted, grinning at him as I pushed open the gate. Rather than iron, it was ice, and it clung to my glove as though asking to be taken away from such a decrepit place.

"Abandoned, maybe?" Luca scurried to keep up as I crossed the once-manicured, now-jumbled yard. Ice sculpture littered the grounds, which had been terraced into the hillside.

"You better hope it isn't," I whispered as we reached the front door. Luca held up crossed fingers, grinning, as I reached for the knocker.

More ice, I realized, thankful that I'd worn thick woolen mittens over my habitual lab gloves. *If they're ice fairies, why not fix the place up with the stuff?*

My question was answered even sooner than my knock. When at last someone appeared, that someone appeared sullen and resentful, as though they'd only opened the door so that they might have an excuse to slam it in my face. Nothing about them screamed "initiative" or "Do-It-Yourself."

"Hi," I said, echoed by Luca. "We're—we're here to interview you."

The pale face looked up at me suspiciously, and I tried not

to sidle. Of all the things we'd discussed on the way to Poole, Luca and I actually hadn't covered what our cover story ought to be. But I'd realized quickly that we'd need one, and I hoped fervently that Luca would play along.

"Why'd you want to interview *me?*" The fairy at the door, a young woman if I had to guess, remained mostly hidden. But like Snow, she was easy to identify: skin so white it was tinged with light blue, huge crystal blue eyes, and silver hair glinted from the shadows of the house. She seemed to be wearing a fuzzy holiday robe.

My brain, momentarily stalled by the reindeer prancing across the fairy's midriff, failed me. Fortunately, Luca stepped up.

"We're from the paper," he explained eagerly. "The one in Belville. People are clamoring for stories about ice and snow these days! We thought your family would have special insight."

"What, just 'cause we run the ice business in Poole?" the fairy shifted, leaning into one hip. She looked suspiciously as if she thought that people who wanted to read about ice right after a heavy storm deserved to be spat upon. I couldn't help but agree that Luca's cover story was a little thin—but still, it was better than what I'd come up with.

"Yes, we—"

"If I never see so much as an icicle for all my days, it'll be too soon," the fairy declared, interrupting Luca.

"Interesting," I said, doing my best reporter impression. "Can we quote you on that?"

"We'd need your name to quote you, of course," my fellow paper agent added.

Thank all the gods and goddesses for Luca, I thought. If William had come, he'd already have the fairy engaged in a shouting match.

"I'm not the one in charge 'round here," the fairy protested, frowning at Luca. "You'd have to ask Auntie for quotes. Not that she'll give you any. *She'll* want to talk about ice even less than I do."

"Interesting," I said again. "And do all of your family members feel the same? Have any of them branched out?"

"How could they, when they all live right here?" the fairy snorted.

I nodded and acted as if I was making notes. And in my head, I was: *So, the Frost family doesn't seem to know about Snow's existence, if this woman thinks all her relatives live right here. But they could still be interested in the mine for business reasons.* "In that case, what's next for your family?" I asked, though I knew it was repetitive. Maybe she'd just take me for a dogged reporter. "If ice has been your business, but you're getting out of it, then—"

"I didn't say we were getting out of it, did I?" snapped the fairy. "That was *my* idea, to leave it altogether, but no one listens to me. Auntie and Uncle and my mum, *they're* the ones on the board. Running the company into the ground, they are. Who needs fresh ice all the time when everyone has an ice box to keep things cold?"

"You mean," Luca said hesitantly, "because people's cold containers are more effective than they used to be, say a hundred years ago, your business has dried up?"

"And here I thought reporters were fools." The fairy cracked the door open a little wider, giving Luca an appraising look. "Wait, you look like a scholar."

"It's a, um, it's a disguise," Luca said hurriedly. "To, um, make people pay more attention—"

"Iceboxes have been around a long time, though," I interrupted. "Surely the ice business would have felt that by now?"

"Look around you," the fairy sneered at me. "You think we've been living in the pink these past decades?"

I slid a glance at Luca, who was still fidgeting nervously. "So the family's thinking of branching out, huh? Into what?"

"They aren't. I told you. I told 'em they ought to go for stuff that doesn't melt. Like silver, everyone needs silver. And these mountains have all kinds of ore in them. It would fix all our problems!"

Luca fidgeted again. Desperate, I stomped discreetly on the hem of his robe. "So, um, you're waiting for your family to agree to—"

"Waiting for them to die, more like," the fairy interrupted again. When both Luca and I, distracted from all fidgets, looked at her aghast, she had the self-consciousness to add, "What? It's just an expression. Fairies basically live forever—everyone knows that. Why are you still here, anyway? I told you I wasn't giving out quotes."

And with that, the front door slammed in our faces. I flinched, and Luca coughed in the icy dust.

"Oookay then." I turned slowly to my partner in crime. "I don't know if we've solved any *existing* mysteries yet, but if one of the Frost clan ends up murdered, I know where I'm telling the police to look first."

14

Social Graces

Luca and I loitered around the mansion for a little while after we'd been dismissed, but no other family members showed up. Personally, I found that rather relieving. Eventually we decided to head back into Poole, even though we still had several hours before Tomte would be free to pick us up.

"So," Luca said, shuffling carefully lest he slip and slide down the steep streets, "that was probably, what, Snow's cousin? Or possibly her half-sister, if they share a father."

I snorted. "No wonder half-siblings get such a bad rap in fairy tales."

"You can't say that, Red," Luca protested, sputtering even as he grinned. "Besides, it's *step* siblings usually, not half siblings. Not that either one is bad! But you ought to know better than to categorize someone according to their story. The Scholars Agreement of Brass says that no one should be penalized or profiled according to impersonal evidence!"

"Is that the actual wording? I never heard it before. I just know my moms used to call me a lazy reasoner if I relied too much on old tales," I joked. Whether it was put in scholarly terms or simply the creed of a family of Seers, the fact was, most people in Beyond considered profiling characters according to old stories—or according to race, as well—to be very poor taste. All around us, stories played out every day, with infinite variations. Just because Snow was a dead ringer for a certain fairy tale didn't mean that we could make any assumptions about the people around her. Just take her "huntsman" as an example: rather than an uneducated serf of the family, Sir Rowan seemed to be—if I had read between the lines right—their very fancy and martially-inclined butler.

The thing about stories is that they're difficult to pin down until they've ended. So most of the people in Beyond, in addition to being headstrong enough to write their own endings, had to be patient.

"Your parents sound so cool," Luca said. "You grew up on the Isle of Kairoi, right?"

My heel skidded underneath me and I almost ended up on my butt on the snowy sidewalk. *Why don't they put in more stairs around here?* "Uh, yeah, I did," I admitted. "I try not to tell everyone—"

"Don't worry, your secret's safe with me," chirped Luca. He cocked his head as he watched me instead of the road. "But why is it a secret?"

"It's not a secret," I protested lamely. "It's just—I don't know—a different part of my life. It's not relevant to what I do today. Like, two separate chapters—two books, even," I added, groping for a metaphor that could explain the fact that while I loved my family dearly, I didn't feel like having a conversation about mystics and lineage.

"I know what you mean," Luca said quietly.

I almost slipped again when I realized that *of course* he knew what I meant. In fact Luca could probably have filled three or four separate books with the different phases of his life. *How come I keep putting my foot in my mouth with him?* I wondered, a bit desperately. *The last thing I want to do is hurt him, or be insensitive. Why can't I seem to look beyond my own nose? I can't believe he still—*

"I don't know about you," Luca was saying as I berated myself, and something in the seriousness of his voice caught my attention. "But for me, feeling that—that separation between chapters of my life—it's like a very deep scar, running right through me. Actually I *hope* that's not how you feel. I guess it might be different, because you chose to pursue your own path, and I—well, it was kind of forced on me."

"Oh, my goddesses, Luca," I finally managed to say. "I'm so sorry, I didn't mean to—"

"No, it's okay," he interrupted, turning to put his hand on my arm. "I didn't finish yet. See, what I was going to say is, yes, it feels like this really deep rift. But, I don't know, that feeling kind of eases sometimes. It doesn't bother me as much, when I'm with you."

I stopped dead in the street, blinking. Suddenly the sunshine on the snow around us was way too bright. My eyes stung. "Luca—are you saying *I* make you feel better? But I'm always saying the wrong thing!"

"I know *you* think so," Luca said, chuckling. "But I don't think so. It's like you were saying earlier—we always figure things out, eventually. I'm just really glad we can talk about things like this, Red."

"I'm—um—me too," I mumbled, scraping at my eyes with the back of my mittens. Unable to process the warmth and kindness of what Luca was saying to me, my thoughts jumped to a neutral subject. "Oh, but—poor Snow. It just occurred to me, she probably feels this way, too. But I wonder if she can talk to the dwarves about it? If any of them understand? Or how much she carries forward with her, from her childhood?"

Luca accepted my only-slightly-relevant babbles with grace, walking companionably along as I started moving again. After a while, he mused, "Research suggests that what you begin life as continues with you, in one form or another, throughout your life. I mean, not about people, that research is about types of paper actually, but still, I think the basic idea is the same. I think people always have a little core of them that remembers. Like when I was imprisoned, working for Owl as Jade—"

"You don't, um," I interrupted. I hated to repeat my mistakes, especially twice in a conversation. But the thought of what Luca might know of Jade's memories also mortified me.

Luca watched me, his eyes solemn beneath his hood. I sighed and did my best to let go of my mortification—how important was it, really, in the face of everything Luca had been through? And despite all that, he was still the sweetest person. Hurting him was the worst feeling in the whole world.

"*Do* you remember everything, from being Kalos, and then Jade?" I asked finally.

"Not everything," he answered. "It's all kind of hazy. Probably because there was magic and curses involved. Snow's memories of growing up and being sent away from home are probably much clearer."

"Uh huh." I was torn between focusing on Snow and the mystery, and abandoning all pretext of investigation and quizzing Luca on what he meant by 'not everything.' Neither course of action seemed quite right. "I'm hungry," I announced, a bit too loudly. Snow slid off a nearby roof with a *whump*. "Are you hungry? How about cold? Want some hot chocolate? I'm buying."

Luca glanced at me with an amused look that suggested he knew all about my internal struggle. But I was grateful when he simply agreed and picked out a cafe down the street.

The cafe was cozy and charming, and soon I had a porcelain cup—really more of a bowl—filled to the brim with thick, rich hot chocolate in my hands. Just breathing in the chocolaty goodness was enough to remind me to hit the "reset" button on my mood. The mountain of sugary whipped cream and crystalline sprinkles atop my drink didn't hurt, either.

"Here, Red, let's sit at the bar along the window," Luca called as he weaved between tiny tables and overstuffed chairs. "We can keep watch!"

I shrugged at the kindly dryad behind the counter, as though to say, *he doesn't mean it in a creepy way, promise!*, and followed. The counter top along the window was inlaid with blue and purple mosaic tiles, so pretty I almost regretted setting my overflowing cup on it. But I had to in order to shed my heavy cloak, which I hung on a hook in the nearby corner before sitting on a plush purple stool.

Luca had already claimed his seat, not to mention half his salted caramel-topped drink. At first I thought that the sugar rush had made him jittery, but I realized as I settled in that he was still quietly laughing at me.

"You got something on your nose," he said, pointing at his own just in case I'd forgotten where mine was.

"Hm?" I wiped at my nose and my hand came away slathered in whipped cream. "Oh, jeez. I'm surprised I don't have a beard as well," I chuckled.

"Maybe you do, and I just haven't said anything yet," Luca said, clearly doing his best to maintain a straight face. In this case, his best wasn't very good.

"Well," I said, grinning, "I guess that'll be my disguise, then, if any angry Frosts show up."

Luca burst out laughing, and I had to reach for his cup to keep him from spilling it. "That's one of the things I like about you, Red," he said as he recovered. "You always make the best of things. It's like you paint everything around you with a golden brush."

"*Me?*" I set my cup down, surprised. "What about *you?* If I have a golden brush, then you have a pink one."

Luca tilted his head at me, still chortling. "Pink?"

"Yeah, like roses, you know?" I was *trying* to allude to rose-colored vision, or something of the sort—but the words wouldn't come. Instead, like a pair of punch-drunk pixies, the two of us dissolved into giggles again.

"This is what you call keeping watch?" The new voice cut through our merriment.

I looked up to the speaker—someone I recognized from Belville, though she'd been gone for several seasons. Short, stocky, with tipped ears and slanted eyes that suggested elven heritage, the word she immediately prompted in my mind was *leonine.* From her intense brown gaze to her curly auburn hair and glowing amber skin, everything about her suggested competence and power. And I knew from past experience that was entirely accurate.

"I—I was joking, promise," said Luca, swallowing his laughter.

"Leo? You're back?" I asked, instinctively leaning forward.

Leo, or more accurately, Mary Jane Leonine, Belville's one and only reporter, glanced between us, a shrewd, calculating look. Then, with a smile, she slid onto the stool beside Luca. Onto the counter she placed her order, a chocolate croissant and a steaming latte. Luca swiveled and scooted toward me to give her more space.

"Nice of you to remember me," Leo said. "I hope you'll understand if I don't shake your hand, though. I hate using the prosthetic when it's this cold outside."

Leo dipped her right shoulder at us, ruffling a chic woolen jacket. The sleeve was tucked up and I recalled that her arm ended abruptly, just shy of where her elbow might have been. All kinds of prosthetics are available in Beyond—some are said to be even better than organic limbs. But if Leo didn't want the fuss of dealing with one under her heavy garments, I certainly could understand that.

I still wondered what she was doing in Poole, though. Last I'd heard, she'd been off on an in-depth investigation of a tropical fish smuggling ring. Meanwhile, Luca leaned toward me, and I could tell what was on his mind: *is this some kind of karma for having pretended we were reporters earlier? Does she know?*

I doubted she did. But either way, Leo was giving us little opportunity to explain ourselves. After a tiny sip of coffee, she went on, "Didn't think I'd meet Red the alchemist and Luca the bookseller way out here in Poole, though. Isn't it a bit early in the season for holiday sightseeing trips?"

Luca began, "No—" and ended quickly when I poked him in the back, hidden from Leo's eyes.

"Never too early," I said firmly. I respected Leo, but we'd never been close enough for me to suppose that she valued my privacy more than she valued her paper.

"I suppose you'll only get busier as the holiday approaches," Leo conceded, watching me over her pastry. It looked heavenly. My stomach growled, reminding me that I actually *was* hungry and that hot chocolate, as thick and rich as it might be, did not count as a meal.

"Are you out here for a story?" Luca asked, fiddling with his empty cup.

Leo watched him like a cat debating whether or not to pounce on a catnip mouse. "I'm on the way back from one, actually," she said. "But I can never pass by Poole without stopping here. I was at Lake Greendale this morning," she added, fully assured that we'd been dying to ask the question.

I was hooked. "Greendale? Why'd you go out there?"

"Word on the street is, the Greendale deal with the mine is about to fall through," Leo answered. "There could be shady business involved."

Luca shifted on his seat. "I didn't realize they had a deal with the mine. What do you mean, 'shady'? Like bribes and stuff?"

"Got it in one," Leo said with a smile. "Although in this case, there *is* a little more than that. Turns out Lake Greendale is in jeopardy. It was made centuries ago with a dam, and that dam is worse for wear these days. Interesting, don't you think?"

"So, they need money to fix it up?" Luca scrunched up his nose.

Leo laughed, tipping her head back, her voice robust. "You're not wrong. But in this case they want gravel. My sources say they're hoping to restructure their deal with Lark, and she's not playing along. Too many other things going on at the mine, if you catch my drift."

"A *gravel* deal?" My mind had stuck on this point. There was some esoteric magical ore to be had at the mine, and Snow's old family was fixated on the mine's waste?

Leo watched me, her eyes alight. "I love talking over my assignments with fresh eyes," she commented to Luca. "That's how I find the best angle to write about. Our local alchemist thinks the rocks are most interesting, does she?"

"I—I just think it's strange," I said.

"Everything is when these big contracts are changing," Leo said with a shrug. "Unless you have some inside information, perhaps?"

I hesitated. To be honest, I was looking for a distraction. Some local deity must have seen fit to answer my unspoken prayer, because as I glanced out the window, I caught sight of someone in uniform striding purposefully down the street.

There was no mistaking that uniform.

While I continued to hesitate, the police officer burst into the cafe, snow swirling around his boots. Leo and Luca both turned to look as well, all questions of mines and information forgotten.

"I'm looking for one Cinnabar Sunset," said the officer, an older night-elf with electric purple eyes. His gaze on me suggested that, even though we'd never met, he already knew he'd found who he was looking for.

"Call me Red," I stuttered, rising from my chair like a guilty child in school. "Why do you need me?"

"Not me," the officer corrected, snapping his boots together. "Officer Thorn of Belville's sent out an emergency communication requesting your presence at her station."

"What, now?" I asked, thinking sadly of the lunch I was about to miss. "Do you know what's happened?"

"At your earliest convenience," the officer said, with a furrow in his brow that suggested *now* was when I would need to make it convenient. "The nature of our communication did not allow for details."

I looked down at Luca. "Can you get in touch with—"

"We have already located Tomte," the officer interrupted. He gestured with one gloved hand at the street. From the center of town, I heard the jingle of the sleigh bells approaching. "It was he who suggested we look here for you."

"I guess he knows me well," Luca said as he rose, shooting me a nervous smile. "It—it must be a really big deal, right?"

"We can't be sure what it is," I said, refusing to worry prematurely. Leo waved us on, and the officer gestured impatiently at the door. I sighed and grabbed my cloak. "Let's go find out."

15

Poisoned Pen

As the sleigh shivered and shook its way along the old mountain roads, I had time to think. Luckily for us, Tomte had brought some extra lunch along. Chowing down on falafel sandwiches kept him and Luca busy, and as I ate mine I savored the silence.

At the station, I knew, it'd be mayhem and noise, as usual. Of course if something truly awful had happened, like another murder, then perhaps that chaos would be merited. But as a shopkeeper used to traveling solo—aside from one grumpy magical familiar—I still hadn't gotten the hang of doing things as loudly and as collaboratively as possible, which was the way Officer Thorn liked to do them.

I hadn't even realized that she *had* an emergency communication system. But of course, she would; it only made sense that all the nearby police stations, perhaps even all the stations in Beyond, ought to be connected. Thinking about it, I could admit to myself that part of me had viewed this trip to Poole as a respite. How short-lived that hope had turned out to be!

I can understand why someone might want *to be at the bottom*

130

of a lake, I thought wryly to myself. *Or, perhaps, on top of a mountain in a mining gang with a bunch of dwarves.*

Appealing as it might be to "leave it all behind," I knew I'd never be able to. I had too many good friends to worry over—not to mention a certain snow fairy I was feeling more and more sympathetic toward.

***

"Are you sure, Red? I could go with you," Luca offered for the eighth time.

I smiled despite my impatience. *What was it I was thinking about leaving things behind?* "Luca, I told you, there's no need to be worried yet. Officer Thorn only asked for me, and besides, you have a shop to run." I gestured at said shop, which was waiting stolidly right behind Luca. Tomte and his sleigh were already rattling out of town, having deposited us on the bookstore's doorstep.

But apparently, Luca didn't want to go in.

"I promise that if anything serious is going on, you'll be the first person I come to. Aside from William," I added. *And Gloria, who will probably be waiting for me outside of her shop. It takes a village to solve a mystery, I guess . . .*

"Alright," Luca said reluctantly, drawing out the word. "But, Red?"

"Yes, what?" I'd already turned to leave, but paused.

"Just be safe, okay?"

"Sure," I said, gearing up to run to the station.

"And—Red? Thanks for letting me investigate with you. I had fun."

At the earnest note in his voice, my consternation evaporated. Thorn and her catastrophes notwithstanding, I stopped and turned back around. "Luca, it's me who should be thanking *you*. You were great. If it had been just me, the Frosts probably would have thrown me out before I finished saying hello."

Luca beamed. As I turned to go, for real this time, I couldn't help but think that this was a *much* better note to leave things on.

I whipped through the streets of Belville, not pausing by my own store. I couldn't help but notice, though, that everything looked normal around town—aside from some strange new posters tied to the trees in the Square. No one would be barbarian enough to nail anything into the bark of the old maples and oaks—some of which I suspected of being sentient; it was hard to tell with trees—but occasionally, important notices or festival decorations would be secured around their trunks with string.

Time for 'sightseeing,' as Leo would put it, later, I told myself. *I doubt Officer Thorn's emergency has to do with harmless posters.*

That, however, turned out to be untrue.

I burst into the police station to find Officer Thorn hunched behind the front desk, deep in a hand-wavey conversation with Trent, the local Witch. For reasons lost to time, every small town in Pastoria has one, and only one, Witch. They were assigned and distributed by some unknown power. Unknown to us layfolk, that is; I'm sure the system made perfect sense to the Witches involved in it. I'd always figured it must be something like Thorn's police guild or my alchemical apprenticeship. The Witches went through training and then, when another Witch died, would be assigned to a town accordingly.

I might not have been a fan of magic on the whole, but I liked Trent, who—having arrived in Belville just after William and me—had become a sort of younger brother to me. If I was Thorn's Unofficial Assistant Number One, Trent was surely Number Two. His charms and scrying skills often came in handy. Not to mention the fact that his unflappable demeanor served as a great counterpoint to Thorn's tendency to leap to conclusions. Seeing him in the station, leaning casually against Thorn's heavy desk, made some of the tension between my shoulders release at once.

"Hey look," said Trent, as cold daylight poured into the station behind me. "It's Red. Hi, Red. Can you talk some sense into Officer Thorn?"

"Red!" Officer Thorn looked up at once, crumpling a piece of paper on the desk before her. "What took you so long? And how come you never told me your real name is Cinnabar?"

At once, I saw what had happened: Officer Thorn, in looking for me, had gone to William. William, in turn, had made free with the personal details. *Maybe there was something about the police communication spell that required real names.* I made a face as I shut the door behind me. "An alchemist named Cinnabar? Come on, that's just a pun waiting to happen. You don't need any encouragement as it is."

When Officer Thorn looked confused, Trent leaned over and explained, "Cinnabar is a rock that makes mercury. You know, like alchemists use? Right, Red?"

"It's a mineral," I answered on autopilot. "Is someone going to tell me what's going on?"

"There's been a sighting," Officer Thorn declared. "An *attack.*"

At the same time, Trent said, "The miners made an ancient

dragon mad."

I looked between the two, unsure whether to laugh or be concerned. Officer Thorn's long black hair, usually perfect, stuck out at odd angles from her head. Trent, meanwhile, was his usual pale, human-looking self. The purple streaks in his shoulder-length hair were a bit stronger than last time I'd seen him, but that was it. His jeans—Trent was the only person I knew who wasn't a gnome and yet wore denim—and black-and-blue tie-dye t-shirt were covered in smudges, suggesting that Thorn had interrupted a winter cleaning effort.

"Start at the beginning," I suggested. I pulled a wooden visitor's chair out from the wall and leaned against it, not wanting to sit again so soon after the sleigh ride.

"I was up at the mine, making Lark aware that I'm officially treating Raven and Heron's deaths as murders, when it happened. Lark had assigned the Flock to find the vein the new ore came from—and they found it. As soon as they identified the correct branch of the mine system, a roar was heard. Minutes later, there was a dragon flying over the mine and camp, and several miners got injured in the scuffle," Officer Thorn said, *thump*ing her open palm against her desk for emphasis. "It was an unprovoked display. Ignore the Witch; we're having a difference of opinion."

Trent scoffed.

"Lark's shutting down anything to do with the new ore," Officer Thorn continued, her teeth clearly gritted. "And she wants protections on the rest of the mine. And so do I. In fact, I want them on the whole town. On page two hundred and forty-eight of the Guild handbook, it clearly states that sightings of extra-large or larger magical creatures with presumed malicious intent is cause for an emergency!"

Extra-large echoed in my mind, as did *emergency. They really have seen a dragon on the mountain now. And it was supposedly so safe! Oh, boy, what I'm going to do to Sir Rowan when I see him!*

But I did my best to set aside my fear and anger, and to focus on what was before us. Officer Thorn was toying rather viciously with a paper on her desk, one that looked an awful lot like the notices I'd seen in the Square. "And how does that play in?" I asked, pointing to it. She whirled it around for me to read. In bright red paint on white canvas-like paper, someone had drawn a crude set of crossed pickaxes. Underneath, they'd written,

> *First they come for our jobs!*
> *Then they disturb our peace!*
> *THey bring MURDER and DRAGONS into ur homes!*
> *The dwarVES must LEAVE!*

"Someone is using the dragon attack to stir everyone up against the Flock," Officer Thorn said, as though Trent and I were slow as snails in the mental department. "This is a classic example of ostracizing a subverted or foreign group!"

Trent crossed his arms. "It wasn't an *attack*. The dragon just flew by and people got scared, that's all. Also, did you memorize that whole guidebook?"

Despite my nerves, I hid a smile behind my hand. It *was* strange to hear Thorn using such officious language.

"It's a recruit's first assignment. But that's not the point," Officer Thorn insisted. "How can you say there isn't any danger? Half a dozen of Lark's miners are up there in the mine infirmary!"

"Yeah, with bumps and bruises and *sprains,* because they

took one look and ran," Trent challenged. "It's not like the dragon came out breathing fire or something. Has it occurred to you that maybe the dragon wants to talk?"

Officer Thorn glowered like a smushed and smoldering jack-o-lantern. "It *roared*! I heard it!"

"Sure, but only when the miners were right next to its lair, most likely," Trent shot back. "As long as we stay away from it, we should be fine—exactly like Belville's been fine for centuries up til now!"

Breathless, the two turned to me.

"Well, it's good that the dragon just flew overhead and then left," I said diplomatically. "That *is* what happened, right? But now Lark is concerned? That makes sense. And where is Maeve?"

"Where *is* Maeve," Officer Thorn repeated with emphasis. "Isn't that what we'd all like to know these days!"

I glanced at Trent, troubled. "Do you really not know?"

"Oh, I know, all right." Officer Thorn shifted in her chair, making the stout wooden legs groan and creak against the hard floor. "She's in the basement. Filing reports. *You* two stay here. I need to show you something else."

With that, she rose and made for her office, each step shaking the station's timbers. In her wake, I raised my eyebrows at Trent.

"I didn't even realize there *were* filing cabinets in the basement. Why does it sound like Maeve's been made to go sit in the corner?" I whispered.

Trent ducked his head, a lopsided grin on his face. "Because she has. From the sound of it, she's been spending too much time 'investigating' on her own up on the mountain."

"I can hear you, you know," Officer Thorn declared as she

came back into view. "Are you two going to help me, or are you going to be joining her?"

Trent straightened, his hands rising as if to say, *this again?* "This isn't school, Officer. You can't—"

"Look," Officer Thorn insisted. With no further explanation, she slapped another piece of evidence down on the desk.

I crossed over to look at it; it was considerably smaller than the poster—little more than a scrap of woven fabric—thickly woven, *like,* I realized, *Snow and the dwarves' vests.* My stomach plummeted to the ground. But it wasn't bloody—just strangely glowy. After a moment, Trent gave in and leaned over my shoulder to take a look, too.

Trent finally shrugged. "So what? Someone tore their shirt at the mine?"

"Snow did," Officer Thorn said heavily. "It was Snow who found the vein that sent the dragon roaring. As they were running out, she tripped and got a bit scraped up. And Maeve found her."

Trent and I exchanged a glance, waiting.

"And then," Thorn continued at last, even more ponderous than before, "Maeve came into the office, where I was still meeting with Lark. Lark keeps to her office, as you know, except when she's doing rounds. She's very punctual. Anyway, the upshot of that is, we weren't outside to see the dragon. We did hear the uproar, but that was it. We were about to go check when Maeve came in, talking about the attack. And, I'll admit, it sounded unbelievable at first. But when Lark expressed doubt as to what Snow and the Flock had seen . . ."

The longer Thorn's voice trailed off, the higher my eyebrows rose. Finally, I had to guess. "Are you saying Maeve jumped Lark?"

I wasn't surprised because Maeve had started a fight with someone in a wheelchair—actually, Officer Thorn and I had once fought with Lark, and she had proven more capable than either of us. What surprised me was that Maeve hadn't been intimidated by the brisk, in-charge air of professionalism that surrounded Lark at all times.

"She threatened to arrest her." Thorn's voice came out half sigh, half hoarse whisper. I realized she probably didn't want Maeve to hear us. "For endangering the miners."

"I thought she's only a trainee. She has no real power," Trent pointed out.

I watched Thorn glare at him as I straightened slowly. I'd never known her to be mad at Trent—not once. Nor had I ever heard her so desperate. *She feels responsible for Maeve,* I reasoned. *So she loses either way. Either Maeve's just a trainee and yet she's not giving Thorn the chance to stand up for her, or Thorn was trying to trust Maeve, and Maeve flew off the handle.*

"Well, I'm sure that wasn't pleasant, but it seems to be dealt with for now," I said. "So really there's just the dragon itself to worry about, and then whoever's spreading these notes. And when you look at this one, it *is* strangely inconsistent."

Officer Thorn was staring at *me* now, hanging on every word. I cleared my throat and pointed out, "The spelling, for example. Why would the note-writer spell 'our' correctly several times, but misspell it as 'ur' in the line about homes? And who would benefit from stirring up rumors, anyway? It clearly isn't the dwarves or Snow, and most of the miners would go to Lark with a complaint before they started putting up posters in town."

"Yes," breathed Thorn. "See? Exactly. So who wrote it?"

Trent caught my pointed look and shrugged. "I could try to

do a tracing spell on it, but—"

"Do it. Take it," Thorn said, thrusting the paper across the desk at Trent. I could tell the Witch had been rubbed the wrong way by all of this, even though I didn't quite understand why. Usually Trent was more than generous when it came to his friends. *Please, please, just go with it,* I thought, my eyes boring holes in his head. Though I doubt he heard, Trent took the paper without complaint.

"I didn't bring any of my stuff," he said. "I didn't have time. Let me gather up some eyebright and mugwort, okay?"

"Anything you need." Officer Thorn sank back into her chair, her elbows on the desk. In response to my sympathetic look, she closed her eyes with another deep sigh.

"You know what's going to be most helpful," I said, "is hosting a town meeting to make sure everyone's on the same page about the dragon. Whether that means protection spells or not."

"The town needs to be protected," Officer Thorn growled.

"Yes, but setting aside the guidebook for a moment," I said, treading on thin ice, "think about it: Trent was right. The dragon didn't directly hurt anyone, and as far as we know, it never has before. As long as we keep our heads, we should be just fine, right?"

For a long moment, Officer Thorn was silent, her head in her hands.

"We can just talk it over with everyone," I added. "And then you can make your case with Trent again. How's that?"

With one last sigh, Officer Thorn lifted her head. She glanced up at me with that familiar glint in her eye. "You're exactly right. And *I* was right for getting you back here. We'll call a town meeting at the smiths' guild tonight . . . Cinnabar."

16

One Taste . . .

The Working Guild of the Smiths of Belville huddled at the end of town nearest the mountain, as though hiding. I suppose being so near to the supply of ores was helpful for a blacksmiths' guild, but the building had always struck me as strangely secretive. It took up half a block, only one street off the Square, a quick five-minute walk from my own shop. And yet I rarely visited—except when a town meeting was called. Even when I went up the mountain, with Officer Thorn or otherwise, I usually cut through the neighborhoods around the guild rather than going right past it.

The smith's guild was one of the few buildings in Belville made of brick. It looked like a huge garage, and in most ways, it was: after all, smiths often repaired cart wheels or whole vehicles. Huge bay doors all the way around the main floor could open up, to let in shipments or clean breezes. Sometimes, when the wind was just right and the bays were open, I could hear the ringing of hammers and smell the ash of the furnaces down at my shop. Above the work floor, there was another story I'd never been to; most likely it housed guild offices, maybe even a canteen. I wasn't sure how fancy smiths got. On the whole, they seemed to be even more distrustful of magic and conveniences than I was.

. . . Though admittedly, much of my feelings about blacksmiths came from the fact that I'd very briefly dated one years ago. *Oh, the folly of youth.*

"Right," said Thorn as we approached. Evening had fallen, and the shops were shut; still under its snowy blanket, Belville was strangely quiet. "Thank you all for coming here early with me. The smiths usually set up for us, so I'll just have you stand by the door to greet people while I talk to the Mayor."

"We're being greeters?" William had chosen to come along with the officer, Trent, and me. He shook himself as he eyed the guild building, which loomed at us across the street.

"Red and Trent are," Thorn said firmly. "You're with me, Chatty. We'll man the west entrance after I make sure the mayor's all set. Trent and Red, you take the east one. Write down everyone who comes in and get a feel for what they're saying."

"But wouldn't—" Trent gave up talking as Officer Thorn turned on her heel and marched across the street. He turned to me, waving one hand in consternation. "Wouldn't it make more sense to just, I don't know, put things to a vote as soon as everyone gets in?"

"It does, and we probably will, but right now I think she's looking for any extra evidence she can," I said sympathetically. "You know how riled up she is over the posters, and . . . the mine."

And Maeve, I nearly said, but held my tongue at the last minute. Earlier that afternoon, when Trent had come back with the results of his tracing spell, he'd been downright snide about the posters, insinuating they were the work of the unfortunate police recruit. "No trace of anything here," he'd said, "except *death*." Officer Thorn hadn't taken that too well.

No wonder she didn't want to greet people at the door with him as her partner.

Trent was already halfway across the street, his shoulders hunched and his hands stuck in his pockets. I hurried to catch up and stand with him just inside the open bay door. At the far end of the building, Thorn and William loitered.

We'd arrived a good fifteen minutes early. Glancing around the cavernous work floor, now quiet and tidied for the evening, I saw that the workbenches and machines had been pushed up against one wall, and a stage was visible at the other end of the room. The only people there were two or three figures huddled in the center—people who looked like they represented the smith's guild. I only recognized them vaguely, but figured Thorn would be the one to deal with them. By silent agreement, Trent and I settled in to wait and see who else came through the door.

After about two minutes, Trent broke. I hadn't realized we were playing a waiting game.

"I didn't really *mean* it," he said out of nowhere, as though I'd chained him to a table and shone a bright light in his face.

I turned from staring out the doorway to look at him. "What didn't you mean?"

"About the whole death on the note thing. I mean, it *was* true. There's something afterlife-y about that poster. But those kinds of traces are really hard to pin down," Trent added, staring at the ceiling while he heaved a sigh that seemed to come all the way up from his toes.

"Then why didn't you say that? Why be—" I hesitated, but decided Trent could handle the truth. "Why be so antagonistic about it?"

Trent rolled his eyes. He wasn't as good at it as Gloria, but he was close. "I'm just tired of hearing about Maeve, okay?"

"Tired?" My eyebrows rose. "She's only been in town what, all of four days?"

"I just don't see why it's a big deal."

"Well, you know how Officer Thorn is," I reasoned. Suddenly helping out at a town meeting felt more like writing an advice column.

Trent scoffed.

This made my eyebrow rise even higher. "What's this about, Trent? You *do* know Thorn. You know she'd be just as shaken up if *any* of us were in trouble or acting out."

"Would she, though?"

"Trent," I asked before I could think better of it, "is there something—between you and Officer Thorn?" I wasn't even sure if they were remotely the same age. I would have assumed Trent was much younger than the officer, but who could say? Stranger things had happened.

In this case, though, Trent lay my suspicions to rest immediately. "Ew, no. I mean, not 'ew' about Thorn, but you get what I mean. It's just—we're—I *thought* we were friends. But if that's just how she is about everybody, then. . ."

"Hey." I reached out, laying my hand on Trent's arm. His skin shocked me, just a little, like a static electricity zap. "She may not be the best at showing it, but I'm pretty sure you're her best friend in town. Aside from me, of course," I added with a light-hearted grin. "Basically, whenever she says 'unofficial assistant,' change that in your head to 'friend that I don't want to admit to having because I'm a scary police officer.'"

"Ha. More like 'peon that I'm using for their skills,'" Trent said. But he grinned in the yellowy lamplight as he did.

I kept watching him, curious. "Is that really what's behind all this?"

"What?" Trent kicked at the ground and stuffed his hands back in his pocket. His grin became wry. "You think I'm gonna say I have this big crush on Maeve instead, or something?"

I shrugged. "More power to you if you do, but I think it's pretty clear that her affections are engaged elsewhere."

"It's not about that. I haven't met them yet."

"Excuse me?"

Trent sighed. No doubt he was wondering when people would finally start showing up for the meeting, but I have to admit I was interested. "It's a thing for Witches. They don't want us running around causing drama and then having to leave our towns after we're assigned to them, so we do this thing. One of the first rituals you do shows you the face of your, you know. . ."

"I don't," I said, now fully distracted from the meeting.

"One true love," Trent mumbled. It was hard to tell in the lamplight, but his normally pale skin looked pink. "It's a . . . thing. Every Witch believes in it."

"Okay," I said, charmed by the idea of grungy Trent as a hopeless romantic. "So who's yours?"

"I can't *tell* you," Trent protested, sounding very much like a child laying out the rules of wishes. "Besides, they aren't here yet. I think—I think it's going to be a while."

"And in the meantime, you don't want to feel like you're entirely alone?" I guessed.

This time it was Trent's turn to shrug. He stared resolutely at the door.

"You aren't, you know," I insisted.

Trent's mouth scrunched up like he was trying not to give me the satisfaction of smiling. "There's people coming," he mumbled.

I turned and peeked out the door. Dark shapes moved at the end of the block. "They aren't going to be here for at least another minute," I said, crossing my arms. "So, what are you going to do if everyone wants a protection spell?"

Trent shifted, the tension in his pose releasing. "I don't know, honestly. That's kinda why I was arguing with Thorn. You can't just set up a force field around a whole town, not overnight. It'd be a whole lot easier to just not engage with the dragon at all."

"I see your point, but people don't often take the easy way," I said, feeling my age. Travel and experience broadened horizons, but they also taught caution.

In companionable silence, Trent and I waited to see who would show.

And we only had seconds to wait. The dark shapes from down the block materialized into the grocer and his boys, who filed in without even looking at Trent and me, despite our greetings. At the other end of the room, a rumble indicated the arrival of miners—not *all* the miners Lark employed, but a majority of them, if I had to bet. More townsfolk streamed in past Trent and me, and I gave up hope of saying hello to each one, hastening to write them in a little notebook taken from my hip pocket. Trent made eye contact and even said hi to some of the incomers, but it was clear that everyone was anxious about the dragon sighting and ready for answers. Remembering Sir Rowan's advice about making no noise, I did my best to fade into the shadow of the door frame.

Before we knew it, the guild hall was full.

"I don't get it," Trent whispered to me. Rather than watch the door, he'd pivoted to stare at the people milling about the floor. "The dragon didn't even fly over town—just the mine. Why is everyone so worried?"

"Well, it *was* a dragon," I said reasonably. "A large one, by the sound of it. And besides, Lark's mine is basically part of town at this point. What time is it?"

"Ten past 6:30. Don't you have a pocket watch or something?"

"I *do*, but I'm busy," I said, adding to my notes. "Have Thorn or the mayor stepped up yet?"

"No. Wait—there they are. Here we go," Trent said. He grabbed my shoulder and tugged me further into the room. "Come on, it's starting."

Officer Thorn started things off, her confident voice quelling the murmurs and shuffles at once. Everyone stood shoulder to shoulder listening in rapt attention as she described the basic facts of the sighting—pretty much the same speech she'd given me earlier, though she left out specifics about Snow and the dwarves. As she spoke, I looked around for them, but didn't see them in the crowd. *Maybe those posters got circulated around at the mine, too,* I thought, the cold, hard feeling in my stomach growing larger. I'd tried not to think about it during the afternoon, but with Lark shutting down any investigation of the ore and the mine facing a *dragon*-sized threat, it was starting to look like there was very little I could do to help my new friends.

Or Sir Rowan. He, I noticed, was standing still as a statue beside the opposite door.

Thorn turned the meeting over to Mayor Marguerite and the town council, and they started discussing options—namely, whether to enact some kind of magical defense or not. When they opened up the floor for public suggestions and concerns, they were met with a wave of comments ranging all the way from "we should hunt the dragon down!" to "why haven't we sent away the dwarves, since they're the ones who made it angry?" and everything in between.

"This is so weird," Trent whispered, leaning over to me. "It's like an alternate world or something. You think there's something in the air making everyone act so extreme about all this?"

"What, like a poison?" I frowned. "Not in the guild hall, specifically, if that's what you mean. You and I've been in here longer than most of these people, and all we talked about was your love life."

"Point taken." Still, he elbowed me all the same. My grin was brief.

"Why aren't you up there telling them what magic you can or can't do?" I asked him, as the comments went on and on in front of us.

Trent dug his hands into his pockets, looking uncomfortable. "Honestly, I didn't think I'd need to. I didn't think people'd be this worried. But I guess you're right—maybe I should."

"It'd make sense to limit expectations a bit, at least," I said. Amid the heavy cloaks and coats, my eye caught sight of a spot of pitch black. My heart leapt. In the next minute, to my relief, William emerged from the crowd and came to us, unnoticed by anyone else.

"William, what's going on?" I asked at once, while also appreciating that maybe my canine companion had much better sneaking skills than I did.

"Orders from Thorn," he panted and turned to Trent. "She wants you up there on stage."

"We were just talking about that," I said, looking up at the Witch as well.

Trent shifted from foot to foot. "If they ask me to do anything, though, they'll be disappointed. It's not like I can do something here and now that'll be strong enough. Unless, maybe, if you amplify it."

"You?" Me? I shook my head. *Does he really mean William?*

"We'll cross that bridge when we come to it," William growled.

I looked down at him in surprise. "I don't think I've ever seen you agree to help a Witch before."

"Yeah, well, needs must," the familiar grumped.

Together, Trent and William made their way forward, joining the council and Thorn on the makeshift stage at the other end of the room. Despite being young and relatively new in town, Trent commanded more respect than he probably realized: a second hush fell across the crowd as they saw him.

"Listen," he said, his hands still deep in his pockets, when the mayor gestured for him to speak. "I can't do anything *right now* that's going to stop a dragon. I still think, personally, that the best thing to do is just let it be. And if we want to set up some town-wide protections in the future, we can talk about that later. But . . . if you all want something for tonight . . . Me'n William here can at least put a protective charm on everyone here. It isn't much, but you could think of it kind of like a little bit of good luck. Dragon-avoiding luck, am I right?" Trent smiled a bit nervously at the crowd, which chuckled. As Trent's shoulders eased, so did the tension in the room. Clearly, a decision had been made.

I watched, smiling, as Trent made his preparations. He sat down cross-legged on the cold floor, his hand buried in William's fur. Watching, I couldn't help but think, *Maybe fear is a bit like poison, and that little bit of laughter was enough of an antidote.*

William began to glow, deep starry blue. And to my surprise, Trent began to sing. In fact, he began to sing a spell that sounded a bit like a ballad. He had a surprisingly nice voice, too. And the tune was so light . . .

Even as I felt a warm sensation wash over me, the combination of William and Trent's magic, my own thoughts turned sour once more. Thinking of antidotes made me think of my own power in the present situation—which, despite all of Trent's protests, was even *less* than the Witch's. I'd thrown myself into the mysteries of the ore and the dwarves' deaths because I'd thought I could protect my friends. But when it came right down to it, what could I really accomplish? What could a lone alchemist do against a *dragon*, or even against some unknown murderer?

Trent's song ended with a soft trill, and William's glow faded. Around me, townsfolk began to move and murmur again—but they sounded much more positive than they had before. In fact, some were even smiling.

I sighed as I watched the crowd shift and break. Luca was up near the stage, talking to William, and the sight of him just made me feel even *worse* about the whole situation. Just as I was tugging on my ponytail, wondering how in Beyond everything would work out, I glanced across the right side of the room and noticed some familiar curly auburn hair.

Leo.

<h1 style="text-align:center">17</h1>

Home is Where the Hearth is

Officer Thorn's natural exuberance had returned with the successful conclusion of Trent's spell. She joined Trent, William, and me on the street corner outside the guild hall, watching the satisfied townsfolk leave.

"I'll take your list," she said to me, holding out a hand. "I'll send Maeve 'round and talk to them all tomorrow. Just have a follow-up, make sure everything's alright."

"And keep her from the mine," William sniffed.

For a long moment, Thorn looked at William. Then she just sighed. "And Lark," she acknowledged. "She'll be getting a report about tonight, of that I'm sure. But maybe you and I should pay her a visit. Her and the dwarves," Thorn said, addressing Trent.

Trent nodded, though he swayed on his feet. Clearly, placing such a charm on the townsfolk had taken its toll.

"Here," I said, giving her several pages of my notes. "And why don't I bring dinner over to the station tomorrow? Since it sounds like you'll be busy." *And since that seems like about all I can do,* I thought, and immediately reprimanded myself for being so glum.

"Thanks, Red." Officer Thorn beamed at all of us one more time, and then she took her leave and started off alone.

"Are you just *trying* to come up with excuses not to be in the shop these days?" William demanded of me. "I need half a dozen sticking potions and a custom growth order and we're all out of gold powder, and now you're going to take an afternoon off to cook for *Thorn*?"

"I'm going to go talk to her about tomorrow," Trent announced, and took off.

"I didn't say I'd be cooking all afternoon. She likes pasta, and I have some dried, so it'll be quick to make," I told William absently. *It'll be good for Trent and Thorn to talk,* I decided. "Come on, let's head home too. If you're that worried, I'll get a start on restocking things tonight."

"*Someone* has to be worried. About the shop, that is." William's paws crunched in the days-old snow as we walked down the now-empty street. Lights from snug windows cast irregular glows on the blueish white expanse before us, making me think of the Frosts' ruined statue garden. When William spoke, I had to ask him to repeat himself.

He growled. "I *said,* we don't really think Maeve put up those posters like Trent suggested, do we?"

"Oh—well, he admitted to me that he might have exaggerated that," I said. "But I'm not sure who else it would have been. Although also, I doubt she'd want to run Snow out of town. Unless it was to keep her safe . . ."

William huffed. "She hasn't even been here a week, for sky's sake."

"True. But it's pretty obvious—at least it was to me—that she fell in love with Snow at first sight."

"Your point?"

"Sometimes people in love get all twisted around and do strange things."

William gave me a look. "Like get sucked into mysteries involving *dragons,* and then go gallivanting off to interview potentially murderous fairies? You never did say what you learned from that, by the way."

"I told Thorn," I protested. "I told her I thought the Frosts *might* be involved with Lark, maybe looking to expand their business, but that it didn't seem like they had enough money to be paying off Raven. Maybe someone set them up. Anyway, investigating that wasn't strange. It was helping."

The wide, dark expanse of Market Square met this statement. I paused, looking at the tree-dotted park and wondering why, if my actions weren't strange, I was feeling so adrift.

A startled bark from William interrupted my thoughts.

"Sorry, sorry!" A laughing voice—Luca's—rang out from the corner beside my store. As I ran to catch up, I remembered belatedly my promise to keep him updated.

"Why can't you read a book at home like normal people?" William accosted Luca. The magical glow from his ruffled fur, weak from his spellwork earlier, faded slowly.

"Luca," I asked, finally joining them on the corner, "were you sitting on the step reading? In this weather?"

"I was practicing," Luca corrected. As a demonstration, he merged so completely into the nearest shadow that I lost sight of him for a moment. Then he reappeared with a grin. "But yes, I was also reading. I left the meeting ages ago and didn't see you. I didn't know how much longer you'd be out!"

Is everyone *else better at being sneaky than I am?* I shook my head with a chagrined smile. If he had found a way to enjoy his shadow powers, leftover from the curse on the Drus, then that was a good thing.

William muttered something about "layers of creepy," and I kicked some snow at him good-naturedly. Before he could retaliate with a sweep of his tail through the snow drifts, I hustled everyone inside.

We went around the shop and entered through the back door, which opened into my lab. Because I still had some intention of fulfilling William's orders, I continued to hustle my two companions until they sat safely on the other side of the interior window, in the shop. From their stools behind the sales counter, they could see me just fine. I shook the snow from my boots and hung up my cloak before firing up a small burner to heat some water.

"Tea or cocoa?" I asked through the window.

"Information first," said Luca, with unusual determination. Well, I *had* left him with quite the mystery to ponder. As the kettle rattled and began to boil, I filled him in on all the behind-the-scenes information on the posters, the mine, and Thorn's predicament with Maeve. William offered minimal commentary. When I offered him a cup of rose and lavender tea, he accepted it, but the tilt of his furry nose made it clear he was still miffed at me.

"I'm glad no one was seriously hurt, at least," said Luca. He leaned heavily on the window frame, hands cradling a bright orange earthenware mug. I'd turned on the lights in my lab, but the shop remained dark, giving the impression from my angle that Luca and William were puppets in a show.

"Only their pride," William rumbled. He lapped at his tea, making the pink bowl I'd given him tilt dangerously from side to side.

"Well, yes, that." Luca shrugged with the easiness of someone who didn't have much pride to begin with. I smiled: I liked that about him. "I mean, I do feel really bad for Officer Thorn, and Maeve, too. And all the dwarves! But at least they're okay. The way everyone was talking about the dragon, I was worried something really bad had happened."

"Sorry I didn't get back to you earlier," I said as I began pulling ingredients off of shelves and tools out of cabinets.

"I figured you'd gotten swept up in the moment," said Luca. Though he said it lightly, something in his tone suggested, *as usual.*

"What?" I straightened up from where I'd been rummaging below my workbench. "I'm not that bad, am I?"

William snorted. "A charging dragon couldn't break your focus."

"Focus is a good thing when you're used to working with flammable materials," I returned, though I felt a little pang at his choice of words.

Luca chuckled. "Well, anyway, I also wanted to tell you something. I checked into it—Leo's story about the dam, I mean."

A pause ensued while we caught William up on our encounter with the reporter Leo, who, it turned out, William already knew was back in town. Because of *course* he'd know about gossip like that.

"Looks like it's true," Luca resumed. "The last repairs to the dam were practically a century ago, and there's plans on file with the town of Greendale to strengthen and expand what's already there. I'm not big on engineering, so I didn't really follow it all, but it seems like a massive project. I can see why they'd want to bring in a bunch of material for it, and these days, Lark's mine is the biggest one around."

"So the stakes are high for both families," I mused, measuring handfuls of prickly nettle pods into glass cups. It took skill to do so without getting tons of the little stickers stuck in my gloves—skill I had *almost* mastered. I still had a way to go, but at least I was better at that than sneaking.

"*So,*" said William, repeating my word with emphasis, "if we're looking for murderers, it could be anyone trying to coerce the dwarves or Lark into doing what they want. The Frost family looking to make a deal for new money, or the Greendale clan looking for a *different* deal, a gravel deal, to save their home. Or it could be someone who just hates dwarves, like one of the trolls at the mine."

"I don't see how that's a strong enough motive for murder," I pointed out. "There hasn't been any real anti-dwarf talk at the mine that we know of—aside from the posters today."

"And if someone was hoping to use the dwarves to get at the new ore, they were stymied by the appearance of the dragon today," Luca said thoughtfully. "Also, what about that knight? Is *he* a suspect too?"

"No," said William, as I said, "Yes."

We stared at each other through the window, a brief battle of wills.

"He said himself he was here on behalf of the Greendale clan," I reminded my star-struck familiar. "And Snow said there's a chance they might resort to murder."

"*And* he told Red there wasn't a dragon," Luca said, looking very stern over his mug. "He's been causing trouble ever since he got here."

"*Or,*" William said, more to me than Luca, "maybe he's in a tough spot, and he's just been trying to keep everyone safe—

like how he stood up for Johann. Have you already forgotten about that?"

"Maybe a bit," I admitted. "But I still want to hear his excuse for sending me after ore that has an ancient and fire-breathing guardian attached."

There was a pause after I said that, and I looked up to find them both watching me. Luca swallowed some tea and asked, "Are you okay, Red? About finding out about the dragon, and everything, I mean. You just seem a little—grim."

"I am a little grim," I said, slightly surprised he'd noticed. "This case feels like it's gone out of our hands. I just want everyone to be safe, but—it doesn't seem like there's anything I can do. Even though I was literally hired—under suspicious circumstances now, but still hired—to help out. Plus, I—I'm worried about Snow."

"Of course you'll end up worried if you're going to go around thinking the worst of everyone," William pointed out.

I bit my lip. "I'm just trying to keep an open mind, is all. I guess the problem is that we don't have enough evidence."

"I think you have *too* much," William mumbled.

"Red," said Luca, "I agree that it's important to be safe. But you shouldn't be so hard on yourself, either. Even if the ore is off-limits for now, I think there's always something you can do. After all, you and Snow are friends, right?"

"Of a sort," I agreed, chuckling despite myself. I gave it some thought. "Well, Officer Thorn's going to be busy tomorrow with the miners. So maybe in her stead I'll go up and talk to Snow during lunch. She might have some insight about the sighting, and besides—it's only fair to tell her everything else we've found out."

"I'll shadow Leo," Luca offered, perking up at the chance to help. "Just during lunch, like you, but I might be able to find something out. I'll let you know if I do."

"Better you than me," I acquiesced, grinning.

"Yeah, because you have too much work to do," William reminded me. "You better get all those potions done before you go running out to play detective again."

18

Cold as Ice

Your word is your bond, my mother liked to say. Usually, she said this when trying to get me to promise to come right home after gymnastics lessons or to help clean our house. Even as a child I could see that. Still, I tried my best to live up to my mother's expectations in most ways—even if I couldn't be a Seer, I could certainly be honest.

Most of the time.

I slipped out of my shop just after eleven the next day, a small smile on my face as I thought of William's chagrin when he discovered I'd only powdered four vials of gold, not the ten he'd requested. I'd told him everything was ready. And, category-wise, it was . . .

Can't be helped, I thought, giving myself a free pass on this one. No one around town could really need that much powdered gold, anyway, especially at the price it sold for. And if I didn't leave now, I might not catch Snow on her break.

I set off running through the streets toward the trail. I'd learned at least one lesson from last time, and worn a lighter cloak. This one was a rich pink woven with yellow sunbursts,

158

one of my favorites. My thighs did still protest as I hit the mountain slope, but I told myself it wasn't as bad as it could have been.

Taking the shortcut Maeve had shown Officer Thorn and me, I poked my head above the ridge and into Snow's campsite in no time. As I walked in from behind the tents, I counted the forms sprawled around the fire pit: five dwarves and one snow fairy. Everyone present and accounted for. And, if my nose was any judge, they were enjoying a particularly spicy chili.

"Hello, everyone," I called as I emerged between the tents. "Sorry to drop in on you like this."

"Red!" Snow spoke loudly, and she almost overturned her wooden bowl. The dwarf nearest her, Pigeon, looked concerned, but the others viewed me with only mild—if perhaps fearful—curiosity.

"Just here to compare notes," I said, holding up my hands. "I hope that's okay?"

"Actually, I was supposed to go back to Gloria's," Snow continued more normally. "Right after this. I guess the infirmary needs more soap and stuff."

How much soap can one operation need? I wondered—but in the next moment, reminded myself that they *were* working at a mine, after all—a mine which had recently had a very busy infirmary. "Oh, makes sense. Want me to go with you again?"

Snow hesitated, then nodded. "I don't really . . . I just don't like towns. It'd be better if you came."

I smiled, glad to feel useful.

"What d'you have to say?" asked one of the dwarves. I recognized him, mostly by his voice: this was Goose, the first dwarf I'd met. He was wearing a lavender vest, something

I noted carefully in order to help me tell the dwarves apart. Their faces betrayed very few differences when they weren't expressing strong emotions.

"Mostly, I was curious about what *you* think about what's been going on," I told him. This seemed to be the right thing to say. As the dwarves shifted again, this time in a more welcoming manner, I settled onto a nearby stump. "Who do you think is behind all this?"

"Who else could it be but the other miners," said one of the dwarves. His voice sounded like a sled pulled over sharp rocks, giving me new perspective on the adverb *brokenly*. As I focused my attention on him, he belatedly introduced himself as Robin.

A few of the other dwarves nodded in agreement with Robin's statement, looking down at their neglected meals. "Only the trolls would be strong enough," one agreed, adding, "I'm Albatross—just Tross, actually."

"The trolls are the only ones as strong as us. That's what I was tryin' to tell you yesterday, Pigeon," Tross continued.

Pigeon stamped at Tross, who immediately went quiet. *Definitely the leader,* I thought. Pigeon said only, "It's no use stirring up trouble where there is none."

"But do you think you might still be in danger?" I asked, worried for them.

"We're much smarter now," Goose assured me. "We always stick together, everywhere we go."

"And we keep a lookout," Tross added. "For strangers."

Seeing as I was basically a stranger and I'd just strolled into their camp, I was skeptical of this, but didn't call him on it. "Well, just be extra careful," I said, biting my cheek. "Do you think it's possible the murders had anything to do with the ore, too?"

"We only know for sure that one of them was murder. Raven could've just walked off," Pigeon pointed out. *He really is trying to keep them in line. Grief affects people in different ways,* I thought, trying to conceal my own disbelief.

"Who knows. The truth is there's hate everywhere," said Robin, the first speaker, with a shrug. "It wouldn't be the first time we've seen it."

"First time someone's died, though," said Snow.

"About that," I said slowly as the dwarves hastened to comfort the fairy. "Snow, I wanted to tell you that I've done some poking around, looking for who else is involved here. And it looks like *both* sides of your . . . your old family might be."

"Both?" Snow looked genuinely surprised. "Who's that?"

"What's this about your old family, Snow?" Robin asked, leaning up from a side-hug to look at her properly. Pigeon, too, looked curious.

I hesitated. As I looked around the circle, I remembered suddenly that Snow had said she hadn't told anyone about Sir Rowan.

"Nothing, it's nothing," Snow protested. She'd collected herself enough to glare across the fire at me.

"Sorry," I said again. "I meant—just with the mine, that is. There's a chance they might be making deals with Lark. Both the Greendale clan and the Frosts," I added purposefully, trying to get the information to Snow without raising more alarm.

"We knew that," the dwarf beside me said gently.

Snow looked startled. "What do you mean, Parrot?"

"We knew lots of big names would be in on this. Not our

ore, but the mine. We came here because it's famous," Parrot reminded everyone. I hadn't realized Lark's operation was famous. Perhaps in mining circles, I could see why it would be.

"Famous for bad luck," Robin said sadly. "We should've listened to the stories 'bout it being haunted."

"We shouldn't ever have come at all. But we're here now," Snow said, standing. With another look at me that I found impossible to read, she added, "It's time to go get the soap. If we wait any longer, Lark might start to wonder."

And with that, she started off down the road. Robin and Pigeon leapt up at once to clean up her abandoned bowl. Even before the rest of the dwarves had stood or I had a chance to follow Snow, I heard hasty steps and the *whap* of a slammed tent flap behind me. I stood and turned and found myself face-to-chest with Maeve.

A breathless, very angry Maeve.

"You made her run off?" Maeve asked me, her shoulders heaving, her hat askew.

Well, now I understood why Snow had felt the need to yell about my presence! She'd been warning Maeve to stay hidden. I took a step back, trying to look Maeve in the eye. "I didn't mean to. In fact, I'm about to leave with her. But you—"

"Did you ever think you're causing her more harm than good?" Maeve interrupted.

I faltered, partly in surprise.

"That's the problem with all of you tromping around investigating instead of listening," Maeve added as she brushed past me.

"That's not very kind considering how worried you've made Officer Thorn," I retorted, but I was merely yelling at a shadow.

Maeve had bolted down the road toward the mine, away from me and the dwarves—and away from Snow, too.

***

I caught up with Snow quickly, and the first thing I did was apologize for bringing up the fairy clans.

"It's fine," she said, brushing away the words. "I just was surprised, that's all. The—the other family—my father's family—it's the Frosts? You're sure?"

"Pretty sure, from everything we've found, and what Sir Rowan told us," I said, nodding as I walked along beside her. "What do you think?"

Snow shrugged and looked away. "I always kind of figured. But my mother would never tell me for sure." After a moment, she added, "Have you talked to them? Did you—meet any of them?"

"I met one of them, yes," I said, trying to be gentle. "A woman, maybe your age. But that's all. They didn't seem particularly interested in talking to me."

"Yeah. That's no surprise." Snow let out a breath and then, in one of her rare candid moments, she added, "I don't really want to meet them—not any of them—not yet. There's just so many other things to sort out."

"That's fair enough," I agreed. "For now, let's just focus on Lark's soaps."

Snow nodded, and for a moment, she seemed almost grateful. We slipped easily into silence, not speaking again until we reached the salon.

There we found Johann enjoying the last of his lunch—a leftover shepherd's pie from Lavender's tavern, if my nose was any judge. Despite his preoccupation, he set down his fork and smiled as we walked in.

"Here for more, are you?" he asked Snow. "Lark sent word this morning about the new order. Just hold on one moment, and let me bring it out of the storeroom for you."

He hadn't specified what we wanted *more* of, and I was amused when Snow turned her attention directly to the mirror hanging by his desk. It seemed she wanted more time for self-reflection, and I certainly wouldn't begrudge her that.

"Oh, Red, it's you," Gloria said, poking her head out into the waiting room. "I heard Johann and thought it was a walk-in. Brought her back, have you?"

"I have," I said, smiling as I gestured to Snow. The young fairy ignored us, but from Gloria's sympathetic glance, I could tell that was okay. "How are you doing? Didn't see you at the meeting last night."

"I knew Officer Thorn would calm everyone down," Gloria said carelessly. "We've been just fine here. Nothing to complain about. Unlike some, eh?" she added in Snow's direction.

This time the fairy turned around. "I think you're right," she said, apropos of her own thoughts. "It does change. The reflection in the mirror."

"Told you," Johann said, smiling as he reappeared with a heavy box tied with string. "I'm almost never wrong. Just ask my partner, he'll tell you I'm insufferable."

Gloria grinned at her assistant, then turned more solemnly to Snow. "Changed for the better?"

Snow took a step toward us, leaning a tentative hand on the desk. "When I saw that dragon yesterday, all I could think was, *she's so powerful.* And what if *I* could be powerful like that? I know everyone worries about me," she added, glancing my direction. "But what if they didn't? What if I could take care of myself?"

"It's a good start," said Gloria, nodding.

"Except I'm *not*," Snow continued, in a characteristic contradiction. "I'm not powerful at all." She glanced back at the mirror and quickly away.

Johann was watching her carefully from his side of the desk. "An appearance can't tell you everything," he said, his age and experience evident in his voice. "Even if it's a magical reflection. Take those miners who hassled me the other day, who you've replaced. They appeared to be all united, acting powerful because they had numbers on their side. But that kind of appearance isn't always true. In the same way that appearing weak isn't always true."

"Yeah." But Snow seemed uncertain.

"Snow," Gloria said, stepping forward, "I want you to know that it does get better, and stay better. It'll still look dark, sometimes. But never for as long, or as bad as it did before."

"But why?" the fairy asked pointedly.

"That's the part you have to figure out for yourself," said Gloria. "For me, a lot of it was because of her." She pointed at me. "Just because of a friend—that's all. And you have a lot of friends. The hard part is that you have to figure out who they are—and then listen to them. Give them a fair chance."

19

Poisoned Words

As Snow and I left the salon, myself still blushing from Gloria's heartwarming advice, we encountered a distraction.

"Red! Hey, Red!" It wasn't Thorn, but Luca who yelled. I pivoted and spotted him running awkwardly over the snow to meet us.

Have I ever seen Luca run? I wondered, distracted from my thoughts about Gloria and Snow

"I'm okay now," Snow said, before Luca arrived. "I'm going to head up with the soap. You can stay here."

"You're sure?" I asked her.

"Yeah." She nodded, then glanced up at me and almost smiled. "I've got a lot to think about. The walk will be good."

She turned and left, and as she did, a wave of icy wind and spraying snow hit me.

"So glad, I caught you," Luca panted, flailing to a stop, his hands on his knees. "Need, your help. Leo, print, story—"

"What?" I shook my head, baffled by the sudden switch in gear. "What story is Leo printing? About the dam?"

"Not dam," Luca said, straightening with an effort. "That was—cover. She actually wrote—about Snow. Snow's family. Apples. Red, you—you have to come with me and stop her!"

* * *

Without Luca, I wouldn't have had a clue as to where to find Leo. He led me back across the Square, directly opposite my shop. For a moment I thought we were going to the artists' supply store. At the last minute, though, Luca ducked around the side of the shop and up a staircase I'd never noticed. It turned out, the second floor of Art For All was a full-blown print shop. And in the middle of said print shop, covered in splotches of ink and surrounded by humming machines and drying sheets of inked paper, was Leo.

Her face was flushed and her eyes were bright—as, no doubt, were ours, after our sprint through the snow. But while we were exhausted and frantic, Leo was clearly jubilant. Hers was the air of an artisan in their element, right at the final leg of a project, when the end is in sight and they know they have a masterpiece on their hands.

"Sorry, no time to chat!" she called when she turned and saw Luca and me piling through the door.

Luca leaned against the wall to catch his breath, so I spoke first. "Leo, what's going on? Luca said you're writing about Snow."

"Of course I'm not. You think I'd get this excited about the weather? Oh." Leo's eyes widened as she caught the misunderstanding, and she turned again to grin at me. "*That* Snow. Yes. Yes, in fact, I am."

"But—why?" I asked. I had to speak loudly to be heard over

the waist-high printing machines, which populated the open room like a string of blocky islands. "Don't you think she's been through enough already?"

"Oh, who's to say what's enough?" said Leo, with a casual wave of her hand. Rather than skin, burnished gold gleamed at her wrist, where her work gloves ended. *Nice prosthetic,* I thought, momentarily distracted. And in that moment, Leo took the chance to add, "Besides, I think Belville *deserves* to know about her family's murderous history, don't you?"

"What?" I gaped, speechless, at Luca.

And thankfully, Luca had finally recovered himself enough to speak. "Tomte *told* me this morning you were printing something scandalous, but I'd hoped he was mistaken. Is any of it even true?"

But Leo was not interested in his question. "That little gnome went around talking, eh? That's what I get for asking his take on the story. All the more reason to rush to print!"

With a wave of her hands, Leo increased the speed of the printing machines. Letter stamps and damp sheets of paper were flying everywhere, it seemed. I tried desperately not to wonder if it was magic, or magitech, or some combination of both that allowed her to control her production line so easily.

Over the growing noise, Luca repeated at a yell, *"Is—any—of it—even—TRUE?"*

At last, Leo stalked toward us, weaving through her machines with the experience of a hunter through the trees. She held her head high, and still that victorious grin teased her lips. Coming right up to Luca, she poked him in the chest.

"I like you two," she said, glancing over at me as well. "So guess what? I'll give you an advance copy. In fact, take two. My only rule is you have to read it *outside*. There's no room in here for loiterers, and besides," she added, pressing barely-dry papers into our hands, "anyone reading the news in public is advertising for me."

* * *

With ease and efficiency, Leo pushed us out of her rented workshop. In a daze, Luca and I made it down the stairs before standing on the street corner with our noses glued to our respective papers, like tourists making sense of upside-down maps.

"Have you found it yet?" Luca hissed to me.

"Right column, upper side," I hissed back, even though I wasn't entirely sure why we were talking like two-bit spies. "I haven't read it yet. Let me focus."

As one, we took it in:

Two miners dead, suspicious ore found at the mine. Could the Greendale curse be descending on Belville?

New evidence suggests an age-old link between the dwarven mining team and an all-out fairy war.

Both murder victims so far, dwarves named Raven and Heron, came from the same team contracted to do work on the mine. Why should these outsiders be killed here, in our town? Because they have a connection with the mysterious ore.

Industrious investigation has revealed that the Greendale clan, a wealthy family of water fairies whose daughter is even now at work in our mine, has a history that they've been trying to cover up. Over four hundred years ago, they were at war with the clan now known as the Frosts (current residence: Poole). This was a family struggle at its worst, and the reason? A magical ore that could be used to enhance fairy magic.

All those years ago, the Greendale family wanted that ore so badly that they went so far as to kill their neighbors, the Frosts. Whole family units, grandparents and parents and children alike, were murdered over this ore. Finally, before the Frost clan was annihilated, a neutral third party swooped in to remove the ore to a safe hiding place.

But they didn't take it far enough.

Sources say that the new ore discovered in Belville's mine has some of the very same qualities as the ore that the Greendales MURDERED for years ago. What a coincidence that their daughter, Snow, should have been the one to discover it!

With two of her companions dead already, there's no saying what Snow or her family will do. Some ancient sources recently found in Poole suggest that the Greendales are cursed, and have been ever since they resorted to violence over the ore. The ore itself, they say, is out to wreak its revenge on the Greendales.

And if these sources are to be believed, it seems the bloodshed isn't over yet. Perhaps this magic ore was powerful enough to summon down a dragon, after all!

Protection charms may not be enough. For up-to-date reports and vital information, purchase a newspaper subscription!

"Oh dear," said Luca. Always the faster reader, he finished slightly before me.

"Oh dear is right," I agreed. As I folded my paper—not eager to provide Leo with the "free advertising" she'd mentioned—I noticed something that made me feel even worse.

Sir Rowan was striding across the Square toward the tavern, most likely intent upon joining the late-lunch crowd.

"Luca," I said, taking his shoulder and pointing out Sir Rowan. "We can't let him see this article or read it out here, in public. He might try to confront Leo—and make matters even worse. We have to get him to my shop. In fact, we better keep him there so we can ask him some questions . . ."

Sir Rowan stopped beside a stand of what looked very much like fresh-printed papers provided for Lavender's customers.

"Well," said Luca, reasonably, "We can tell him that if he comes and talks to us, we'll talk to him about our visit to the Frosts. He'll probably be wanting any and all gossip, right about now."

20

Antidote

Despite Luca's subterfuge—because really, I was in no condition for making mild-mannered reports to anyone about the Frosts, or our trip to Poole—the plan worked out. And, eventually, what had begun as a disastrous day slowly eased into something almost civil.

Sir Rowan cleared his throat. "Miss, if it's not too much trouble—"

"It's no trouble," said William.

"Thank you, sir," the knight bobbed. "I would very much like—"

"Well, it *could* be trouble," protested Luca.

"I am sorry you think so, sir," the knight bobbed again. "I only wished—"

"If all of you will ever be done bickering," said I, "I've got another tray of fried cheese right here. The pasta we'll have when Officer Thorn shows up."

I grinned at the group already clustered in my apartment. It had been a rough day, sure, especially when we finally let Sir Rowan read Leo's article, but I was amused by the result.

The knight now sat at my dining table, primly tucked into the chair in the corner. Flanked as he was by two dark windows, and overflowing flower pots, he looked like he was in some kind of fey jail. And in a way, he was: William had perched in a chair next to him and was panting all over his cloak (which Sir Rowan had refused to remove), while in the opposite chair, Luca sat with his arms crossed. William was the guard who'd toss the prisoner the key in an instant. I never thought I'd see the day when Luca played bad cop.

"Thank you, miss," said Sir Rowan as I placed the appetizer tray on the table. "That is precisely what I wished for."

"Did I hear my name just now?" With a little of her old energy, Officer Thorn tromped up the back stairs and let herself in. I went to greet her, closing and locking the door behind her.

"Go and have a seat, Officer. We all have a lot to talk about, and I doubt any of us have eaten, so I figured we'd have dinner while we're at it."

"I got your note," Officer Thorn told me, though her presence at my apartment had already told me that. While I started filling ceramic bowls with creamy pasta, she crossed over to the corner of my studio that I'd designated the "dining room." Taking a stool we'd added to the dining set in order to make room for everyone, she ran a keen eye over Sir Rowan. "So you're the knight who goes around starting fights, are you?"

Sir Rowan cleared his throat, swallowing a bite of cheese. "I feel, Officer, that we are starting off on the wrong foot."

"If that's the case, then you only have yourself to blame," Luca muttered.

"We're eating together, so let's try to be civil," I said to all involved. I'd had enough teary confrontations to last me a year. "Here, start passing bowls around. Salt and pepper are on the table, as is salad. Officer, we invited Sir Rowan here to talk to you."

Officer Thorn grunted. "Here's hoping it comes to more than my day did. This smells perfect, Red. Rowan, is it? We'll start with you. What's your story?"

As the rest of us settled in to eat, Sir Rowan gave Officer Thorn the same story he'd told us—roughly. The main difference this time came toward the end.

And Luca was the one to help it along. "What about Leo's article?" he prodded, as Sir Rowan finished explaining Snow's origins and his own allegiance to Greendale.

"Ah. Yes." Sir Rowan fiddled with his napkin for a moment before saying plainly, "If there is more than an ounce of truth in it, I will, as the saying goes, eat my hat. But there is no denying it makes for compelling reading, and in the broad strokes, it is not a complete falsehood. I have full faith that it will mean an end to my employment."

William, whose nose had been buried in his bowl, jerked his head up so fast that pasta went flying. "What?"

"For goodness' sake, William!" I scraped sauce from my forehead; Luca and I, seated across from my canine companion, had gotten the worst of the pasta blast.

"I am certain of it, in fact." Sir Rowan nodded politely, if grimly, at William's surprise. "That the dispute between the family of Green Dale and the Frosts of Poole has been, at times, a violent one is not up for debate. The details about the ore are patently false, of course, but Snow's identity and association with the murders—these are details the Matriarch never would want known. They will naturally see this exposure as a failure on my part to do my duty."

"*Did* you fail to do your duty?" Officer Thorn asked between bites.

"I—I have been delayed in carrying out my duty," Sir Rowan admitted, "which is much the same thing."

William was still spluttering. "But surely—"

"But nothing," Luca said. "If the article's even *half* true, not to mention the *dragon* sighting, then he sent Red after an ore that's really dangerous!"

This time Officer Thorn turned to me, curious. "That so, Red?"

"Well," said I, doing my best to be reasonable, "he did come to the shop, like I told you, and he commissioned me to look into the ore—or rather, the Tree of Life, which we *do* still believe affected the ore, right?"

"I can no longer say," said Sir Rowan. "I honestly did not believe that the Tree of Life would be associated with a dragon."

"But you knew about the old stories, and many of *them* mention a guardian," Luca argued.

"Fanciful embellishment, naturally added over time," Sir Rowan replied, though for once, he looked perturbed.

"Anyway, so we're still at square one regarding the ore, and now Lark's made it off-limits," I concluded for Officer Thorn's sake. "I had planned to investigate only after we'd settled up Raven's death, and I told Sir Rowan so at the time."

Even as Thorn nodded approvingly, Luca sputtered. "No matter what it *is*, if the Greendales really wanted it all that much, and you *had* it, Red, then—"

Sir Rowan coughed. "No doubt the family is aware of the ore, and that much I *did* conceal, I concede. But it is not, as I understand, at the root of their disagreement with the Frosts. Furthermore, I had complete faith that Miss Red and her friends would be perfectly safe. In fact, it was my opinion that finding the ore would be the most expeditious thing to do for everyone involved."

"Snow said she'd outright told Lark that she and the team wouldn't leave until they knew what the ore was," I added, again for the officer's benefit.

Sir Rowan had finally taken a chance to eat, so Luca beat him to commenting. "That part makes sense, if you think about it, since she found it. But still—"

"He lied, yes, we got it," Officer Thorn said to Luca, not unkindly. "But it seems to me that's worked alright, considering. Unless you've also been hiding information about the investigation?" she added with a sharp look across the table at Sir Rowan.

Sir Rowan looked up, swallowed, and dabbed at his face with his napkin. "As a matter of fact . . ."

The four of us leaned in, breathless.

". . . I must confess . . ."

William nearly fell off his chair.

". . . That I was the one to put up the posters regarding the dwarves. Not my best nor most thought-out work, I must admit."

Officer Thorn went rigid, and suddenly I feared for my table. "*You* were behind those rumors? And you framed Maeve?"

"*That* I did not do, Officer," said Sir Rowan with remarkable calmness considering that only a small round dining set kept him from a very angry half-orc. "I put up the posters, because I saw an opportunity to draw this entire affair to a close. I did nothing to frame young Maeve. Although, the police recruit has been spending a good deal of her time at the mine, and it would be wise to keep her . . . out of the way."

"That's my business, and mine alone," Officer Thorn said. She'd settled back into her chair, but the growl remained in her voice. "And anyway, you could have done a better job with the posters. Red saw through them at once."

At this, Sir Rowan looked interested. "Did you, miss?"

I waved my fork modestly. "I didn't know it was *you*, exactly. But when I looked at the one Officer Thorn had, I did think some things about it were off."

"I never got to see it," William pouted.

"Trent said it had something of the afterlife on it," I added, ignoring my magical canine. "That's why we thought of Maeve."

Sir Rowan sat back, tilting his head as though I'd accused him of something he'd never considered before. At last, he said, "I will be honest with you—with all of you. No doubt it is clear that my heritage is . . . mixed. My father was of the same clan from which Snow comes, but my mother was—something else altogether. I am, therefore, very close to immortal. And I have served the fairies of Green Dale for a very long time.

"However," he added, as Officer Thorn and I exchanged a glance and metaphorical heart-shaped fireworks went off over William's head, "as I have said, those days will surely come to an end due to Miss Leo's article. I am therefore at liberty now to share whatever I choose—and to aid whomever I choose. If you will condescend to accept my offer, I would be glad to help the four of you in your efforts to clear up *all* the mysteries which you currently face."

William's tail wagged. "You want to help us?"

Luca, meanwhile, crossed his arms. "Why stay here if you don't have to?"

"A valid question, sir. But I think you will understand if I say that I feel personally responsible for much that has happened," Sir Rowan said. "And I would very much appreciate a chance to set it right."

"You know," said Officer Thorn, "I could charge you for spreading malicious gossip."

"I believe you could, Officer. However, would that be as productive as solving the crimes and officially clearing young Maeve's path to happiness?"

Bold move, I thought, one eyebrow raised. But once again, he had a point. Everyone at the table focused on Thorn and her reply; her verdict was the one that mattered.

She looked around at each of us, then sighed. "Oh, so be it. But you'll have to be in charge of him, Red. I have my hands full dealing with Lark."

"I thank you. If you would like," Sir Rowan said, "*I* could deal with the mine—"

"No! No," Officer Thorn declared. "Between the murders and the dragon, Lark's demanding high security these days, and that's my responsibility. Pick something else to do."

This time everyone looked at me. I swallowed the last of my pasta and shrugged, thinking aloud. "Well, aside from clearing up the murders—which, yes, we know you and Maeve are dealing with at the mine, Officer—it seems to me that, when you really get down to it—ignoring any commissions or anything else—the most important thing here is supporting Snow, who's facing some really hard choices. I think she's just starting to find herself, and now that her family might take a step back," I glanced at the knight, who inclined his head, "she has a chance to actually make a choice for herself, for once. Except for this whole thing with the ore. I know that the vein is clearly associated with a dragon, but that still doesn't tell us what the ore *is*."

"Red," said Luca, a warning clear in his voice.

"Hear me out," I protested, putting up my hand. "I don't have to go near the vein. We don't have to deal with the dragon at all—although for the record, I don't think Trent was *totally* wrong about trying to talk to it."

"Easy for you to say," muttered Thorn. "You didn't see how scared the miners were."

"True. But that's kind of my point," I replied. "The miners still have a chunk of this ore somewhere. All I have to do is look at that, and then we can clear up answers everyone wants and move on to more important things."

"A wise decision," Sir Rowan said—*not too surprising,* I thought wryly, *since that's what he wanted in the first place.*

"But Red," Luca protested again, "that's the exact *opposite* of what you were saying before."

"I know, but now we don't have to worry about Sir Rowan putting pressure on Snow," I reminded him. "And there's not much else I can to help the investigation as a whole."

"Lark won't agree to it," Officer Thorn said. "And it isn't my place to make her." But I noticed she didn't say not to proceed.

"We've been to Poole—we could go see the Greendales," Luca said, still upset.

"I wouldn't advise approaching the family now that the article is out," Sir Rowan told him. "They will feel a certain need to . . . protect their privacy, shall we say. Any questions you have about them and their affairs, I could ask of a friend of mine in the kitchens; it would be the surest way of getting answers discreetly. In the meantime, Miss Red's suggestion is most expedient, and requires only that we borrow the ore in question for a short time."

Clearly, I thought, *Sir Rowan heard that little hint of permission from Officer Thorn, too. And he's ready to run with it.*

And, admittedly, I was ready to run with it too. After my despair the night before, it felt good to be truly useful again.

Officer Thorn got up. "That's my cue to extract myself from the conversation. Get it?" She eyed the four of us with a hint of her old chuckle as she savored the mining reference—not quite a pun, I thought, but she *had* been under strain, after all. I smiled back at her. She added before she left, "I'll expect a report tomorrow night."

21

Reckless Deeds

Naturally, Luca still had his reservations about my idea to pursue the ore. As he protested, it became clear that no amount of conditions could convince him that the mine was a safe place to investigate. And he wasn't entirely wrong.

"Even if you *don't* anger the dragon, how will you even find the ore?" he pointed out. By that time I'd cleared the table and everyone sat around nibbling—or gorging—on cookies from a central plate. "They've probably hidden it somewhere for safekeeping by now."

"I could sniff it out," William suggested, helping himself to his fourth snickerdoodle. "If it's magical, that is. Magical things always have a kind of smell."

"A very astute point," Sir Rowan said, prompting another tail wag from William. "However, as we are not sure if the ore is magical or not, I think it best to limit the number of persons involved. I propose to speak to Lark myself, presenting myself as an interested party in brokering a deal."

"Why would she want to deal with *you* when she's told

everyone else the ore is off-limits?" Luca was quick to ask.

"Actually," I said, the thought occurring to me as I thought about what might set Sir Rowan apart, "you are a *knight*, after all. Why not say you want to look at the ore to, I don't know, learn about the dragon or something?"

"Or even go *after* the dragon?" Luca mused, with a rather violent undertone for someone who'd just been telling me to stay safe.

For his part, Sir Rowan looked surprised, like he'd forgotten he was sitting there in full chainmail. "I suppose I can see how appearances would support that suggestion, Miss Red."

"I bet she'd buy it," Luca declared, in yet another surprising turn. "She wants the dragon gone, after all, and she's always been helpful in the past when I need to check records or research."

"*Helpful* might be a stretch," I muttered. I was surprised Luca didn't remember his first trip to the mine with me, a trip in which we'd ended up riding a rogue mine cart and fighting a zombie. *Although, none of that was Lark's fault exactly.*

"I think it's perfect," William said, panting up at Sir Rowan.

I hid a smile behind my hand. All merits of our plan aside, it looked like Maeve wasn't the only one harboring a bit of a crush this winter.

* * *

"I don't like it, Red," Luca said for perhaps the fourth time. I'd ushered him and Sir Rowan downstairs, and only Luca had lingered. He shifted from foot to foot on my back patio.

I sighed, leaning against the door frame. It was dark, and so cold my breath stood in the air like a tiny cloud. "I know,

182

Luca, but there's not much else I can do. Aside from ferrying Snow around town."

"Yes but that doesn't mean this is a *good* one," Luca protested. "Just because we couldn't think of anything else doesn't mean we have to do this."

"So what," I asked, exasperated, "we should just sit tight and wait while someone else might get murdered, or even worse, a bunch of people could get hurt by chasing after Leo's cursed 'arcane prize'?"

"At least let me go with him instead," Luca insisted rather than answer me directly.

I frowned at him. "You don't think I can handle myself? Just because I can't fade into shadows doesn't mean I'm totally inept."

I did manage to sneak around the mine once already, I added silently. It wasn't the best argument. In fact the whole defense was pretty weak. Part of me knew that Luca was right, and that he was the better choice for a sneaky mission.

But *no* part of me was about to let him wander off around the mine.

"Of course you can, Red, I know that," Luca sputtered. "I'm just saying I—I mean—we can't even trust him, not really, not after everything—"

Luca waved his hands without filling in the rest of the sentence. I crossed my arms. "I *know* all that, Luca. And I know how to be safe."

"Yes, but—"

"But nothing. You have a shop to look after," I reminded. "And you don't have a William to cover it while you're gone."

"No, but I'm getting one," Luca muttered through clenched teeth.

"Look, I know you like to be involved, but the truth is some things are too dangerous—"

"You think *that's* why I'm upset?" Luca stared at me, his eyes round in the moonlight. Finally he threw up his hands. "And now *I'm* the one who can't look after myself. Fine. You know what, Red, you can just—just—good luck, that's all I have to say."

"Fine," I echoed, watching him go. Something inside told me I'd made a mistake. But I couldn't quite put my finger on where it had happened.

* * *

The next morning, Sir Rowan and I met behind my shop just after breakfast. Huddled in our cloaks in a faint snowfall, overhung by dark rumbling clouds, we looked like a pair of vultures.

Or illegal dealers, I thought humorlessly as we snuck out of town.

Sir Rowan's plan *was* our best bet, though. He'd go and present his case to Lark, and I'd be waiting in the wings in case anything went wrong. I was back up, essentially.

And given that I was back up, and therefore not meant to be seen, I'd worn my darkest clothing. As a child of Seers devoted to vivid colors and sparkly decorations, I actually didn't own much dark clothing. Had Luca and I parted on more friendly terms, I might have asked him to borrow one of his robes. Instead, I'd donned an old forest-green cape over dark brown leggings and hoped for the best.

I looked like a child playing the part of "Tree Number Two" in a school play.

Sir Rowan, naturally, was too gallant to comment. In fact we said very little as we ascended the mountain, waiting until the last moment—just outside the mine—to confer.

"I expect to be taken to the main office," he murmured, turning back to me. "I trust you know where that is, miss?"

"Sure," I said, thinking "main office" was an awfully nice name for another hut. "I'll circle around the side and be under one of the windows. Everyone's working in the mine already, so it should be pretty easy."

"Hmm," said Sir Rowan, with only the briefest of glances at my stiff snow boots. "Remember to look out for sticks, miss."

Did he just make a joke? I hesitated, and in that moment, Sir Rowan rounded the corner and approached the guards. I listened to him greet them; they definitely recognized him. But then, who wouldn't? In a matter of seconds, they were escorting him into the mine grounds.

Time to go, I reminded myself. I leapt around the corner and dove behind a stray boulder before the remaining guard glanced my way, then awkwardly crab-walked through the shadows until I was near the hut.

As I sidled up to the ramshackle structure, I could already hear Sir Rowan.

"I thank you for seeing me on such short notice, my lady." His voice floated quite clearly through the window. I settled onto a rock to wait.

"It's no trouble. But I warn you, the ore you've come to ask me about is highly restricted, after the attack two days ago," Lark replied, her voice as clipped and polished as ever. "And I will allow no entry into the associated branch of the mine at all."

"Of course," Sir Rowan said, and added mildly, "I understand you are no longer interested in determining the properties of the ore, or making it available on the market?"

"No," Lark answered very definitely. "This is not an academic operation, you understand. What is the point in spending time evaluating an ore, when to mine any more of it would simply put my miners in danger? There are some boxes left unopened. I am sure you know what I mean, Sir Rowan."

There was a slight shuffling sound, like paper sliding over wood, and in the meaningful gap between sentences, I realized that Lark must be pointing out a copy of Leo's article. *Of course she would keep up on all the gossip in town*, I thought, *especially at a time like this.*

The knight cleared his throat. "I do indeed, my lady. Though, as you surely noticed, that particular box is open and the secrets have flown. But it is not about the family of Green Dale that I have come to. I feel it as a . . . personal duty, one could say, to investigate this dragon myself. I feel that my expertise in the matter might go some way toward righting what wrongs I have, until this point, been a part of."

"A suitably noble goal," Lark observed. "And you feel that examining the ore might help you in this? Well, I'm not in a position to turn away anyone who thinks they can . . . deal with . . . a dragon so close to my mine. Skar, show Sir Rowan the sample."

Skar and Skaab were the names of Lark's troll advisors— and bodyguards. *Clever*, I thought, *having them hold onto the ore. What place could be safer?*

There was a heavy, ponderous scuffling, which I assumed was Skar presenting Sir Rowan with the ore. The knight very politely thanked somebody, and then there was a silence. For a moment, I thought Lark was going to let him take it away for a *real* examination, and that my presence wouldn't be needed at all.

Ha. Hadn't I learned yet that my luck on this case wasn't so good?

"Belville's resident scholar might have been of more use to you," Lark began, her voice smooth but slightly ominous in the silence. "Unless, of course, you have more expertise in minerals than your appearance suggests."

Sir Rowan coughed, a small, polite sound. "Actually, my lady, I find it useful to be knowledgeable about many things."

"Do you?" I could almost hear Lark's smile—and it put me on high alert. "And yet here you are, at loose ends. Seeing as you're so knowledgeable, I half thought you might come *here* for employment."

"While I appreciate the sentiment, I do not think I would be suited for your line of work, my lady."

"No," Lark agreed. "You haven't got the force necessary. And you aren't quite as cunning as you think you are, either. A knight doesn't need the assistance of rocks to track down dragons. And that means there's another reason for your visit today. Skar, Skaab, let's find out what secrets the knight has been keeping, shall we? You know how I *hate* surprises."

By this time I was on my feet. "High alert" had become "heart-pounding alarm." Had any of the people in the hut looked out the window, they would have seen my head. But they didn't: they were focused on Sir Rowan. That's why, when I looked *in*, it came as a surprise when a rock flew *out* at me.

In total confusion, I let out an *eek* of shock and bewilderment which was only barely covered by Sir Rowan's raised voice from within the hut. "I can see that it is time to leave . . ."

"Yes," said Lark, "Past time, I think."

The rock. It had nearly hit me square in the goggles, but I'd caught it just in time. And now, in my hands, I cradled a specimen of the much-discussed ore. I'd never seen it before, but its faint blue and green glimmer—something I'd never encountered in a normal rock—assured me that it was what everyone was after.

I was also standing out in the open, having leapt back from the hut.

22

Into the Woods

I stood there, stock still in the muddy snow. My gaze was still fixed on the hut. Should I go in and rescue him? But how would I rescue him from two huge trolls and a powerful mine owner? All I had was a rock and some old lightsticks, and if I threw the rock at someone's head then all of this would have been for nothing.

Slime, I remembered. I had a couple vials of acid and slime potion in my tool belt. The acid was too weak to do anything useful now, but I'd once used the slime against the miners to great effect. Of course, it'd give me away, but I only had nanoseconds left before someone discovered me anyway.

I tucked the ore deep in a pocket in the breast of my cape, then ran my hands over the tool belt on my hips. Before I could find the right vial, a *schwinngg!* and some discomfited troll grunts rang from the hut.

So that's what he keeps under his cloak, I thought, realizing at once that Sir Rowan must have pulled a sword on his attackers. *Well,* that *makes sense.*

It also meant that he had the situation in hand. The last

thing I needed was to be involved in a sword fight.

"Who let him in with a weapon?" Lark's voice rang out.

"I'll take my leave now," Sir Rowan said confidently, confirming my suspicions.

"Oi! Who are you?" said a new voice. This one wasn't in the hut—it was behind me. *Curses.*

I turned, gulped, and waved at the oncoming orc. And then I bolted.

* * *

With my speed, I made it out of the mine grounds without being caught. But the guards and miners gathered behind me like a tidal wave; their yells and grunts pushed me along. As I ran headlong for the cover of the trees, I heard the telltale rumble of trolls.

Some of them are going to follow Sir Rowan, I thought, hoping that he had left his horse nearby. *And if they're smart, some will go along the road. So I should . . .*

Well, I shouldn't go toward the Flock's camp, for a start. I didn't want to get them into any more trouble. I cut down across the mine road, sliding in the snow. As I did so I caught a glimpse of my pursuers. They were, indeed, using the road. And some of them seemed to be riding magically-powered sleighs.

As I crashed through the snow, half running and half falling downhill, I knew there was no way to cover my trail. And no way was I going to climb up a tree and wait for it all to blow over. No; my only hope was to beat them to town. Even if the miners followed me all the way to Belville and proclaimed me a thief, I'd still have done my job. Officer Thorn would just take me to the station and have me check out the ore there.

Sometimes it paid to have a police officer for a friend.

Or should I make that "unofficial manager"?

A branch heavy with new snow whapped me in the face, reminding me to focus. The light dusting of snow had become stronger, and the clouds rumbled above.

Wait—was that thunder?

It could also have been trolls, a little voice in my head said.

Or something even worse, I thought, recalling the dragon yet again. No one else had tried to take the ore this far from the mine yet.

My feet faltered and I slid into a tree trunk, yelping as I nearly twisted an ankle.

"Focus," I repeated to myself aloud. But a loud swooshing drowned out my voice.

I looked to my left and saw a toothy face grinning atop a sled that sparkled where it touched the snow.

"No thief as fast as me!" cried the miner.

"Ha!" I retorted cleverly. "You haven't seen how fast I can go yet."

I gave up running downhill. It was more dangerous than it was worth. Instead I veered suddenly right, away from the sled. This caused chaos as I nearly ran right into another sled I hadn't noticed. But with a desperate burst of speed I managed to leap right past him. If he'd been any quicker, he probably could have grabbed my belt.

My belt. As I continued sprinting, dodging trees, I fumbled among my tools. The acid met my hand first: I recognized the angular vial by feel. Frustrated, I flung that one away. The next vial was rounded, larger: slime.

Perfect.

I turned on my heel just briefly, just long enough to get a quick look at the three sleds following me. And long enough to throw the vial against a tree trunk between me and them.

The glass exploded against the tree, its shards blending in with the falling snow. I turned my attention back to running. I knew full well what was going on behind me: I'd practiced for months before finally perfecting that slime potion. It would expand rapidly as it hit the air, covering everything around in purple goo.

Could magic sleds run on sticky slime as well as on snow? I was about to find out.

Shouts behind me, not to mention a sudden crash, told me that the answer was negative.

I hit a clearing and risked another look back. Two of the sleds were in pieces, but one clever driver had avoided the patch of slime. He, too, was looking backward. That gives me a chance. Without another thought I flung myself into the bushes along the clearing.

Turns out, the bushes were growing together along what in the summer months would be a stream. And where I'd hoped to land, that stream went down a small rock fall. During the summer, it was probably very pretty.

I stifled a yelp as I vaulted through icy branches and landed hard on my butt a good three feet below where I'd expected to. Though I felt like I was seeing stars, I held my breath and listened. It sounded like the third sled had zipped right past me without a second glance.

And even if he comes back, he won't see me through the bushes and the slope, I thought. It was cold comfort, seeing as I was drenched in sweat and icy snow and aching to boot, but it was comfort nonetheless.

The bushes crowded around me in the tiny ravine. I could hardly see the charcoal clouds above. As the snow strengthened and my breath slowed, I realized that the forest had become strangely quiet. *I really hope Sir Rowan had Nessie,* I thought. He could be in Belville by now.

And then that voice in my head added, *Luca was right.*

Luca had been right. He had had every reason to worry. Sir Rowan had done exactly what he'd done when we first met him: got me to agree to something without disclosing all the details first. In fact, it was pretty clear that this was how he operated, and I should have listened to Luca about it. Instead, I'd let the knight drag me into a daring plan that he'd only told me half of.

He smuggled his sword past the guards—past all of us. He knew all along he had it to fall back on, but I didn't. He probably was planning all along to throw the ore out the window, rather than try to get it out of there himself. That's the real reason he wanted me to come along . . .

Especially, I realized with some bitterness, *because he already knew how fast I am.*

It wasn't a warm and sunny feeling, being tricked like that. But, I reasoned, trying to remain constructive, it did work. Barely . . .

Not really, that sullen voice in my head reminded me. *You aren't home yet.*

"But I will be," I murmured. The silence muffled my words. Snow was covering my legs and arms, already half an inch thick. I had to move before I became a snow-woman.

I shifted to a crouch, looking around my ravine carefully and listening as hard as I could. None of the bare branches and twigs around me stirred. And yet, it seemed to me that

I could hear a faint thumping, almost like footsteps. But it wasn't on the ground; it was coming from . . .

Above.

I held my breath as I looked up.

Snow obscured my vision, getting in my hair and nose. I tried batting it away, as though it was a swarm of pesky insects, but of course that didn't work. Heart banging in my ears, I squinted hard into the sky.

And there, outlined against the black clouds, a brilliant white form flashed. Iridescent blue and green wings beat, and a spiked tail snaked across the sky. From scaly nose to sharpened, lethal toes, it was easily as big as the tavern in Belville.

I cursed, very quietly, and very badly.

But the dragon didn't seem to take an interest in me. As best as I could tell, it circled among the snowy clouds, and then—it vanished.

23

Magic in All Things

Of course, Sir Rowan beat me back to the shop. I found him and William sitting in the tea nook quite cozily while a few of my regular customers browsed. Doing my best to be friendly and not at all suspicious, I nodded politely at everyone—well, maybe less than politely at Sir Rowan—and walked straight through the shop, into my lab, and then out the back door.

I stood there, my back pressed against the door frame, breathing deep. The air was cold and it was still snowing, faintly, but I felt more at ease when I could see the sky.

As long as it's just the sky, I thought to myself, *and not any murderous, winged, humongous guardians . . .*

A dragon. For a moment I was very still, just letting that sink in. I thought back over all the risks I'd already taken: running up and down the mountain alone, getting myself caught in all kinds of places, not telling Thorn what I was up to, not even telling William where I was, sometimes. I hated to admit it, but Luca had been right to worry.

Luca had been right about a lot of things.

195

"What are you doing? You know that's the wrong way to make a snow person, right?"

I jumped about three feet in the air at the unexpected voice, and turned to find Gloria looking at me speculatively. She stood on her side of the little alley between our shops, her head and shoulders visible over all my winterized, potted plants. A slight angle in one arm suggested that she was carrying something—that perhaps she'd come out to empty out a recycling can.

Not to scare me like I was a mouse under a hawk's shadow.

I shivered. "Hi, Gloria. Yeah, I know. I just . . ."

She settled into a familiar pose, leaning on one hip. "You saw it too, huh?"

I said nothing, and she went on, "Just had a customer in who saw it on the way here. Do you really think it was the dragon? The one from the mine?"

"Yeah. I think so," I said, drawing another shaky breath. "You don't seem too worried, though?"

Gloria shrugged. "I didn't see it. If I see a dragon, I'll worry about it then. Right now, I've got a salon that desperately needs cleaning. And half the town has the benefit of Trent's protection spell, anyway."

"True. Good luck with the cleaning," I said, as it was clear she was headed back inside. As her door snapped shut behind her, I found myself smiling faintly.

Gloria's right, I decided. *We do have some protection, at least. And it's time to get to work.*

* * *

After changing my clothes and thawing my hands—not to

mention sending detailed notes to both Thorn and Luca—I finally settled into my lab. Customers still hummed and chatted out in the shop, and William and Sir Rowan still occupied the armchairs. The earthy smell of their tea wafting in through the interior window was calming, at least. I took a deep breath and focused on the ore in front of me.

When placed on a ceramic tile on my workbench, it didn't look like anything to get too excited over. The white of the tile *did* enhance that strange green-blue glow, but other than that, the ore just looked like a lump of slightly iridescent black rock. I pulled my goggles down over my eyes and began to observe it systematically, making notes in a tired old lab book:

<u>Unknown Ore</u>
    Appearance: shiny, but somehow matte at the same time.
    Hardness: Medium—definitely less than diamond.
    Edges: rough cut by an ax, otherwise rounded, no distinctive shape . . .

After I'd filled half a page with observations and sketched out a little picture to boot, I decided I was ready for testing. I stood up from my stool, reminding myself to stretch, and went to the shelving unit along the back wall of the lab. There, I kept things that were for me, rather than the shop's customers: raw ingredients, backup tools, and a series of acids and solutions designed specifically for testing unknown objects.

Unknown, potentially magic objects, I thought, shaking my head as I sat back down with my mineral-testing kit in hand. *Honestly, maybe this would be a better job for William.*

Inspired by that thought, I decided to run a test for magic affinity first. Using diamond-tipped tools, I was able to separate a small piece of the ore and transfer it into a dish. From there, I bathed it in a handy little solution my old alchemical master had designed: the liquid would detect magic in the ore, and turn a different color depending on if that magic was elemental, fairy magic, elf magic, and so on. All I had to do was wait an hour for the test to have its full effect.

I let the little chunk of ore steep and turned instead to tidying, then rustled through my notes for the key to the solution's color changing so that I could know what my results actually meant. Just as I was about to sit down and congratulate myself, a head popped around the window frame in front of me.

"Are your experiments going well, miss?" Sir Rowan asked.

"Pretty well considering that a few hours ago, I might have been dragon food," I replied, frowning at him.

"Did you see it too, then? William's friend—a Mister Dusty— came in and appraised us of the dragon sightings above town. I confess I had thought them idle rumor."

My frown deepened. "*Rumor?* Aren't you supposed to be able to—I don't know—*sense* dragons, or something, since you're a knight?"

Annoyingly, Sir Rowan chuckled. "I would not ascribe such powers to myself, miss. I merely deal with the things I see."

This sounded an awful lot like what Gloria had said, and I was momentarily unable to argue. In the silence, William's head popped up too: he'd scrambled atop the stool behind the sales counter.

"Sir Rowan *does* have good sales powers, though," William informed me. "He helped me sell some of your new candles. I bet you didn't even notice, did you? You had your nose in the ore."

"How nice of you to make yourself useful," I observed to Sir Rowan, though I was still reserved. To William, I said, "Hey, maybe you can be useful too, as far as this ore goes. Want to take a look and see if there's any magic on it?"

"There is," said William, without looking. "I could sense it when you came in the shop."

"Then why not say something?" I asked, exasperated. "What kind of magic is it? It must be really strong, if you could sense it even without trying. Right?"

"It isn't Apple-y, if that's what you're asking," said William. Sir Rowan looked on with interest.

"That isn't helpful," I retorted. Any further reply was cut off by a shrill beeping from my workbench—my little timer was going off. I'd set it to remind me about the magic test on the ore, and it turned out I had needed the reminder. "Hold on a moment, I have to see what my test says," I told my little audience, and continued talking mostly to myself. "Um, let me see here, the solution has turned purple, with pinkish overtones—and if I check on my key, that color means . . ."

I looked up, confused. "Pixie magic?"

"Thought so. But it was a little hard to tell—there's pixie magic all over the place around Belville, even though the pixies themselves stay hidden this time of year," said William, his tail thumping against the stool he sat on. To Sir Rowan, he added conversationally, "I *hate* pixies."

* * *

As Luca had pointed out before, pixies—small, brightly-colored, fairy-like creatures, usually no more than one foot high, prone to flying around on dragonfly wings and turning the occasional hapless traveler into a tree for amusement—had been present in Belville for a *long* time. They weren't a day-to-day occurrence; most of them lived in a little community outside the town, hidden by magic. But they liked the bustle of having the town nearby, and often were said to spy on people or interfere in little things. Trent, in particular, had a habit of blaming anything that broke or got lost on the pixies. I myself had no strong feelings on the matter—at least, not as strong as William's. In fact, I often forgot about pixies altogether.

"I just don't understand why they'd care about a rock," I said, perhaps for the fourth time, much later that evening. I'd done many more experiments on my ore sample, and during the course of my work, my annoyance with Sir Rowan had faded. He'd helped William run the store, and eventually close it up, too. In exchange, we offered him dinner.

"You'd think they'd be bored by it," William agreed, clambering into his usual window seat. It was after dinner now, and the three of us gathered near the small fireplace in one corner of my apartment.

"You are certain there was nothing present *aside* from pixie magic, miss?" Sir Rowan asked tactfully. He was the last to take his seat, and he brought with him a tray bearing three mugs of hot chocolate—an indulgence he'd insisted on making for us himself.

"Positive," I said, taking a mug and breathing in the rich aroma. I passed another to William, then went on, "I ran that magic test two more times, just to be sure. And the ore didn't respond to any of my other acids or solutions. The only *really* strange thing was—"

"Yes?" prompted Sir Rowan, sipping at his own mug.

"Well," I said, wondering how exactly to explain myself

without sounding odd, "in a few of my tests, the ore gave results that would be similar to something *alive.* Not sentient, like an animal or person, but—something I might expect to see from a plant, for example."

"Strange, indeed."

"Do you think that could be because of the influence of a magic tree?" asked William. "Maybe this really *does* all come back to the Tree of Life."

"But it wasn't apple-y, as you said," I reminded him. "It was more . . . mossy. I tested for traces of things you might find with fruit, like sugars, cyanide. If there's a physical connection, I'm not seeing it. If there's a metaphysical connection, that's ultimately up to you. As far as I can tell, I've got a lump of black agate that seems to glow from within."

William snorted. "Then maybe it's all just a joke the pixies are playing on us."

"Except for the dragon." I looked at Sir Rowan; after all, he had the most riding on this. After a moment, he seemed to sense my attention, and looked up.

"I do not doubt you, of course, miss," he said. "I was merely thinking. What a cruel irony if, as William points out, all of this misfortune comes down to a magical illusion?"

"It's not an illusion—the ore *is* weird," I said, not sure if that was a comfort or not. "And anyway, maybe all the misfortune was about something else entirely—tensions at the mine, for example. Or the Greendales' gravel deal. Maybe all this ore talk just ran us off course."

"Like Atalanta," said William, perking up. "That *would* be apple-y."

Sir Rowan, too, seemed to brighten, and for a moment I let them enjoy their discussion of ancient myth. But I could only take so much before I tried to get us back on track. "I'll turn the ore over to Officer Thorn tomorrow during lunch," I said, clearing my throat. "It's too late today, I think. In the meantime, Sir Rowan, what are you going to do?"

"As I said, I trust your judgment, miss," Sir Rowan answered steadily. "But even so, this matter is far from over. I will remain and see it through to the end. Not for my former employers' sake, naturally, but—for Snow's, as you so articulately pointed out last night. I cannot help but feel responsible for her fate."

I watched the knight carefully, thinking. From everything I'd heard, it sounded like Sir Rowan *was* responsible for Snow's circumstances—at least in part. He'd been the one to suggest sending her off to live in the woods. But a lot of other people had been complicit in that. And then, of course, there was Snow herself, who had chosen her new companions, and chosen her new way of life.

When, I found myself wondering, *is the poor girl going to be able to live her own life, and have her own decisions recognized without someone else taking responsibility for them?*

24

Best Kept Secrets

Even before I opened the shop the next morning, it began.

"Oh, hey," said Gloria as we unlocked our doors at the same time and hauled out signboards. "So you're Belville's latest thief, huh?"

"I heard some weird stuff went down at the mine yesterday," Dusty said shortly afterward, making me jump as I poured out spiced tea. "You wouldn't have any idea about it, would you?"

And so on, and on. Everyone from Lavender's errand-runner to the vampiric florist three doors down to the local schoolchildren on holiday seemed to know all about what had happened at the mine. And even if they didn't, they sure thought they did. What they *didn't* know was what the ore had turned out to be.

And because of that, Red's Alchemy and Potions was the most popular shop in town. Gossiping customers crowded the aisles, knocked over my displays, and colonized my book corner. I half expected Leo to drop down from the chandelier

203

at any minute, demanding a story.

"Looks like you could use some help," Trent observed. It was after lunch by then—or was it before? I'd totally lost track of time. On the pretense of fulfilling some custom orders for winter fertilizer and bright blooms powder, and maybe finally working on that ink for Luca, I'd finally managed to slip away from the crowd and lock myself in my lab.

I leaned against the door, wiping my arms over my face, knocking my already askew-goggles nearly off my head. "How did you get back here?"

Trent grinned and shrugged. He was seated on the small kiln-master's stool right beside, you guessed it, the kiln in the corner. It was running today: I needed to make some new crucibles after the ones I'd used on the ore. That meant Trent had scored the warmest seat in the entire building. Normally I would've been upset, but the crush of people out in the shop had raised the building's temperature quite a bit.

"But really," I protested at Trent's silence as I dropped down on the bench beside my lab table. "No one should be back here."

"You were busy, and I didn't give William time to disagree," Trent explained, his lopsided grin still in place. "Is he okay out there by himself?"

"For a few minutes he will be," I said firmly, needing it to be true rather than believing it. "If anyone gets snippy he'll probably just bark at them and besides, most of the people here are after gossip, not potions."

"They say all publicity is good—"

"Don't even start with that," I said, holding up a hand to interrupt Trent while simultaneously chuckling at him. "People with more than one shop assistant can say that all they like, but it's not true here, that's for sure."

"I could make you more," Trent suggested, straightening up on his stool. "Maybe an animated broom to look after the spills, and a coat rack at the front door—"

"No! No. Again, don't even start," I laughed.

Trent shrugged once more. He knew exactly what my feelings on animated objects were: namely, that they were a bucket of trouble, whether or not they actually had *been* buckets before some spell-happy Witch got hold of them. Animation seemed to be one of Trent's specialties, or at the very least, a persistent interest of his. On that subject we simply had to agree to disagree.

"Your loss," he declared. "But I could have had a shovel or something steal that ore for you, you know. Why didn't you ask me?"

"Because the thirty-odd miners working in that mine wouldn't have taken kindly to a flying, thieving shovel," I joked. Sitting helped me recover my wits. I began to look around the cabinets, partly for fertilizer ingredients, partly for tea. "But really, Trent, you should be glad you weren't involved. I haven't been so wet and cold in . . . forever, I think."

"Again, I could have helped with that," he insisted.

"Well, next time I'm planning to do something basically illegal, I'll look you up," I promised, exasperated. With a quick smile his way, I added, "Now what do you think Officer Thorn would think of that?"

Trent smiled back, so I assumed he'd patched things up with our mutual friend. "Maybe she'd realize she's not the only one around here who needs unofficial assistants."

A thought struck me. "You haven't actually met Sir Rowan

yet, have you?"

"The knight dude? No, I keep missing him." Trent leaned over, trying to look out the window into the shop. "Is he here?"

"No. I was going to ask your opinion of him, but never mind," I said. My searches turned up no more clean tea mugs, so I resigned myself to working on the fertilizer. I began with my mortar and pestle.

"What's Luca think of him?"

I paused, pestle in midair, and looked suspiciously at Trent.

"What?" He put his hands up innocently, a look he had perfected, despite the "tricks > treats" t-shirt he wore. Briefly I wondered exactly how much trouble Trent had got up to in school. Given how persistent he was about being included in future robberies, I was willing to bet it was a lot. "I just think, like, he has good insight into people. He deals with them every day."

"So do I," I said dryly, returning to my work. I didn't want to admit that Trent was right. For reasons I couldn't quite put my finger on, Luca's intuition was often better than mine. But that didn't mean I wanted to relive a fight with one of my best friends. Luca himself still hadn't been by the shop, which wasn't so unusual, but still—I hated to dwell on it. "So, Trent, did you sneak into my lab for a reason?"

"Curiosity," Trent admitted blithely. He made a show of looking around, as though I might have set the stolen ore out on a shelf, like a trophy. "I was surprised William let me in. Do you think he likes me better now that we worked together?"

"I wouldn't count on it," I said, knowing from years of experience that William's opinion of Witches would take a monumental effort to change.

Trent's reply, whatever it might have been, was interrupted

by a knock at the door. A knock at the *back* door, not the door to the shop. I swiveled. Trent was staring at the door with his mouth still open.

"What, did you think it was just for show?" I chuckled. "Open it, would you? I've got ground potassium all over my gloves."

"What if it's Lark?" Trent said, not moving.

I hesitated. I hadn't realized the obvious, that Lark knew exactly where to find me and her lost ore. What if she'd sent the trolls after me? Was all that running through the snow for nothing? What if she broke into my shop?

The knock sounded again, rapid and insistent.

"Well, too late now," I decided aloud. "Just open it, would you?"

* * *

Trent stood and opened the door as though the polished brass doorknob was a snake, pulling his hand back quickly and balancing on his toes, at the ready.

"*Finally.*" Maeve spilled in through the doorway, trailing huge snowflakes from her ragged uniform. She was bent half over, and I couldn't tell at first if that was because she'd had to duck to get through the door or because she'd been so eager to get inside.

I'd also never heard her speak so aggressively. Well, aside from the time I made Snow upset, of course.

"Uh, hey, Maeve," I said. Trent stood back and merely grunted. "Is everything okay?"

"Of course it isn't okay." Maeve pulled herself upright and began brushing at her uniform. I soon realized, though, that the gesture was more for her nerves than for actually cleaning the snow from her lapels. In fact, she looked like she might cry. "There's been another—there's been another—"

"Robbery?" I guessed hopefully, because it was on my mind and was better than the alternative.

Maeve shook her head violently, sending her beret—slick with melted ice—right into Trent's chest. *Seriously,* I wondered, *is it storming out there* again? *I thought the snow had died down this morning.*

Trent, who had not deigned to catch the beret, also did not deign to pick it up.

But Maeve didn't even seem to notice its absence. "Poison," she gasped. "They think it might be poison. He had a—seizure—Thorn said—get you—they're all—they're all—"

"It's okay, just breathe," I told her, although this seemed like useless advice since her breath was already coming in huge gulps.

Maeve shook her head again. "You have to come—have to come—"

"Just spit it out already," Trent suggested, also unhelpfully. I glared at him and he said, "What? So someone's been murdered with poison and they want you to take a look. What more does she need to say?"

"Not murdered," Maeve said. Without looking at Trent, she pulled her chin up and snapped her heels together in a gesture highly reminiscent of Officer Thorn. "Red, Tross has been—has been probably poisoned, but he didn't die. He had a seizure at the mine just now and the Officer has him at the station and medical personnel is flying in. But she wants you to help identify the poison. Just in case."

"One of the dwarves," I said for Trent's benefit, although in my opinion he was being a bit of a pill. Trent, not the dwarf, of course. I stood and began to shed my existing lab gear for cleaner accessories.

To his credit, Trent shifted, whistling in a low, grave tone. "I guess that mine really is bad news, huh?"

"Not the mine," Maeve contradicted again. She flushed when we looked at her. I think she was struggling more with her own difficulties in communicating than Trent's attitude. "Maybe not the mine, I mean. Or the trolls. I thought it was trolls, but maybe it wasn't. What I mean is, there's a—a possibility that the dwarf wasn't the target. Because the lunch he ate was—it was actually Snow's."

25

Lead Down the Path

"**B**ut why would someone murder Snow?" Trent asked. After hastily donning a cloak and shouting at William through the shop window, I'd followed Maeve outside, and Trent had followed me. It seemed he had every intention of coming along to the station.

In the wind and ice, though, he had to speak directly into my ear to be audible. I glanced at Maeve, cutting a path through the street ahead of us. There was no way she could hear, but I still worried.

"I don't know," I replied at last. "Maybe someone realized how important she is in deciding whether the dwarves stay. She really wanted to know about the ore."

"I thought everyone wanted her," Trent said, shaking his head. "I mean, obviously not like *that*. But like, not dead."

Not like 'that' indeed, I thought, still watching Maeve's gray coat. "Maybe someone got frustrated that she kept saying no," I theorized. As I did so, I couldn't help but think of Sir Rowan, too.

"Or someone's been after her all along." Trent said this and

210

then pulled away as we neared the station and entered single file. Maeve seemed to have forgotten about us, and Thorn wasn't at the front desk, so once more Trent was able to slip in where he technically shouldn't have been.

It's official, I thought, my mind happy to focus on anything except the grim scene awaiting us. *Everyone in town has better shadowing skills than me.*

* * *

Options in Belville's police station were limited. Thorn had opted to use the station's back room, often a basic morgue, as her infirmary. What might have been quite morbid actually had a strange charm to it: as I stopped at the doorway, I saw five faces looking back at me. Apparently, not even Officer Thorn had been equal to the task of keeping Snow and the remaining four dwarves at bay.

Fortunately, Maeve quickly pulled Snow and her friends into the station's main room. This was good thinking on her part, since I wasn't sure the back room had enough air in it for any more people. Once the team had left, leaving the space around the main table clear, Officer Thorn proved my suspicions right by heaving a great sigh.

"Good work coming so fast, Red," she said. She stood at the head of the table, Tross's head resting between her large hands. His eyes were closed and for the moment, he looked stable. "I got a rest potion into him. Standard guild issue. It won't fix anything, but it'll stop any ill effects and buy us a little time. What're *you* doing here?"

As I'd stepped into the room, Trent had become visible behind me. He crossed his arms over his chest rather than resorting to his usual shrug.

Officer Thorn pursed her lips and looked down again. "Never mind. Saves me the trouble of searching for you, anyway. Go and keep an eye out for the med team, will you? Someone's supposed to be coming over from Pine. Don't know who they're sending, but you can be sure they'll be airborne."

Mutely, Trent saluted and left.

That meant Thorn and I had the unconscious dwarf all to ourselves. I looked down at him uneasily. Even his cheery yellow vest looked drab and sad under the circumstances.

"Officer," I said, when it became clear she'd run out of orders for the moment, "you don't think this could be because of the ore, could it?"

Officer Thorn paused, and in the silence I could hear the wind whipping around the building, and muffled sobs out in the main room. Inside my head, a growing sensation of guilt was deafening.

"That'll depend on the exact method of the attack," she said at last. "We don't have enough facts yet. Isn't that always what you say?"

"Sure." I gave her a small smile, acknowledging her attempt at sympathy. "Okay, so what do we know so far?"

"Suspected poison," Thorn said at once. Like Maeve, she sounded a bit like she was giving a presentation at the police guild. That was how I knew that this danger at the mine had taken a toll on her, too. "No evidence as of yet. The others say he was normal all morning, maybe a bit slower than usual, nothing out of the ordinary for such a cold day. At lunch, he ate Snow's meal, as she said she wasn't hungry. About an hour later, the fellow working closest to him—Goose—said that the victim seized up and then suddenly collapsed. Goose called to the others and managed to catch him before he fell. Nurse on site at the mine confirmed this as seizure and ensuing muscle weakness, but she's only equipped for, as she put it, 'bloody injuries.' We'll need the med staff to know anything more."

"Okay, so the symptoms so far are sudden seizure and then muscle failure," I said, thinking. "Honestly I'd have to talk to him to be able to narrow it down. It could be any number of things. We can't even be one hundred percent sure it was something he ingested at lunch."

"Seems most likely," said Thorn. "If you want to poison someone, you do it in food."

"I suppose, but it could also have been in the air or—"

Officer Thorn shook her head. "No one else felt any effects. And remember, this was probably meant for Snow, who's much smaller than Tross."

I raised an eyebrow. "So?"

"So, a fatal dose for her might only have been enough to cause a seizure in a dwarf," Thorn explained.

A very good point, I thought. My mind raced through a list of all the poisonous substances I worked with or was aware of.

The front door of the station banged open, announcing Trent's reentry. Officer Thorn and I both paused, waiting for him and the mysterious medical help to make their way to the back room.

However, the pair of white-coated strangers didn't *need* to make it to the back room before I understood why Officer Thorn didn't call on them more often.

"It's a poisoning! A *poisoning!* Why didn't you bring the stretcher?" one yelled at the other.

"We gotta act fast! There isn't time to argue!" the other

argued back.

"Oh, goddess. The tall one's Hunter," Officer Thorn grunted in my ear, motioning to an older man who seemed, if I wasn't mistaken, to be a werewolf. The shaggy gray hair and facial tattoos were a giveaway. "The burly one's Spruce," Thorn added, gesturing now at a slightly shorter but much wider person. A pin on their lapel proclaimed them as "were-bear and proud."

"They're actually quite good, but they're *always* like this. They get it right in the end, I suppose," Officer Thorn continued. She was able to get away with this running monologue because, during this entire time, Hunter and Spruce continued arguing with each other like the rest of us didn't exist. Even as they set up their kit around Tross.

"Isn't all that negativity bad for the patients?" I whispered to Thorn.

She snapped her fingers. "That's a good one. I'm going to remember that and ask them about it next time they're *really* getting on my nerves."

"You," said Hunter, turning to me. "You're the local expert?"

"Not exactly," I said, though I stepped up all the same. "I've just been thinking. I think we're dealing with some kind of heavy metal poisoning. I don't know how much resistance a dwarf might have to that, but it fits with the symptoms, and possibly the timeframe. I doubt it was a potion or any kind of spell—those would have had either a much quicker, or less dramatic, effect."

Meanwhile, Spruce was checking over Tross—very carefully, it must be said. At last, the preliminary diagnosis came: "Muscle weakness, elevated blood pressure, signs of digestive distress. No foreign substances to be found. No injuries."

"Oh no," I said aloud. Officer Thorn turned to me at once, and the other two followed her gaze. "All those things together made me think. There's a kind of corrupted lead that sometimes occurs naturally in mines exposed to magic. It has effects similar to normal lead, but they take root much more quickly, and with a much bigger impact on people's health. If it was powdered, and added to his food—I think that would explain exactly what happened."

26

Plumbing the Depths

Thursday the waiting room started up again.

"What d'you mean, 'corrupted'?"

"Are you saying this is another accident?"

"Do we all have it, then?"

"What about someone trying to get Snow?"

Finally, Officer Thorn broke in. "Listen! I understand you have questions. We all do. For now, I want all five of you—yes, Snow included—to go into my office, one at a time, and get tested to see if you have it too. Those of you not being tested can line up outside my office door. We'll all know more when this is done."

As the dwarves scrambled to comply, jostling each other while they lined up along the wall like overgrown kindergartners, Thorn pulled me and Trent aside.

"Let's take this chance to ask some questions," she began.

I interrupted. "You realize that's about all I can do, right? I can't test them for lead without taking blood. Unless Trent has some kind of spell, maybe?"

"Actually, I could try if you want," Trent said, rubbing his chin thoughtfully. "Maybe a tracing spell, especially if I could get my hands on a piece of lead first . . ."

"We'll keep that in mind," Officer Thorn told him, though it was clear he'd lost himself in magical musings. While Trent continued muttering to himself, she turned to me. "Mostly we just need something for the dwarves to do. Keep 'em quiet, soothe some fears. How much of a chance is there that they're all poisoned, do you think?"

I surveyed the miners along the opposite wall. While the dwarves shifted and mumbled to each other, Snow stood quiet at the end of the line, with Maeve beside her. "Everyone seems to be acting normally, as far as I can tell. I don't see any signs of strange pains or weakness. But again, I have to stress that I don't know them all that well. I can't say what's totally 'normal' for any of them. But it *is* conceivable that if there was a dose in his lunch—or Snow's lunch—it was added to the others' too."

"But if they were equally exposed then why aren't they all paralyzed?" Thorn countered.

"I don't know," I repeated, frowning at her. "Maybe Tross had some kind of susceptibility to it. Or maybe he got a double dose, since he ate Snow's lunch too."

"Hmm." Thorn paused to think this over, casting a glance over her shoulder to the backroom, where the med staff still tended to the fallen dwarf.

I took the opportunity to remind her, "You know I don't have medical training, right?"

"Still better than those two," Thorn muttered. I almost wasn't sure I'd heard her. Before I could ask, she went on, "Okay, Red. Tell the dwarves we haven't decided yet if it's an accident or not. All these deaths could be accidents, when you get right down to it. Maybe it's just a case of terrible luck."

"You don't really think—"

"Get them talking," Officer Thorn said firmly. She clapped me on the back, sending me stumbling toward her office. "I'm going to keep an eye on that medical team."

"Red, you don't have any lead on you, do you?" Trent asked. He was behind me now, leaning over my shoulder as Officer Thorn strode away. I sighed.

"No, Trent. Do you really think I'd carry poisonous metals around with me every day?" I grinned at him and rolled my eyes. "If you really want a piece, William can help you find some in the shop. I keep it on hand for magitech batteries, not that there's much magitech around here."

Trent wavered.

"What might be *more* helpful," I told him, seizing another opportunity, "is if you'd sit in on these interviews with me. Maybe just do a normal health spell or something?"

Trent grinned. "You really have no idea how magic works, do you?"

"Not a clue," I grinned back. "That's William's job. Come on, we've wasted too much time already."

* * *

Trent perched atop Officer Thorn's immaculate desk while I drew up a chair alongside it. The first dwarf to come in and sit in the chair beside the door was the one who had been especially worried about Snow a few days before. While I racked my mind for his name, Trent just came out and asked him.

Suddenly I felt even better about my decision to have Trent join in on the "tests."

"I'm Robin," the dwarf informed him. "That's what they call me, you know we all have bird names. We did it a long time ago. Sign of being in the team, and all. Snow never wanted one though we told her maybe owl, like snowy owl—"

"Makes sense," Trent said quickly, cutting Robin off before he rambled until bedtime. I leaned forward.

"Robin, let's start off with how you're feeling. Physically, I mean. I know this has all been very upsetting emotionally," I said as kindly as I could.

"Well I do have this terrible pain in my arm . . ."

"Your arm?" I hesitated. "Is there a chance your arm has been exposed to something?"

"The cold," said Robin, quite reasonably, since all the miners wore vests rather than real shirts.

"So it could be the cold causing the ache?" Trent suggested.

Robin shook his head slowly. "No, I don't think it's that."

"Is this accompanied by any dizziness or confusion?" I asked him.

"Well . . ." Robin looked far off in the distance as he thought. "I guess I did feel pretty confused about why I'd wanted to move that boulder all by myself. I shoulda just waited. But I was in a hurry to expand the camp once I realized we'd be here a while."

I blinked. "Just to be clear, are you saying the sore arm is from—moving a boulder by yourself?"

"Yeah. I've been pretty sore ever since. That's not a sign of poison, is it?"

***

Quite a while later, Trent and I welcomed the next dwarf into the room. This time I recognized my friend from the campfire, Parrot.

"I feel better about it knowing you're the one to do these tests, Red," Parrot said, starting off on a friendly note. His bright teal vest stood out against Thorn's dark wood paneled walls.

"Thanks, and I'm glad to see you again," I told him, smiling, "though I'm sorry for all this trouble. Now, we just have a few questions. Can you start by telling us how you're feeling physically?"

"Aside from any work-related aches," Trent suggested.

I pursed my lips at him. "It's helpful to know everything . . . although, yes, if you know the reason for any ailments, definitely share that too."

Parrot didn't have to think about it. "I feel perfectly fine. That's the funny thing about it. In fact, I was telling Robin just this morning that I think this is one of the nicest sites we've worked at, since even when you're outside the mine it's a pleasant temperature. That's setting aside the dragon and poor Raven and Heron, though."

"Uh huh." Parrot and I clearly disagreed about "pleasant," but it made sense that someone who worked underground would prefer cooler temperatures. "Okay, that's good. Have you noticed anything strangely sweet in your food or drink lately?"

"Sweet? No. You're saying lead tastes sweet?" Parrot shook his head. "Never really thought much about how rocks taste, myself."

Lead wasn't really a rock, particularly when it was corrupted by magic exposure, but I pushed that detail aside. "Have you noticed anything strange about any of the ores you've worked with around the mine?"

"No," Parrot said at once, "except that ore Snow found, 'course. Was it you who got a look at it yesterday, Red? Everyone up at the mine's talking about it. Tell me, what did you find?"

"Uh . . ." I glanced at Trent, and at the open door. "I can't say anything about that ore at the moment."

"Are you sure? After all this trouble, we'd awfully like to know."

"I know. I'll let you know as soon as I can," I hedged, and soon thereafter sent Parrot on his way.

As the dwarf left, Trent stared after him. "Pretty insistent, huh?"

"Well, it's understandable—"

"Or suspicious."

"Oh, come on." I didn't want to think that the most friendly of the miners might also be the most deadly. "Let's just focus on the task at hand, shall we?"

* * *

The next dwarf in was Pigeon. I recognized him not only as the leader but also as the most concerned dwarf of the group, and the interview with him didn't prove me wrong.

"What exactly is this test? What're you going to do? Is that a Witch?" He peered at Trent doubtfully.

"Pigeon, please just sit down," I said. My nerves were wearing thin. "We're just going to ask you some questions."

"What's the use in that?" Pigeon sat, and pushed the wooden chair all the way back against the wall. "How can you tell if there's corrupted lead in me from questions?"

"Would you rather we take your blood?" Trent challenged him.

Pigeon crossed his arms. "I'm scared of needles."

"That's enough," I told the two of them. "Pigeon, let's start by talking about how you're doing physically. Any unexplained pain or weakness, or anything like that? The weakness might feel like fogginess, or even make you seem a bit jittery."

Pigeon's stony gaze slid between Trent and me. "Maybe."

"Maybe what?" Trent said, already exasperated.

"So I get jitters. So what? Lots of people do," said Pigeon self-consciously. "Who told you I get jittery? Did someone tell you I dropped my ax?"

"No one's told us anything about you," I replied soothingly. *Okay, chalk one up for jitters and paranoia, too. He and Tross did seem close . . .* "How about any confusion?"

"No."

"Any headaches at all?"

"No."

"Hmm." I sat back, trying to remain friendly. "Have you noticed anything sweet in your food?"

"I hate sweet stuff."

Yeah, what a surprise. I heard Trent snort beside me and knew he'd thought the same thing. "Alright, Pigeon, thanks for your help."

"What about the test? Am I sick?"

I bit my lip. "You're going to be fine, Pigeon. But if anything gets worse, let one of us or Thorn know, okay?"

With a grunt, the dwarf left. *Two to go, including Snow,* I thought. My stomach rumbled. *Here's hoping we get out of here before dinner . . .*

* * *

Goose, my cliffside-singing buddy, was the last of the dwarves to come in before we got to Snow. I wasn't looking forward to having Maeve, Snow, and Trent all in one room. But Goose made me smile no matter the circumstance.

He sat in the chair with his legs drawn up, obscuring his bright green vest.

"Hi, Goose," I said. "How're you doing?"

"I'm okay," he said. "Except for, you know, everything."

I nodded. "Is anything bothering you physically?"

Goose paused to think. "My throat's a bit scratchy."

"Scratchy?" I repeated.

"Yep." The dwarf nodded. "From the talking. And crying. And singing."

"Oh, of course." I smiled at him gently. "I think Trent might be able to help with that."

"Huh? Oh, sure. I'll make up some special peppermint tea for you and have Thorn send it up to the camp," Trent promised.

As Goose nodded his thanks, I asked, "Have you noticed anything strange about the ore, the mine, or around the camp?"

"Mmmmm," Goose tilted his head as he thought. "No. Everyone knows Tross has a sweet tooth, though."

I hesitated. "Pardon me?"

"You said it was sweet," Goose explained. "The corrupted lead. He'd like that. Everyone knows he likes anything sweet. Even the other miners."

And if the other miners knew, then the trolls knew too. And, I made myself add, *Sir Rowan.* "Thanks very much for your help, Goose."

223

* * *

The moment I'd been dreading came. Snow drifted into the room, with Maeve close behind.

Maeve seemed to have appointed herself the keeper of Snow. While at first this had seemed very unorthodox—no matter how understandable—I soon realized that it was more necessary, and more useful, than I had thought.

I started off the same way I had with the others. "How are you feeling, Snow?"

And, had Maeve not been standing right behind Snow's chair, I think the interview might have ended there. Snow's answer was a flurry of tears. Tears from a snow fairy were just as frozen as one might expect. In an instant, the room was dusted with ice crystals.

But Maeve hastily brushed off the nearest surfaces and had everything under control. "It's okay, Snow," she said quietly. "She doesn't think it's your fault. None of us do."

Trent grunted. Snow hiccuped.

I realized that Maeve was right: Snow was overwhelmed by guilt. Were I in her shoes, I might be too. Heck, I felt guilty just for my part in holding up the ore proceedings. "That's right, Snow," I said firmly. "You know that I know there's a lot going on here. *None* of it is your fault. People who hurt others have only themselves to blame."

"B-b-but," whispered Snow, "You know—my family. Either one of them could have—either one—"

"Yes," I said, not entirely sure what connection she was drawing. "Your *old* family, you said." *Not to mention that the Frosts, if that's who she means, don't seem to know she exists. They may have heard about her in the paper by now, but still, they aren't beating a path to Snow's door. If they were involved with Raven or Lark, it was probably just for business deals—a coincidence.*

Snow dissolved again. Maeve cleared her throat and clarified. "She feels like, if she had never stayed with the dwarves, they wouldn't be in this danger."

"So she thinks her old family did it," Trent concluded. He hadn't spoken yet, and his tone wasn't quite friendly, which earned him the attention of the room. "So, that's good, right? That means we know where to look."

27

Writing on the Wall

In the wake of Trent's practicality regarding the Greendales—harsh as it might be—the rest of our "test" with Snow was unremarkable. Once we were done, Officer Thorn had Maeve escort Snow and the rest of the dwarves back to their camp. In fact, her very words were:

"Go, enjoy your dinner, and look out for each other. I'll let Maeve know as soon as I have any news about Tross."

Apparently Maeve's stock with the miners was pretty high, because they all accepted this without protest. The six of them trouped out of the station and into the dark, stormy evening. I watched them go, not envying the cold blast of air that met them at the door, but definitely envious of the dinner they'd be eating soon. *I doubt Thorn's going to let us stop for food.*

But in the next moment, she proved me wrong. Officer Thorn beckoned Trent and me over to the desk in the front room, which sported a new tablecloth, several loaves of bread, a dressed salad, bowls and utensils, and a steaming tureen of Lavender's famous stew.

"Eat, sit," Thorn said, waving her hands at some stools she'd probably pulled out of the storeroom closet a moment before. Trent and I followed her suggestion mutely and gratefully. "The medical team needs my office to write their report, anyway. Don't think you need to leave leftovers for them, either."

While I shook my head at Thorn's selective hospitality, Trent swallowed a huge bite of bread and asked, "So is Tross stable now?"

Officer Thorn nodded as she ladled herself some soup. "He is, and much quicker than he might have been otherwise, thanks to Red here. Your idea about the lead was spot on," she said to me. "It saved them a lot of time in diagnosis. Sounds like we're out of the woods. They expect a full recovery in a few days."

"That's great," Trent told his bowl of soup, which obscured the lower half of his face.

"A few days?" I mused, soaking a bit of crust in my own bowl. "That seems a bit long if they were able to treat it so well."

Officer Thorn leaned her elbow on the table and pointed at me. "I thought so too. Chalk it up to Pine's med staff, right? But no. Turns out, this was a *lot* of lead. We're talking like an entire pipe's worth in his interior plumbing."

Trent snorted a laugh, but I was alarmed. "Good thing we caught it, then. That can be fatal, you know, especially when it's corrupted lead to begin with," I added, swatting the Witch.

"I know, I know," he said, sobering. "And I guess, since everyone else was fine, this proves Tross was a victim."

Thorn's ears pricked up. "Everyone else was fine, huh?"

"Well, Pigeon admitted to some jitters and weakness," I reminded Trent. "Those are potential symptoms."

"Yeah, symptoms of being a nervous hypochondriac," he retorted. To Thorn he said, "They had some stuff to say about Tross having a sweet tooth and being really interested in the ore, and Snow's convinced her family is behind all this, but other than that they were totally fine."

"Which side of the family?" Thorn eyed us.

"The Greendales," I said, thinking how inconsequential the Frosts seemed these days. "The other thing is, Goose said that not only did Tross have a sweet tooth, but everyone at the mine knew it. And I'm willing to bet that the corrupted came from somewhere on the mine's grounds—after all, we know there's another magic vein there already."

Thorn sighed. "None of this is helping narrow down the suspect list."

"Don't you have a checklist for that?" Trent asked her with a grin.

"Checklists don't help when influential members on staff of that mine have known anti-dwarf feeling," Thorn said, chucking what was left of her bread at him.

I knew she meant Skar and Skaab, but I stayed quiet, thinking. Something about the murders felt more personal than out-dated, shallow racial prejudice.

When Officer Thorn started staring at me, I realized she wanted me to speak up. "It seems to me that one of the best things we can do is follow up on the lead," I said at last. "And for that, I guess we need to go back to Lark."

"Extend the olive branch, eh?" Thorn grinned. "I'll support that. First thing tomorrow, I say. Although . . ."

"Although what?" I asked, scared that Lark had barred me from her property or some such thing. She would have been well within her rights to do so, I had to admit.

Officer Thorn swallowed another large bite of bread. "I never did get my report yesterday."

"Oh." Relieved, I told her everything I'd discovered about the ore—along with William's and Sir Rowan's thoughts.

"What I'm hearing from all of this," Officer Thorn said, tipping her chair back as she thought, "is that dragon's guarding more than just a valuable vein of rock."

"It sounds like a sanctuary of some kind," Trent put in. "You know, living magic, possible Tree, pixies, dragon? Maybe there's some kind of big cave underneath the mountain that we were never meant to find."

"A refuge," I agreed slowly. For some reason, something Trent said—*we were never meant to find it*—reminded me of Snow's life with the dwarves, which had been so tranquil until Sir Rowan and, by extension, the Greendales found her. *No wonder she said she identifies with the dragon.*

"I don't have any interest in finding it," Thorn reminded us. "As long as it doesn't have anything to do with breaking the law, I don't care. Let the dragon stay there, I say."

"I think Lark feels mostly the same," I said, thinking of what I'd overheard the day before.

"That's because Lark's sensible. Unlike you and your friends," Thorn said to me.

"Hey," I protested, but I had to laugh, too. "You have to admit that it's good to know about the ore. It means we can focus elsewhere for the murderer. And after we talk to Lark tomorrow, I think we should talk to Snow, too, and tell her all this. I had meant to today, but, well—"

"Another attempted murder occurred," Officer Thorn finished for me, stroking her chin. "Whoever's doing this hasn't been satisfied—not by the removal of Sir Rowan from the picture, and not by the appraisal of the ore. Oh, I know you hadn't had a chance to report to anyone yet, Red, but everyone knew you'd figured out what it was."

"Well, 'figured it out' is a little generous," I murmured, picking at the remains of my salad.

"My point is, the murderer must have known that an answer about the ore was coming—and, to add to that, that Lark wouldn't be selling, since you had to steal the ore to get a look. But they murdered again," Officer Thorn continued over my vague protests. "So what's the motive that ties all three murders together?"

"They seem random to me," Trent chipped in. "Aside from the fact that it was all dwarves."

"It can't *really* come back to that, can it?" I asked. "I mean, that kind of racial hatred, it's so crass. Maybe centuries ago it would have made sense, but not today."

"Murder is crass," Officer Thorn reminded me. "We can't assume we know anything about someone capable of crimes like this."

"Spontaneous crimes, if you think about it," added Trent. "None of it was planned out very far in advance. Pushing someone over a cliff, a cart collision, feeding someone a poisonous rock from the nearby mine? It's all pretty convenient."

"But at the same time, nobody really benefited," I couldn't help but point out. "Nothing's come of the murders. Even the whole thing with the ore being put off limits was because of the dragon, not the deaths."

"The Greendales have benefited," Officer Thorn mused, her hand back on her chin.

Trent beat me to a snort of disbelief. "By having a wild article written about them, that accuses them of being bloodthirsty and greedy to boot?"

"Set that aside," Thorn challenged, "And you can see a few ways they'd benefit. First by throwing suspicion on the Frosts, their rivals, with that promissory note Red found. Then by weakening Snow's circle. And in the long run, what they really want is the gravel deal—and that's been expedited. Lark was telling me yesterday," she went on, in response to my surprised look. "She—Lark—said she needed something productive for the miners to focus on. And despite what you think, Red, the deaths of the dwarves *did* have an effect on Lark putting the ore off-limits. And two of those happened before the dragon showed up, you'll recall. Had Lark proceeded with the new vein as soon as Snow found it, and scaled back production on the gravel, the Greendale's dam would have suffered for it."

I traded glances with Trent. "I had no idea."

"And that," said Officer Thorn, rather smugly, "is why it pays to be in charge."

28

Queen of the Mine

The next morning dawned with a familiar vehemence. As was quickly becoming usual, I hadn't slept very well—my dreams were full of flittering dragons and bursting dams. And during the long stretches when I was awake, I kept imagining bumps and thumps and fumes, as though my apartment housed a ghost who wanted to poison me.

When I rose, the snowstorm continued to rage outside the windows. I stood in the tiny kitchen making my morning tea, and as the kettle heated, I looked out between the paisley curtains. Nothing but gray shadows and curling white snowdrifts met my gaze.

At least the window patch is holding up, I thought, making a mental note to touch base with Dusty later that day. It was a Rest Day in Belville, meaning that my shop—along with all the others lining Market Square—would be closed. The mine would be open, though, especially after the recent disruptions. Officer Thorn had decided that I and Maeve should come along with her to meet with Lark just after breakfast. Thorn didn't know yet that William planned to come along too; I'd left that to be a pleasant surprise.

William stirred in his corner, and I called out, "You better get yourself ready, you know. I expect this meeting to take a while, since Lark will no doubt want to talk about the ore—and how I got it. I want to check on Snow and the dwarves afterward, too. In fact," I continued, more to myself, "I'm going to bring along some snacks." I'd spent too much of this investigation hungry.

While William wordlessly stretched, yawned, and shook himself all over, I began collecting food. Black pepper biscuits, some smoked cheese, an apple, and a little pouch of dark chocolate all went into a special charmed bag my mother had given me long ago. Blue satin, covered in bright yellow flowers and crystals, it was the kind of bag that could hold anything without leaking and could squish down to incredibly small sizes. For a moment I paused, my focus wandering as I traced the old patterns. Then I chose my largest traveling mug and made some extra tea, pouring plenty of honey in once it was done. When at last I donned my tool belt, tall boots, and thick purple cloak, I had to admit I looked exactly like the poster child for "winter adventure" that the desert-dweller in me found totally alien.

Officer Thorn's habitual knock on the back door reverberated around the house. William huffed.

"Come on," I told him. "If we're lucky, we might be able to put an end to all of this today."

* * *

The wind raced through the streets, skimming over several

233

feet of snow and plowing through snow banks like an army of kids on sleds. As soon as William and I locked up the shop, I was glad I'd worn my thick cloak. I was even gladder when, with an old yellow scarf, I belted it around my body, leaving the minimal amount of give for my arms to move. Cloaks are great, but I've never understood why more people don't want to *close* them against the cold.

Officer Thorn had already retreated into the street, where Maeve was waiting. Even she had bowed to the weather: a standard-issue shawl curled around her shoulders and covered her up to the chin. Above that, her eyes glinted as she eyed us. I wasn't sure if she was silently judging my fashion choices or unhappy about my loudmouthed companion.

And, for once, Officer Thorn didn't opt to explain her thoughts. "She knows we're coming," she said, turning and tromping off down the street as soon as we'd joined her. Maeve, with her long legs, snow-treading capabilities, and no doubt anxious heart, was already several steps ahead. "I had Trent send a message up last night right after you left."

For a moment I was surprised Trent hadn't insisted on coming too, but then I remembered how early it was. I nodded along, sticking one arm out through the upper half of my cloak to sip my tea.

"You warned Lark that Red was coming, huh?" William followed in my footsteps, taking the path of least resistance through the wind and snow. "You must be serious."

"I am," Thorn snapped, "so none of your jokes."

"*You're* the one who's always making terrible pun—"

"Do you really think that she won't be really upset about the ore?" I asked, interrupting William's retort.

Officer Thorn hunched her shoulders. Instead of a walking

stick, she'd opted for her club, a gnarled weapon about as big as Dusty. It swung through the snow like a hot knife through mounds of frosting, lending an ominous air to her words. "I don't know what she'll do. But someone as savvy as her will know better than to put up too much trouble in an official police meeting. I told her I'd notified the guild and everything. And between you and me," she added, her voice falling below the storm, "I think she *did* want to know, just a little bit."

After that, there wasn't much more for any of us to say. We quickly fell into line: Maeve in front, then Thorn, me, and William taking up the rear. I put my hood up and kept my head down. Something deep inside me told me that we weren't alone, that someone was watching. Whether that was someone lingering between the dark, shivering trees or some dragon surfing the storm overhead, I couldn't say.

Maeve only turned back to us when the guards stationed at the mine entrance wouldn't let her proceed. When we caught up to her, I noticed a strict look pass between Thorn and her rather rogue assistant. *Let me do the talking,* it clearly said. Maeve fell back with me and William but didn't respond to my sympathetic glance.

In the time it had taken us to walk up from town, the miners had begun their work. If anything, the storm was thicker up on the mountain, making it difficult to tell what time it was. But clearly, Lark had insisted that business continue as usual.

I will say, it was nice not to have to sneak through the miner's camp. I followed the guards with my head held high. Our little group filled up half of Lark's little command hut, herself and her trolls taking up the other side. I'd never actually been in it before: in contrast to its rustic exterior, it was clean, well-appointed, and even luxurious. Geological maps lined the walls, with very useful-looking desks and cabinets beneath them. There were no chairs, however. Lark watched us from her wheelchair like a queen receiving foreign dignitaries of unproven worth.

It occurred to me that she kept her headquarters small on purpose. The look in her eye was intimidating up close.

Thorn returned the ore, and launched at once into her official explanation of its properties—and my actions. Just as easily, Lark decried them. I shuffled, looking at the maps. Even though they were discussing me, I'd always been of the opinion that Lark and Thorn, when in a room together, were best left alone. They seemed to speak their own language, something too much like three-dimensional chess for my straightforward mind to keep track of.

". . . however the information comes to us," Officer Thorn was saying, and she nudged me into paying attention again, "there's no denying it's useful. And it underscores your decision to leave that branch of the mine untouched."

Lark's mouth was pressed very thin. Then, with a graceful wave of her hand, she shrugged at Thorn. "Your associates are very zealous, as always. And I am very busy. So I will save us all some time." She turned to me. "Everything the Officer has told me is true?"

I nodded. "It's a kind of corrupted agate. I wouldn't even say it's particularly useful or valuable, aside from being so unique."

"And you don't seem disappointed by that," Lark observed as she eyed me. "In which case, why bother to steal it?"

"I—well—we wanted to borrow it," I said, under the pressure of a stern look from Officer Thorn, "because it seemed so much simpler just to *know* what it was, rather than leave everyone guessing. And, if I'm honest—I wanted Snow to know. So that she and the dwarves would feel free to leave."

From the way Maeve was glaring at me, she considered this too many details to share. But I held Lark's gaze, trusting her to understand.

And, in fact, she did. After considering me for a long moment, she smiled. "You've let Officer Thorn act for you, in returning the ore. And by reflection, that means that the officer stands with you. I'm glad to hear that you, and the officer, stand with Snow, as well." Lark shifted to include all of us. "My mine was not supposed to be a place where outsiders are in danger and information is kept hidden."

"You've only done your best," Officer Thorn said, with a gentleness I found surprising.

"But they *were* in danger. They still are," Maeve burst.

"You're young," said Lark, turning to her, "and not as practical as a police recruit training with Officer Thorn ought to be by now." This stunned Maeve into silence, and in the ensuing pause, Lark went on. "I have operated under the assumption that *all* of my employees were, and are, in danger."

"And they could be," I agreed, stepping up. "Not just because of the dragon, I mean. That's the other thing we wanted to talk to you about. The way Tross was poisoned—we think it was corrupted lead. It probably came from somewhere near that exposed vein."

Lark's eyes narrowed and her lips pressed down once more. "It seems there is more than one reason to block off that section of the mine, then. I will have that investigated at once."

"Thank you," said Officer Thorn. "In the meantime, I don't suppose you've noticed anyone hanging around the area?"

"It's been under guard since the dragon sighting—the *first* dragon sighting," Lark clarified, with a censorious but also, I thought, slightly amused glance at me. "I've had no reports of anyone causing trouble. But you are welcome to question the guards yourself, of course. There is a shift change at lunch time."

"We'll be there," Officer Thorn said at once. "And we'll let you know if anything else comes up."

"I am sure," said Lark, with one more glance at me, "that you will. After all—it would only be fair, wouldn't it?"

29

Waiting for My . . .

Officer Thorn, showing what I considered to be a great deal of restraint, allowed us to be escorted discreetly from Lark's office. As soon as we'd been deposited on the road outside the mine, she turned to her assistant with hands on her hips. "Lark was right," she said. "That was completely impractical. And irresponsible."

Maeve wavered. Standing on top of the snow around us, she towered above us all. "B-but—"

Thorn rounded on me. "But that's not to say you should go bringing up vulnerable people in everyday conversation, either."

Maeve continued stuttering, and William sneezed. "Red was right to come clean, though. Finally."

"Hey," I protested. I'd been about to say something much more grateful but William ruined it.

Officer Thorn sighed. "Maybe we're all too close to the case. It's gone on for too long now, that's for sure. Come on, Maeve, let's stop by the station to record the meeting while it's fresh, gather our thoughts, and then get to questioning the guards

239

when it's time for the shift change. Red, will you swing by the Flock's camp and update them, when they show up for lunch? William, you go with her, just in case."

"Sure." William's tail thumped in the snow. He grinned a doggy grin up at me. "I keep telling you that you ought to be escorted everywhere."

"You hush," I told him, rolling my eyes. Even though I grinned, I had an uneasy feeling in the pit of my stomach. *Thorn's right. We're way too involved in all of this.*

"That's that, then. One of these days, you all will learn that when you're dealing with an operation as big as Lark's mine, you have to show respect and proper care." Without any further words, the officer and the recruit strode away down the road. The swirling snow soon swallowed them up.

"I wondered why she was so eager to involve the guild all of a sudden," William said as he watched them go.

"For all her bluster, Officer Thorn knows what she's doing," I said. "And she and Lark have been frenemies for a long time. Or really, I suppose, more friends than enemies—not that either one of them ever admits it. Come on, the dwarves' camp is this way, along the ridge."

"So that crosses Lark's trolls off the list, if the lead's been locked away by their boss," William continued musing as we fell into step side by side. "Who's left?"

I'd been so focused on the dwarves' plight that I hadn't thought about the actual murderer. "The Greendales. Or even Sir Rowan," I said, remembering my first suspicions.

"Please," William said dismissively.

"Just because you like him doesn't mean—"

"If Sir Rowan was the murderer," William interrupted, "the murders would be way more cool. And consistent."

"William," I replied severely, "murder is never 'cool.'"

"Whatever. So who is *actually* left? One of the miners working on their own? Or maybe someone else working for the Greendales or the Frosts?"

"It does seem possible that the Greendales, at least, would hire someone," I agreed. "But that would make it hard to trace. And we never did hear back from Sir Rowan, about whether or not they were interested in the ore after all, and what they planned to do about the article."

"Maybe *you* didn't," William said, his tail in the air, "but *I* did. He came by yesterday while you were at the station."

"And?" I swatted at him teasingly, but mostly just managed to make swirls through the falling snow. "What'd he say?"

"He said he'd been talking to an old friend of his in the kitchens via a speech spell," William said loftily. "Just like he promised. And his friend said that the Matriarch was super mad over the whole thing. Sir Rowan's definitely fired, just like he suspected, and won't ever be allowed back there again. He said they'll probably also distance themselves from the ore, just to save appearances—not that they were ever interested in it at all, he says. They were always just here for the gravel. But it sounds like they were doing some digging of their own into the dwarves, too. Sir Rowan and his friend think the Matriarch *was* the one to reach out to Raven, and that she tried to pay him for information. Even though she'd sent Sir Rowan to get Snow, he says she didn't trust him to do the job, most likely. But now they're completely done with Snow, it sounds like. She's been 'tainted' by all the bad press, in their opinion."

I shuddered. "What an awful-sounding family."

"Well, it's not like it comes as much of a surprise," William said, shaking snow from his ears. "If you ask me, clans like that, all concerned with appearances, are usually the ones that are the most ugly and fractured on the inside."

All concerned with appearances. It rang a bell in my mind.

"Is that the camp ahead?" William's eyesight, better than mine, had made sense of the shapes ahead of us in the storm. I glanced up.

"Yep. I don't see the fire going, though." But internally, I still mused. *It sounds like something Johann said, doesn't it? When we were looking at that mirror . . .*

"Maybe we're too early. What time is it?"

Distracted, I ruffled my cloak, searching through my belt and pockets for an old time piece. "Just after eleven," I said, squinting to read the clock face through the snow. "I think the miners usually took their lunch around eleven thirty, if I remember right. Let's wait here for a minute just in case."

I dropped down onto one of the snow-covered stumps arranged in a neat circle around the campfire, and it hit me. *Appearing to be united,* that was the phrase that Johann had used. I murmured to myself, "Oh, my gods and goddesses."

William must have heard the undertone in my voice. He whined. "What is it?"

"I think I know who it was. All along, I was thinking it couldn't be possible, because I thought of them all as one unit—"

"Shh," he interrupted suddenly. "I can hear someone coming."

"Oh, no," I said again, standing. "We shouldn't confront him alone."

"There's no time," William insisted. "Red, you need to send off one of your flares."

30

In the Shadows

Back in the fall, when I had accidentally gotten myself stuck at a haunted castle with a murderer, William had shown up less inclined to help and more inclined to murder me himself for running off on my own.

My compromise—rather than offer up my head on a silver platter, or allow myself to be chained to the shop—had been special flares. I'd actually used one at the time. The normal kind: you light it, it flies up in the air, it's bright and colorful and hopefully people notice. Well, that wasn't good enough for William. He had insisted that I invent a *new* kind of flare.

It was actually very clever, if I do say so myself. My new batch of flares combined the alchemical practicality of a mundane flare with William's familiar-magic. As far as I could understand, familiar magic had two major components: an energy source (in William's case it was the stars) and actual familiarity, that is to say, a bond between people. Even though I wasn't a sorcerer, William's bond with me allowed him to sense when I was in danger. And imbuing his magic in the flare meant that the little rocket would fly up into the sky,

243

burst, and send little shooting stars zooming toward other people who also shared a bond with me.

Of course, we'd never tested one in the middle of a blizzard halfway up a mountain. But there was no arguing with William when he had that tone of voice, especially since he'd helped invent the flares in the first place.

In my haste, I dropped my snack bag beside the stump as I leapt up. Darting around the nearest tent to buy myself some time, I drew a flare out of my tool belt and lit it with a striker my old alchemical master had given me years ago. Despite my doubts, the flare went up at once with a deafening crack and fizzle. My surprise actually knocked me backward, and I got a faceful of snow as I watched the burning red light disappear into the clouds.

Glancing back through the tents at William, I saw that he was glowing brighter than ever. "Did you help it out?" I asked.

"We need all the help we can get," William said. "I am *not* dealing with a pack of murderous dwarves alone."

"It isn't all of them," I said with certainty. "It's just one. Who's coming? Curses—they must have heard it. If it wasn't for the dragon, I'd say we ought to run off into the forest right now."

"No," William practically barked. "No going near the ledge!"

William's eyes blazed blue, like twin stars through the snow. I fell silent at once. *He must be really worried if he's using so much magic,* I thought, my spine tingling again. Familiar magic was easily depleted; at some point, William would run out of energy until he could stargaze again. Something told me I didn't want to be on the mountain when that happened.

Rather than argue, I retreated behind the tent again. The camp was at once an excellent, and a terrible place to try to hide. There were no nearby trees or boulders (thanks, Robin) for cover. The storm would help, but at the same time, my vibrant purple cloak would not blend in with the drifts. I could only hope I'd been outside long enough that snow had started to crust over my shoulders and hood.

I couldn't hear anything but the wind. That meant little, though. William's hearing was much better than mine. If he said someone was coming, then he was probably right.

In this weather, the flare was probably only visible to the people it sought out, I thought, trying to calm my rapid pulse. *And if the tests were true, then that was probably just Thorn and maybe— maybe Luca or Trent, although they wouldn't know where to look for me. But no one at the mine would have noticed it. They might have heard the noise, but it's unlikely they saw anything.*

I slipped my goggles on and tugged my hood down over my face. Cautiously, I leaned out along the bottom edge of the tent and tried to see if anything was happening.

The first thing I noticed was my blue satin bag winking at me through the snowfall. *Oops.* Between that and the depression my butt had left on the stump, it was pretty clear that someone had been in the camp. And where was William? I leaned farther out, trying to locate him. It took me several scans before I realized that he was lying right in front of me, next to my vacated seat at the campfire. With the rapidly-accumulating snow covering his fur and his head tucked down, he looked exactly like a log that the dwarves might have hauled over for seating.

Rhythmic crunching sounded from the road. I snapped back into place behind the tent.

"'You're always so worried, Pig!' 'We should just have the local Witch give us a protection spell!' Bah! As if we couldn't fend for ourselves." The voice accompanying the footfalls was muttering, imitating others, but it was definitely Pigeon.

The murderer. I was absolutely certain of it.

"Tross!" Pigeon's footsteps came to a stop and he bellowed. From the sound of it, he was standing near the campfire. I winced. It wasn't the tone of one friend calling out to another. "Tross, is that you? You better come out here!"

My nose wrinkled as I tried to think. *He heard the sound of the flare, and it made him think that Tross was out here? Why would that make sense? His nerves really must be getting to him. Actually, he could have exposed himself to the lead too, accidentally, which might heighten that paranoia—*

But that wasn't helping. In fact, my thoughts were sounding a lot like Luca, which filled me with dread. Suddenly I regretted letting off that flare. Suddenly it seemed like a very bad idea to bring *more* people to a ledge with an angry, murderous dwarf. All I could think was that William and I had to leave.

"TROSS!" Pigeon bellowed again. A shuffling sound began, which sent my heart into my throat. But it never got closer, which made me think that Pigeon was now pacing around the cook fire.

Focus, I told myself. *What do I have that can help?* My fingers ran over the assortment of vials and tools on my belt. I'd used up all my slime during the escape with the ore, and had forgotten to make more. I did have some rope, but my chances of lassoing—and then holding—a powerful miner essentially made of rock seemed pretty slim. I had some smoke bombs, but those worked best in dry situations. *Still, maybe if I got one right in his face and then William and I ran back to the mine . . .*

Why had Thorn let us run this errand alone, again?

Oh yeah, because the dwarves had seemed so diminutive

and cute, with their bird nicknames and their teary eyes.

Making a mental note *never* to trust anyone with team names ever again, I risked a quick look out at the campfire.

My blood went still and jagged as ice. Pigeon had begun walking toward the tents. Toward William.

A smoke bomb probably wasn't the best idea, but it was my only idea, and it was one hundred times better than watching Pigeon stumble over—and then focus all his ire on—William. I fumbled in my haste to free one of the rounded glass baubles from my belt. *Come on, come on, come on—*

"What's this?" Pigeon's mutterings became audible again as he noticed, but didn't recognize, William-the-log. "This wasn't always here . . ."

I lost control of the string which held the smoke bombs in place, spilling them out over the snow. I swore aloud and dropped down to recover them and honestly it took me a minute to realize that I *hadn't* been the loudest one to speak.

Pigeon had shouted.

Forgetting all hope of staying hidden, I looked up between the tents. William was still lying perfectly still. But behind him, practically on top of him, Pigeon was yelling and swatting at flurries of snow.

And yet—it wasn't just snow. There was something there, flitting around Pigeon's face. My initial thought was *tiny dragon!* but once the alarm had subsided, I realized that this newcomer wasn't flying like a dragon. Dragons fly like birds, graceful when they can soar, but awkward at close quarters. In contrast, this creature was buzzing around Pigeon very deftly, avoiding his clumsy fists and keeping him so busy he didn't even notice me staring. In short, it was flying like a bee, or a fairy.

Or a pixie.

Deciding there'd be time to wonder why a pixie had come to our rescue at a later date, I turned my attention to William. "Get up get up get up!" I hissed, reaching out as though to help him. "Let's get out of here!"

William rumbled as he leapt to his feet. "I should've known Thorn'd be too slow."

31

Seven is Stronger Than One

Apparently the sight of a log leaping up, glowing, and shaking off the snow—not to mention talking—was one straw too many for Pigeon. With another yelp, he fell over backward into the empty campfire.

The pixie watched him for a brief moment and then zipped away—down to my blue satin bag.

Hmmm.

But again, I set the pixie problem aside. There was no longer any use hiding, so I got to my feet and emerged from the tents to stand by William.

"You—you—you're not Tross," Pigeon accused me.

"Nope," I agreed. "Care to tell me why you tried to murder him?"

"I—I—I don't have to tell you anything! You don't know anything!"

My eyes narrowed. It may have been only three of us against a buff miner—still not great odds, unless we could keep him unnerved—but I wouldn't stand any bullying. "Fine. You know what? You *don't* have to tell me. Because I think I've got it figured out. I always thought you were the leader, and that it was cute how concerned you were about Snow. But that was the problem, wasn't it? You were so focused on protecting her. You would do *anything*, in fact, to protect her—wouldn't you?"

"I don't have to take this," Pigeon grumbled as he lurched to his feet. He glowered at William and me. "You can't make me! I won't leave her!"

"It was Raven who started it, wasn't it?" I continued, since talking seemed to keep him at bay. "Maybe he'd been approached by the Greendales—or maybe it was the Greendales posing as the Frosts. Either way, he put it together—he figured out who Snow was, didn't he? And I bet the fairies would have paid him well for information about her."

William had clearly missed the 'monologuing murderers don't strike' memo. He shook himself again. "Red, just run!"

"It was a bit odd, wasn't it, that Raven was talking about money right after Snow started worrying about her old family?" I continued, trying to give William a look to convey that I knew what I was doing. "Too odd for you *not* to investigate. And I bet Heron figured out what had happened, too. Maybe he knew that *you* had been around camp just before Raven's death? Or maybe he, too, realized that it might make good financial sense to cooperate with the Greendales. Or did he just notice your 'jitters,' Pigeon? Those were never symptoms of lead exposure—I bet they were symptoms of guilt. Because you couldn't hide that guilt from the people closest to you, could you? They kept on noticing. And asking questions. When I came up to talk to you all after Heron's death, Tross as good as said that he'd been asking you about how that cart had moved—"

"Enough!" Pigeon cried, interrupting my train of thought. He leapt toward us with his hands outstretched. I'm not sure what he meant to accomplish, but believe me, the sight of a solid five foot dwarf coming for you through the snow could send a shiver down anyone's spine.

It was almost as unnerving as the sight, one second later, of a dwarf frozen in midair.

From the hillside above us, somebody coughed. Politely. "I believe it is very poor form to attack an assistant of the local police. Even if that assistant is purely an unofficial one."

"Sir Rowan?" I tore my eyes from Pigeon, who was stuck in mid-leap like a rock sculpture, to spot the knight riding into camp.

"I received your flare, miss," he said very cordially. As if in agreement, Nessie snorted.

"Uh . . ." I wouldn't have considered myself to have any kind of "bond" with Sir Rowan, given that up until half an hour ago I'd still thought he might be a murderer. But, looking down at William's wagging tail beside me, I figured I knew why William had used magic to assist the flare.

"A very clever invention," Sir Rowan continued. "Given the direction and the speed with which it reached me, I was able to make a guess at your location. I am pleased to see I was correct. However, if I may, it would be advisable for you to move. While the iceflower tonic is very effective at first, I'm sorry to say that its effects are only temporary."

"*That's* why you've been gathering iceflower." I looked back at Pigeon. Icicles dripped from him, as though someone had doused him with their drink. *Which, apparently, someone did.*

Belatedly I realized that I was staring and nerding out again.

I quickly stepped over the circle of stumps, joining William and Sir Rowan, who had dismounted.

Dismounted, but not drawn his sword. He caught my look and seemed to understand. "Oh dear, miss," he said. "I rather hoped *you* had some plan for subduing him. I suppose you gathered from my interaction with Lark that I carry a sword. It is, of course, purely ceremonial. Not that Skar or Skaab knew that, naturally."

"Swords wouldn't be much good against such a tough dwarf anyway," William said. "Go on, Red, think of something."

"What? My idea was smoke bombs and running away," I protested.

Sir Rowan nodded. "Not a bad idea, miss, although one must consider the fact that it is difficult to fool someone who has heard your plan beforehand."

My jaw fell open. "He can still hear us? Then why did you say that about your sword?"

"Rrrr," said Pigeon, as the ice around him began to crack.

"Okay, fine." I gritted my teeth and thought fast, since William and Sir Rowan seemed determined to leave me in charge. "On my count, you run. Get Thorn!"

"But what, miss, will *you*—"

"I can't tell you, because that would be telling *him!* Go on three. One—"

"Did you say someone's supposed to get me?" Officer Thorn loomed out of the snow. Her club was at the ready, but she grinned broadly, no doubt at her own entrance.

"Nice try," William told her. "Your cue was earlier. You're late!"

"The broom was weighed down," Thorn said, as though that made perfect sense. A moment later it did, when Trent and

Luca materialized out of the storm.

Even before he saw us, Luca was talking. "I got the flare and I had no idea where to go so I got Trent and we went to the police station and Officer Thorn said she'd sent you to see the dwarves and—"

"What's going on?" Trent asked, more to the point.

"RRR!" Pigeon said again.

The six of us—myself, William, Sir Rowan, Officer Thorn, Luca, and Trent—jumped back around the circle. With a series of cracks, like a hundred tiny avalanches, Pigeon retracted one outstretched arm. Then another.

"That's your murderer," I told Officer Thorn.

"NOT. A. MURDERER!" Pigeon shouted, shaking his head and gasping as though he'd been underwater. With a crinkle and a thud, the rest of the ice around him gave way and dropped him into the snow.

For the second time, Pigeon picked himself up. This time he was a little more circumspect, though. He trod a circle in the snow as he squinted at each of us in turn. I bit my lip. *Clearly William and I weren't enough to scare him, but Officer Thorn has to be intimidating enough to keep him from attacking again, right?*

"All against me," Pigeon muttered. "Don't even know you. You don't know *me*. But *you* started all this when you and your *family* came to get Snow!"

And with that he launched himself at Sir Rowan, who prudently dodged behind his horse, which shied.

"Stop," Officer Thorn declared. She didn't yell, but she definitely used her 'police officer' voice, which was so powerful that I half expected the snowflakes to pause in midair. Pigeon's feet rooted to the ground, his body reverberating like a twanged bowstring.

"It wasn't my fault, Officer," he said. All at once, he'd become a pitiable little sidekick again. "They're setting me up. *They* wanted to get Snow. They wanted to take her away. They were going to sell her out. They can't do that! It isn't fair!"

"What's going on?"

Four short shapes materialized along the road. Peering through the storm, I recognized Snow and her remaining dwarven friends.

Officer Thorn, always quicker on her feet than I could hope to be, addressed them rather than Pigeon. "Can you attest to the whereabouts of this dwarf during each of the murders?"

The other dwarves gasped, their silhouettes portraying horror through the storm.

"Oh, *Pigeon*." The sadness in Snow's voice answered Thorn's question immediately. Around her, the storm seemed to clear. Her pale face showed plainly that the Officer's question came as no surprise—just a disappointment, as though all along a part of her had known it was coming, but didn't want to believe it was true.

"You can't make me confess," Pigeon insisted wildly. He glanced around the circle, but we had him pinned. In desperation he looked up into the storm. "It was all for the best."

And there, through the stillness which had suddenly descended on us, a huge winged shadow swooped.

Pigeon gulped audibly. "I—I—If I *do* confess, you can't do anything to me! I only wanted to protect Snow all along. I just had to keep them from getting her. If I'm gone, then who will be around to do that?"

"Pigeon," Snow said, very quietly, "you have to let me learn to do that myself."

32

Fairest of All

That night, Pigeon was locked up in Belville's jail—really just a cell in Officer Thorn's basement. On the floor above him, Tross continued his speedy recovery. And while Maeve comforted Snow and the other dwarves, Officer Thorn finally had a chance to write up her reports.

After taking most of the day to warm up, I decided a celebratory dinner was in order. William and I—and my little blue bag—took over a corner table at Lavender's tavern. Over steaming cider and shepherd's pie, we began to put some stray pieces together.

"Told you the flare was a good idea," William began by saying.

I chuckled. "You just wanted a chance to fawn over Sir Rowan."

"I do not fawn! I am not a deer!"

"No," I agreed, snatching up my mug before William could knock it over. "But you were just about squished by a raging miner earlier today. I think we owe someone a thank you."

Carefully, well aware that if this didn't work I'd look like a total fool, I opened up my bag and set it on the table. "Come on out," I coaxed. "It's okay."

For a long minute, nothing happened. I looked around the noisy tavern before us. "Darn, maybe it was a bad idea to do this here. Maybe it's too scary to come out."

"Probably," William agreed, his tail thumping against the wooden bench he'd perched on. "Seeing as your little freeloader prefers to work in the dark."

I set down my fork. "What?"

"Come on, Red. *I* figured it out the moment I saw them."

"What, just earlier today, you mean? What did you figure out?"

"The broken stuff, the missing food, the noises in the night," William said, jerking his nose at the bag puddled on the table. "It's all because of this thief."

"I am *not* a thief!" The tiny voice sounded just as scandalized as Pigeon's had earlier in the day. I stifled a yelp, and then a chuckle as I watched a tiny green pixie fly up out of my bag.

This pixie, however, was even smaller than others I'd seen. She barely topped six inches, and yet her hair was flowing white, a color I associated with age. I had no idea if that held true for pixies, but given the archaic nature of her dress—she seemed to be swathed in a sparkly toga—and the faint smell of aged wood that surrounded her, I guessed it did.

"Hello," I said, smiling. The pixie whirled in midair to focus on my face. "I'm Red. And you are?"

Despite the fervor with which she'd contradicted William, the pixie clasped her hands behind herself as though embarrassed by my question. Her bark-brown skin looked a little flushed.

"How about we call you Sugar," William suggested, his tone

only *barely* snide. "Seeing as you seem to like cookies so much."

"I *do* like cookies," the pixie agreed. "We don't have any of *those* around the Tree. Oh, Red, it was so terrible! Not living with the Tree, of course. But when the miners broke through! It was so loud! I got scared. And then I was locked out! And then I came down to town. I never even knew there *was* a town. Then I found you. Your shop smells so good! But I didn't know what you'd say. Or if I should go back!"

This time I couldn't help chuckling. "It's okay. Wait. Are you saying that the magic ore we found *was* touched by the Tree of Life?"

"Oh, yes, but you can't tell anyone!" said the pixie, tiny eyes wide. "The Tree of Life is our home, and we have to keep it safe!"

Aha. So Trent was right about the underground sanctuary. Another question came to mind. "So it *was* you that got in through the window and rummaged around in the kitchen?"

"Yeeees." The pixie drew out the word, looking between me and William, like a child who knew what would happen when the sentence ended and wanted to prevent it. "But I really am sorry!"

William huffed. "Not sorry enough to say anything before I called you out on it."

"William!" I reprimanded. "She was clearly sorry enough to save your hide earlier. You ought to be nice."

"Oh!" said the pixie, as though just remembering her heroics. "I didn't like that angry person! There were so many of them at the mine. Everyone was so mad. That's why I went to town. I wasn't sure how to get home again! But then you said you were going. So I went with you!"

"But you didn't stay," William pointed out.

"Did we not get close enough?" I asked the pixie. "I have to admit, I don't actually know where they found the ore. I'm guessing that's where they broke though, right? I'd take you there, but I'm not sure I could find it."

Or that Lark will ever let me near the mine again, I thought with an inward cringe.

"It's okay," said the pixie. Since she hadn't been forthcoming with a name, I decided Sugar was it. "I kind of don't want to go back. Not yet. *She* isn't back either. So it's fine."

"Who's she?" I asked.

Sugar giggled. "The dragon, silly!"

Ah yes, the dragon. I cocked my head. Seeing as the dragon had scared Pigeon into confessing, and apparently kept company with pixies, maybe that part of the mystery wasn't as distressing as I had thought.

Especially since I had *no* inclination to mess with a Tree of Life. That sounded like serious magical danger that it was better not to get mixed up in.

And maybe—much like Snow—Sugar just needed a little bit of time to figure things out for herself. That much, I could certainly offer her.

"Well, if you're going to stay in town, you're welcome to stay with us," I told Sugar. "You don't have to hide. Just try not to keep me up at night any more!"

"Hey! Who're you talking to?" a familiar voice said behind me.

I blinked, and realized that Sugar had vanished, probably back into the bag. I slid it from the table and smiled at the newcomer—Luca.

"Pull up a chair," I told him, gesturing to the table. He set down his heaping plate and happily obliged. "We were just going over the events of the day. I can't tell you how grateful I am that you showed up."

"Really?" Luca beamed at me over his food. Apparently, the angst over Sir Rowan was gone, and I was happy to let it stay that way.

"Absolutely," I grinned back at him. "And good call going to Trent, by the way. I guess we still have some bugs to work out with that flare."

"The flares are fine," William informed me, before clambering down off of his bench. I watched him, just in case, and was relieved to see he just wanted to join Dusty at the bar.

"Yeah, it worked out fine," Luca agreed. In William's absence, he slid into the bench across from me. "And I'm really glad you sent it, Red. Especially after—you know, everything."

Hum, I thought. *Not so far gone after all.* "Of course," I said, my smile a little more hesitant as I tried to figure out what to say. Oddly enough, no words came.

Fortunately, Luca had words enough for the both of us. "What an incredible end to the story, don't you think? I stopped by the station to drop off all my research for Officer Thorn, for her report. She says you were right: Trent did a spell on that promissory note, finally, and apparently Raven *was* being paid by the Greendales— the Frost insignia was just a charm. We don't know yet if the payment was something about Snow or about the gravel deal, but apparently, Pigeon thought it was about revealing Snow. He argued with Raven and knocked him over the cliff; that much he has admitted to. And then Heron, the second victim, had apparently been talking about teaming up with the family rather than Lark over the ore thing, so of course Pigeon thought, 'he has to go too.' And it seems like maybe Tross saw something when that happened, and so Pigeon was keeping an eye on him, then finally decided he was too risky to keep around. So that takes care of all the violence at least. He sure was angry, even in his interview, she said. It probably was a really good thing you still had that protection charm on you, from Trent. Now, Officer Thorn says, in the future she wants us all to carry flares like yours, and she's putting in her report that . . ."

I smiled at Luca as I turned back to my dinner. Everything, it seemed, was back to normal.

33

The Huntsman at Home

The next morning, after a full night's sleep at last, I went with Thorn to tie up some of the remaining loose ends.

At the mine.

Despite my trepidation, Lark's guards let us through without a second glance. And when we met her in her office and gave her the final report, she was quite cordial.

"Oh, and one other thing," I added, stepping up as Thorn finished speaking. I stood over Lark beside one of the desks; Thorn and the trolls had retreated to the opposite side of the room to watch. "There's—people living down there, where this ore came from. Pixies and the dragon, at least. I've met one of the pixies and she seems quite nice, but still, if you needed another reason to close off that section of the mine—"

Lark smiled coolly. "It's already been done, Red."

My shock must have shown on my face, because she laughed. The sound was like waves bubbling over rocks. "You thought you were the only one facing excitement yesterday? As soon as the storm abated, the dragon herself helped us block off the mine."

At this Officer Thorn, too, stirred. "The dragon, you say?"

"Yes," Lark said. "She is much more reasonable than one might expect."

This left us with nothing to say, aside from raging and slightly improper curiosity about how Lark and her miners had managed to *talk* to a dragon. In our silence, Lark added, "I am rather more fond of justice than you might think. I believe every good leader must be. Otherwise, the people around you start to have . . . unusual ideas." She gave me a significant look. "I am grateful to be included in the conclusion of your case. But I expect that we will not see you around the mine . . . not until you are invited."

I cocked my head at her.

"You are very lucky," she concluded with her most genuine smile yet, "to have such useful skills."

Though I hadn't actually agreed to her terms aloud, I could tell that Lark considered the conversation settled and over. I nodded, and crossed the room to Officer Thorn. With nothing more than a cordial farewell, Lark turned us loose.

"Oh," she called as we stepped outside, "Red, do tell your friend that the same applies to him, won't you?"

"Who's that?" Thorn asked me as we continued walking.

"Sir Rowan, I imagine," I replied. Thinking of his encounter with the trolls made me cringe at first, but that was quickly overtaken by my urge to laugh.

"Oh, him." Thorn looked up at the sky above us. Wispy clouds remained from yesterday's storm, but clear bright blue shone between them. "What's he doing, anyway? Didn't he say he got fired?"

I paused for just a moment until we'd officially left the mine.

Alone on the road, I felt more confident saying, "He did. He told William and me yesterday that he's going to stick around here for a while. Despite the fact that he lives in the woods and continually refers to Belville as a 'village,' he seems to like it here for some reason."

"Any idea what that reason is?"

"He said something about the dragon. I think he feels like it's his duty to—I don't know—confront it or something."

Officer Thorn looked alarmed. "Him, too? But it's already treated with Lark, apparently. Why not just let it be?"

"It's some knight thing, I guess." I grinned. "Although he turned out to be quite a pacifist, for a knight. Maybe he wants to make it a drink."

Thorn snorted. "Let me know how *that* goes."

"Oh, I will. No doubt he and William will be in touch quite a bit," I chuckled.

The officer accepted this cheerfully, and for a while we walked beneath the trees in silence. Finally I mustered up the courage to ask, "So where's Maeve?"

"Back in Pine," Thorn said, as though she was simply commenting on the color of the evergreens or the birdsong in the breeze. "I recommended more training before another field test.

"But that's not to say," she added more seriously, as though worried I'd got the wrong impression, "that I don't think she'll make a good officer. I think she'll make a great one. She just needs some time."

"That makes sense," I agreed. "What about her and Snow?"

"Snow." Thorn sighed. "Did you realize it was her making all those storms?"

That didn't answer my question, but I played along, laughing at myself as I admitted, "No, I didn't. William did, of course. He made fun of me about it last night. Something about her emotional angst calling down the weather?"

"Something like that. Trent tried to explain it to me, too, while we were on that broom." Thorn chuckled with me before finally getting to the point. "She and the dwarves headed out this morning, Tross included. They're going to Pine, too. I wrote them letters of recommendation myself. They're going to work for the gemsmith over there."

"Coalsworth and Co?" I knew the gemsmith in Pine; I sometimes bought minerals or the occasional tool from them. I'd been impressed by their quality, but they'd always been slow to deliver goods. Maybe with five new helpers, they'd get up to speed. I smiled to think of the miners exchanging their vests and pickaxes for aprons and tiny drills. "That sounds like a good idea."

"I thought so." Thorn nodded, pleased with herself. "They'll have to be there anyway for Pigeon's trial. At this rate they might get it done right before the holidays."

I shivered. Somehow, I'd already blocked the murders from my mind. "Huh. Seems like unfortunate timing, but I guess it's better not to wait."

"Of course it is," Thorn said. "It's just like Snow said. She needs to be free of running from things or looking over her shoulder for murderers. They all do. Then they can find what's *really* valuable in life."

And a chance to love themselves, like Gloria was saying to Snow. A chance to be their own protectors, after Pigeon. Wait—I groaned as I really thought about what Officer Thorn had said. "Did you just make a pun about the importance of love and friendship?"

"And rocks. Get it? Since they're miners?"

Between the range of responses to this comment—from "rocks aren't technically valuable, it's the ore that counts" all the way down to pushing Officer Thorn into a snowbank—I couldn't choose. And since we'd just descended into the outskirts of town, I felt like I'd missed my chance. *It probably wouldn't be the best idea to pick a fight with Officer Thorn in front of witnesses*, I decided. *After all, I have to protect* myself, *too.*

It was a thought that warmed me, and made me more inclined than ever to regard the matter with some of Sir Rowan's pacifism.

And yet, somehow, with a *whoosh* that came out of nowhere, there was snow plastered all over Thorn's face.

Officer Thorn stopped dead in the street, sputtering. In my surprise, I wasn't as tactful as I could have been . . . what should have probably been a sympathetic "oh no!" came out of my mouth as a delighted laugh.

And I wasn't the only one enjoying the moment. From behind a fence post further down the road, Trent popped up, cackling. "Nice look, Officer!"

"You'd better start running now, Witch!" Officer Thorn bellowed. People were starting to peer out of windows. Distracted by a noise, I turned. At the last moment, I noticed Luca standing behind a nearby bush. I managed to dodge, just barely, which meant that another snowball implanted itself on Thorn, this time right in the shoulder.

"Sorry, Officer!" Luca yelled, although he also did not sound incredibly regretful. I started laughing so hard I doubled over.

"Not as sorry as you're going to be!" Officer Thorn promised. She knocked me over into a snowdrift—not a difficult feat, given that my eyes were watering and my knees were shaky—

and took off after Trent.

Footsteps crunched through the snow and Luca appeared over me, offering his hand. I accepted it and hauled myself up, still laughing. "Can you believe her?"

"Fair's fair, I guess," Luca agreed, his eyes twinkling under his hood.

"Sure, except that *I* wasn't the one to start the fight!" I protested as I tried to shake the snow out of my hair. "In fact, if we're going to be *really* fair, I think you're the one who deserves to be pushed in the snow."

"Uhmmm, truce?" Luca was already backing away, grinning.

"Not a chance!" I sprinted after him. He was pretty fast, given that he was running in full-length robes. But I knew I'd catch up. Ahead of us, jovial shouts and bellows indicated that Trent was still harassing Thorn.

In a word, all was right with the world.

Epilogue

A note from Snow

To Gloria:

Thanks for saying I could write to you. I figured I'd better at least write to say that me and the dwarves made it to our new home in Pine just fine. We've just settled in, and the rest of them are already raring to go to work. Even Maeve has already reported to the local station and everything!

I figured I had to write, otherwise Red and everyone would bug you, probably. I heard about Sir Rowan staying, too. Don't feel like you have to hide any of this from them. In fact, I thought if I wrote to you, then at least you could tell them I'm fine, and maybe that'd get them off your back.

I think a lot about what I saw in your magic mirror. You were right. There was so much anger I was holding on to, and it seemed like no one could ever see it. No one even believed I could feel that way–like I ought to be too good or too well-bred or too pretty to be so mad. I guess that's what my grandmother always taught me, anyway. And even after I ran away, I was afraid to show what I felt to the rest of the gang. I just never wanted to think about it at all. And then to have to stand there and look at it in your salon . . .

I think a lot about what happened in Belville, too. It's kind of similar to the way I grew up. Like, a part of me thinks that I should be really shocked by what happened, Goose's death and the others. I'm sad about them, don't get me wrong. But–I'm not really surprised at how it all went down. All that time I was trying to hide the depths of my feelings, my friends were trying to hide theirs, too. I wonder if I should have known earlier who the murderer was . . .

Maeve tells me I shouldn't, though. She says I can't take any responsibility for the actions of others. I think I'm okay with that, really. But what hurts is how much they were trying to take responsibility for *my* actions. Even when I ran away from court, people were still trying to control my life.

The dwarves never run away from things. I never really thought about it until now, but it's one of the things I like about them. It's something I liked about mining, too. You stand there facing a big impossible rock wall and you just go *through* it. No backing down or hiding.

I guess that's what we're doing now. The trial is coming up soon, and we're all going to go and give our testimony. We won't try to hide what happened or how we feel. I don't want to go–I'm scared to go, scared that I'll end up creating some kind of apocalyptic snowstorm because it all just makes me so *mad* that anyone had to die and any of this happened in the first place. But Maeve's coming too, so it'll probably be okay. Maybe it will be like finding an underground cave–we'll dig right through this awful wall, and find a new open space on the other side.

That's what I hope, anyway. I know it sounds a little silly. But . . . something about just seeing my anger, and owning it, makes me feel better. I talk about it with the others a lot. Everyone says they understand, that I'm not wrong to feel this way. I've never had anyone say that before. And I don't think I'd ever really listened to how other people feel, either. Actually, with all this talking, I actually haven't created a storm since we left Belville. Maybe the magic was just leaking out because I was trying so hard to hide it. I do feel a lot freer now.

So, you can tell Red and Sir Rowan that everything's fine. We even found a cute little cottage on the outskirts of town to rent. Maeve found a place nearby, and she said I can go over whenever it gets a little too crowded here for me. It's all so—normal.

It's actually kind of nice.

Write me back, if the salon isn't too busy. Tell Johann I say hi, too.

Snow

Recipes

The recipes included here have been submitted by the residents of Belville, collected (and at times translated) by the author. Mistakes might have been made at any part of the process, but with any luck, these will bring a bit of fun and inspiration to you, our readers! Always feel free to experiment with the recipes included. And if you do, reach out to <u>info@ellehartford.com</u> to let us know how it went!

That said, without further ado . . .

Red's Veggie Curry

Feel free to swap out the veggies below according to your own preferences. And if you're feeling extra chilly, consider adding more chili for some warming spice!

Serves four

Ingredients:

- ½ head cauliflower, chopped
- 2 med. potatoes, cubed
- 2 cloves garlic, minced

- 1 Tbsp fresh ginger, sliced thin, or ½ tsp ground
- 2 fresh jalapeno peppers, seeded and chopped, or dried pepper flakes to taste
- 2 med. onions, chopped
- ¼ vegetable oil
- 2 Tbsp curry powder
- 1 Tbsp flour
- 1 can (14 oz) unsweetened coconut milk
- ½ vegetable stock
- 1 tsp salt
- 1 can (16 oz) chickpeas
- 12 oz. roughly chopped fresh spinach
- Black pepper to taste

1. Boil chopped cauliflower and potato until just beginning to soften, about 5 minutes. Drain and set to one side.
2. Add garlic, ginger, peppers, onions, and oil to a large, heavy saucepan and cook over medium heat until the onions are soft, about 5 minutes.
3. Add the curry powder and flour to the onion mix and cook for 3 minutes more. This will deepen the curry flavor!
4. Stir in the coconut milk, vegetable stock, and salt. Bring to a boil over high heat.
5. Add the cauliflower, potatoes, and chickpeas.
6. Reduce the heat to medium and cover the pot. Cook for about 15 minutes.
7. Stir in the spinach and cook until wilted, about 3 minutes.
8. Season with salt and black pepper if desired. Serve over

rice or with some hot naan!

***

Rowan's Iceflower Slushie

The knight in question wishes responsible adults to know that spirited substitutes can be swapped into this minty frozen drink; however, it's arrestingly tasty as is!

Serves one

Ingredients:

- ¼ C clear soda
- ½ tsp lime juice (add more if you like citrus)
- 2 tsp sugar
- 1 tsp mint simple syrup (or commercial mint syrup is fine)
- 6 fresh mint leaves
- 1 C crushed ice

1. Combine all ingredients except soda in a blender, and blend on a low setting until the contents begin to circulate.
2. Pour in the soda and blend until smooth.
3. Garnish with an extra mint leaf, if desired, and enjoy!

* * *

Sugar's Magical Chocolate Bonbons

If you like things especially sweet, swap in sweetened milk and chocolate chips. These bite-size chocolates are relatively easy to make, but you might find that they disappear very easily too.

Makes about 50 small bonbons

Ingredients:

- ¼ margarine, softened
- ½ lb confectioner's sugar, sifted
- ½ C unsweetened condensed milk
- 1 C shredded coconut
- ¼ C finely chopped walnut (optional)
- ¼ tsp vanilla
- 6 oz dark chocolate chips (about ¾ C)
- 2 Tbsp butter
- Water

1. Mix the margarine, sugar, milk, coconut, nuts, and vanilla in a large bowl.
2. Cover and refrigerate until the mixture has thickened, about 2 hours.
3. Roll the mix into marble-size balls (small hands help with this). Place on lined cookie sheets and freeze until firm,

about 30 minutes.

4. While waiting on the filling to freeze, set up your work-station: line a counter or cookie sheet with parchment paper (consider weighing it down so it doesn't fly out of place).

5. Also while waiting: set up a double boiler for your chocolate chips. Fill one small pot about ¼ - ½ full of water and set it to boil. Place a second, heat-proof bowl over the first, so that it's suspended on the edges of the hot pot. It shouldn't be touching the hot water, but it will get very steamy!

6. Put the chocolate chips and butter into the bowl above the hot water, and stir as the chocolate melts.

7. With the chocolate warm and about half an hour passed, take out the coconut marbles. One by one, dip them in the chocolate, roll to coat, and then place them on the lined paper to dry. (If you're impatient and don't mind messes, feel free to speed up the process! The end result will taste the same.)

8. Store leftover bonbons–if you have any–in a reusable bag in the freezer to prevent melting. Enjoy!

* * *

William's Recipe for Peace of Mind: Orion

Once again, we have a unique twist on a "recipe" from our resident star-gazing familiar. Be sure to wrap up warmly!

"This is an easy one," William informs us. "If you're out on a clear night during the winter–or summer, if you're in the Southern Hemisphere–you can't miss it. Look for three bright stars right in a row. That's Orion's belt–like the goofy belt Red was trying to use to keep her cloak closed. Once you've spotted that, you can find the four stars that mark out his shoulders and feet. It makes a sort of hourglass shape.

"Orion was supposedly some great hunter, kind of like an ancient version of a knight. If you have a *really* clear sky, you can see animals around him–like his faithful hunting dogs. Those were the old days when you could just roam about looking for trouble . . . Not unlike some alchemists these days, mind you. Not that I have anything against travel. But in these colder months, it's nice to remember you have a home to go to."

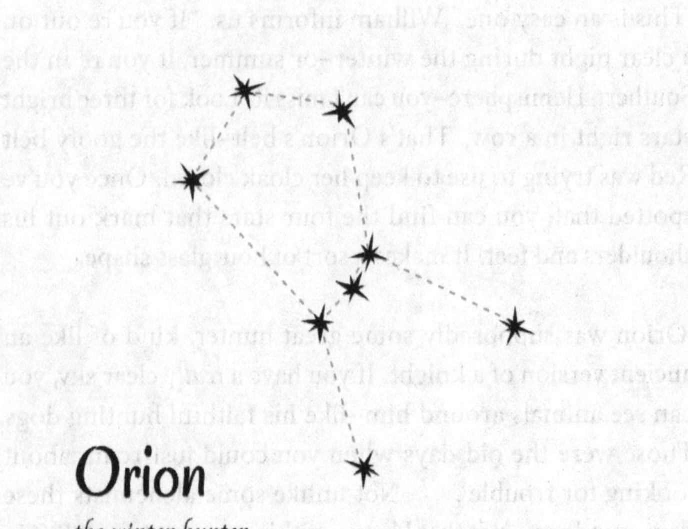

Orion
the winter hunter

Acknowledgments

I'm going to shake up the usual order a bit by thanking my editor first and foremost—a huge shout out to Richelle at Richelle Braswell Comprehensive Editing! Before she came along, this story was a snowy, jumbled up mess, and it didn't even have the right title.

Of course, in a more orderly fashion, I'm also deeply indebted to my family and friends for their support, and to my partner, who dealt with many a stressed-out and hangry moment as I finished up yet *another* round of edits. Many thanks also to the members of my writing club, who put up with my early drafts and also with my erratic cooking. And finally, as always, a *massive* thank you to the other authors who encouraged me, the wonderful book community on Instagram, the Cozy Mystery Book Club, the Cozy Mystery Tribe, and my intrepid ARC readers!

And on top of that, I'm very thankful to *you*. That means you, reading this! I hope your time in Belville has been welcoming and warm. And of course, if you find you have a little extra time on your hands . . . reviews warm even the most frozen of authors' hearts. ;)

About the Author

Elle adores cozy mysteries, fairy tales, and above all, learning new things. As a historian and educator, she believes in the value of stories as a mirror for complicated realities. She currently lives in New Jersey with a grumpy tortoise and a three-legged cat.

If you're interested in what happens next for Sir Rowan (and that mysterious dragon), you can find his adventures in *A Tale of Rowan and Daisy!* When you sign up for Elle's newsletter at her website (ellehartford.com), you'll have access to that ebook for free.

P.S. Just as a reminder, there is an extra special warm place in an author's heart for anyone who takes the time to leave a review. ♥ Even one kind sentence can do wonders!

And if you'd like a taste of book three in The Alchemical Tales, read on . . .

Mermaid for Danger

Chapter One

On the Road Again

"Welcome, welcome! Line for the ferry's to the right. No cutting, or the gods and goddesses of the waves will swallow ye whole!"

"If *I* don't do something worse first," my companion, William, grumbled. He lumbered at my side, his black doggy head as high as my thigh. His magic, a starry blue, glowed faintly as he prepared himself for the transition from land to sea. Though the afternoon around us was bright and cheerful, he clearly wasn't feeling charitable—especially now that our long journey down from the mountains had brought us to the ferry.

"Hush," I told him as he continued muttering to himself. The tiny ferry terminal was awash with people, mostly vacationers and locals, I guessed. Most were dressed in shorts or bathing suit cover-ups, the quintessential uniform of summer in Seaside. And most were also giving William and me curious stares. We carried too much luggage to be day-trippers; in fact, we were in town for a friend's wedding. While I was happy to see and support my friend, as I looked at the strangers in line with us I felt a familiar twinge of, well, strangeness. *Love,* I had once told one of my mothers—and she'd never let me forget it—*seems like such a hassle.* Strangers, vows, big public displays. Even the wiser, older me didn't totally get it.

I re-adjusted the strap of my canvas backpack self-consciously, trying to put my uncertainties about love and its trappings aside. In my year and more of running a shop, I'd forgotten that unique dichotomy of travel: on the road, it's easy to be invisible. But when you roll up in a new town or at a crossroads, you're an object of public interest.

We shuffled along in line as I thought. We *could* have taken a carriage or even caught a magitech hot air balloon from our home in Belville to Seaside, but William had convinced me to walk it "for old time's sake." Judging by William's demeanor now, I was guessing that the old times weren't as fun as he remembered them. Still, I *had* enjoyed a chance to collect a lot of great material along the three-day trip. Just before joining the ferry line, I'd sent a big box of flower stalks and even some malachite ore back home to Red's Alchemy and Potions, and I was already looking forward to getting home and using the ingredients—*after* the wedding, of course.

Come to think of it, Seaside's post office had been crowded too. Maybe that helped explain William's increased grumpiness . . .

I shrugged, letting his attitude remain *his* problem. Instead, I decided to enjoy the view. Seaside was a popular destination for tourists, the kind of city that still felt like a tiny harbor town. Long ago, some enterprising soul had realized that preserving the old wooden harbor, sparkling clean beaches, and vividly painted cabins would bring a lot more visitors. So, they'd had the good grace to hide their magitech train and balloon stations behind the hill that edged the back of town, and I swear they had a team of wizards on hand to ensure that all their window-boxes and tiny, sandy gardens bloomed plentifully. The ferry dock was particularly idyllic, even in line: as we waited patiently, lined up along a low stone wall separating us from the harbor, we could watch the seals playing in turquoise waves and hear children playing at the beach around the corner.

William, however, was looking firmly forward, toward the ferry captain. When two elves rushed up and joined their friends in line ahead of us, he growled.

"Need I remind you that we are in town for a *happy* occasion?" I whispered down to him.

"It's not the wedding yet." A serious undertone of menace laced his words. I rolled my eyes, but kept a more careful eye on the line, just in case William decided to do more than talk.

The ferry captain chatted amiably—and loudly—to each person in line as he took fares for the journey. I gathered pretty quickly that his name was Kye, that he didn't care for magic, didn't hold with technology, and didn't trust the weather, but that he had it on good authority that the wedding next week would be the event of the season. *Whose authority*, I couldn't help but wonder. *His fairy godmother's?* Though the joke made me smile, I hoped he was right.

"Name, destination, type of fare," Kye rattled off the familiar refrain as William and I stepped to the head of the line.

"I'm Red, and this is William. Oh, that's Cinnabar Sunset, if you need my *full* name. Full fare for me, half fare for him."

Kye nodded along thoughtfully, his weathered fingers skimming through his stack of tickets. "And that's William Sunset, is it?"

"Not a chance," William snorted. "Just William."

"And why does 'Just William' get half fare, tell?"

I nudged William with my knee, silencing whatever reply was on the tip of his tongue. To Kye, I said quietly, "He's an arcane familiar."

Usually I didn't like to explain as much to anyone if I could help it. Aside from William being touchy, it brought up a lot of awkward questions. Only sorcerers can create—and therefore own—familiars, which look pretty much like normal animals but often have a bit of magic (and a lot of attitude, in William's case). Technically, a familiar isn't truly alive; it's a spell. I'm no sorcerer, just an alchemist. And I certainly don't own William, as he likes to point out. As far as I can tell, no one does. He'd been with me for years, and never said a word about it. To say this was unusual would be like saying the sea is wet, but William is a loyal and beloved companion, no matter how grouchy he gets, so I never push him on the issue.

Fortunately Kye just nodded again, rather than ask prying questions. "That's alright, then." As he thumbed through his stack of tickets, he asked conversationally, "Here for a bit of sun, are ye?"

I glanced down at William, the shaggy black sheepdog, and then at myself. Underneath my tunic, leggings, and boots, my skin was as brown as ever. Copper, my mother used to call it. I wondered what prompted Kye to think that either William or I needed to work on our tans. Kye himself had gray, leathery skin, and he was so thin I thought he might be some kind of elemental spirit.

"Um, not exactly," I answered at last. "We're headed to the Afolayans' camp. Taiwo said you know where that is? She said you can basically see it from the harbor wall."

At my side, William chuckled. I nudged him, thinking he was laughing about my soon-to-be-married friend Taiwo, who has a tendency to exaggerate. This time he nudged back.

"You, and dozens like you," said Kye kindly. He handed over two tickets printed on blue water-proof paper and asked me for the fare. As I fished in my hidden coinpurse for the correct change, he added, "Don't ye worry. I've added the camp to my route, just for the wedding. Folks've been coming in all week. It'll be our first stop."

I handed Kye my money, thanked him, and shuffled William and our luggage onto the dock. A short walk down the weathered planks took us to the gangplank for the waiting ferry, a boat named *Expedition*. I grinned as I looked over its white trim and blue paneling, thinking of the secrets this seemingly innocuous boat might hold.

"He's blind," William said, pushing past me to claim a spot along the railing of the front deck.

"Excuse me?" I followed, adding, "Hey, if you think you're going to get seasick, you might want to sit in the cabin."

"I'll be fine. It's just the transition I don't like. The *ferry captain*," William said, switching topics seamlessly and speaking as though I was about as quick as a snail. "He's blind."

"Oh. *Oh.*" I glanced back over my shoulder toward the shore, sighing as I rued my comment about "seeing" the camp. "You know I'm slow to pick up on those things whenever we're near the coast. I swear, it's like the light off the water scrambles my brain or something."

William chuckled again. "Sure, blame it on the light on the water or whatever. Even though that doesn't make sense, since you grew up on an *island*. If you ask me, it's because of the wedding."

"It is not," I protested.

"You've been distracted ever since we left Belville."

"I have not!"

"It's because you spend too much time in your lab with your plants and you're scared of *loooove*," William continued, tail wagging, drawing out the word "love" as though he was a child in grade school.

"I am not," I insisted, feeling more and more like a broken record by the second.

"If you say so." William shook his fluffy ears. "It's a good thing Officer Thorn isn't here to ask you to investigate anything, because a criminal could probably walk right past you and you'd be too busy complaining about 'light on the water' to notice."

"Alright, that's enough," I reprimanded him, looking nervously around at our fellow passengers to make sure they hadn't heard the bits about "criminal" or "officer." Officer Thorn was a dear friend, of course, and I'd been happy to help her in the past, but the last thing I wanted was for anything to go wrong for Taiwo.

As though he could hear my thoughts, William snorted. "You better hope nothing comes up at the wedding."

"Nothing will," I said, swatting his head playfully for having tempted ill fortune. "Besides, we're not here for trouble. We're just here to support our friends."

* * *

Find Mermaid for Danger *now wherever books are sold!*

ACKNOWLEDGMENTS

To my Beta readers: Anna Wheeler and Will Nuessle, for trudging through the thick of it.

To my editors: Sean Fletcher and Angel Butts for catching all the plot holes and for sprucing up the verbiage.

To Jenna Moreci, Abbie Emmons, and Alyssa Matesic for providing educational content on YouTube that helped me improve as a writer.

And last but not least, to my family for always encouraging me to express myself in every way imaginable.

9 798987 079904